# ON BORROWED TIME

## ALSO BY DAVID ROSENFELT

# ON BORROWED TIME

DAVID ROSENFELT

Minotaur Books ✠ New York

This is a work of fiction. All of the characters, organizations, and events portrayed in this novel are either products of the author's imagination or are used fictitiously.

Please e-mail David Rosenfelt at dr27712@aol.com with any feedback. Your comments are very much appreciated.

ISBN 978-0-312-59836-5

*To the close friends Debbie and I have made in this "chapter." Carol and John, Karen and David, Ellen and Craig, Annette and Ricardo, Debra and Emmit, Marty and Dan, and many, many others.*

# ACKNOWLEDGMENTS

A sincere thank-you to Andy Martin, Kelley Ragland, Matthew Shear, Hector Dejean, Matt Martz, Robin Rue, Beth Miller, Doug Burns, Scott Ryder, Debbie Myers, and Ross Rosenfelt. They have all been extraordinarily helpful to me, and if there is any fault to be found with this book, blame them.

# ON
# BORROWED
# TIME

**The moment we met is burned into my mind,** and even now I replay it over and over. It's somehow vaguely comforting, and thinking about Jennifer gives her a presence. I've wanted to give her a presence for so very long.

It's not outright denial, but it's almost as good.

It was at a political rally for a candidate Jen was supporting. It's funny, but I can't remember who the candidate was, and I can't venture a guess, based on what I learned later about Jen's politics. In that area, she was always a contradiction: a social liberal who was fiercely in favor of the death penalty, and a fiscal conservative who never met a homeless shelter she didn't want the government to support. But whatever it was she was advocating at that or any other moment, that advocacy was fierce.

I'm a writer, so I had the political "get out of jail free" card; it was a violation of my alleged journalist credentials to even hint at my leanings. I wrote mainly magazine articles, most of them political or business-oriented, but I wasn't there for anything having to do with work. The truth is, I had just been wandering by and stopped to see what was going on.

So on that day we were who we are, or at least as I have always seen us: Jen as a participant in life, and myself as an observer of it.

1

It didn't take a particularly keen observer to notice her. She was light-up-the-room beautiful, even though she was wearing a New York Yankees cap. I hate the Yankees, always have, always will, but I quickly rationalized that I'd never really felt any animosity for their caps. So I went over to her and introduced myself.

"Hi. I'm Richard Kilmer. I'm a journalist."

"How nice for you," she deadpanned. Journalists were not necessarily her favorite people.

"Yes . . . I wanted to ask you a few questions. About the rally . . . the candidate . . ."

She smiled, and it was the first time I had ever seen a smile that had nothing whatsoever to do with the mouth or lips. This smile was wholly in her eyes, and I later came to realize that this was part of her ability as a smile ventriloquist. Just by being in the vicinity, Jen could make everything and everyone smile, without letting on that she was doing so.

"I really don't know that much about him," she said. "But if you want your questions answered . . . Carl, come here a second?"

She called over a young man standing a few yards away. Carl was unshaven, balding, and maybe twenty pounds overweight. Not a horrible-looking guy, but not really my type.

"Hey," Carl said, proving that if nothing else he was a charming conversationalist.

"This is Richard Kilmer . . . a journalist. He's looking for some information." She went on to tell me that Carl knew far more about this particular candidate than she did.

"What do you want to know?" Carl asked.

"Well, to be perfectly honest," I said, "I was more interested in the female point of view."

Carl frowned his disdain at me and walked away.

"You should have said so," Jen said, scanning the crowd. "Then let's see what we can find for you."

She was playing with me, no doubt looking for some female shot putter to stick me with. "I was interested in your point of view," I said.

"Let me guess," she said. "You're particularly interested in my point of view coupled with coffee, drinks, or dinner."

"That's uncanny," I said.

"Why didn't you say so in the first place?"

"I only use honesty as a last resort."

She thought about it for a few moments, as if weighing it. Then, "Coffee."

# I hated that look.

It was a look that said, *You're full of shit, Richard. You know it and I know it, so let's move on, shall we?*

My problem with the look, and with Jen, for that matter, was that it and she were always right. In that case, I had just tried to tell her that we should drive to her parents' house in upstate New York on Monday, rather than Sunday. I had lamely claimed that we'd hit less traffic that way, but she knew it was really because I wanted to watch the pro football games. When it comes to football, I'm somewhere between a fanatic and a lunatic.

"You want to watch football tomorrow," she said. It wasn't a question, but rather a statement of fact.

"Football?" I asked. "Tomorrow? God, the week flew by; it never entered my mind. Where do the days go?"

She laughed, and asked, "What time are the Giants playing?"

"The Giants? The Giants? The name sounds familiar. . . ."

"Richard . . ."

"One o'clock. They're playing the Redskins at home."

She shook her head in amazement. "Redskins. How can a team have a name like that in the twenty-first century?"

I nodded vigorously. "Exactly. They are politically incorrect pigs. Which is the main reason I want them to be defeated tomorrow. Somebody has to take a stand on the side of decency, and they will leave Giants Stadium tomorrow having learned a moral lesson. And it's about time."

There was that look again. It was time to come clean.

"The winner makes the playoffs. The playoffs, Jen. That's three wins from the Super Bowl. I really want to see it."

"Then why didn't you just say so in the first place?"

I shrugged. "Honesty? Last resort? Remember?"

She smiled. "Tell me about it." That was sort of a catchphrase she used whenever someone told her something she already knew, which was pretty often.

Jen agreed that the game was not to be missed, so she called her mother and told her we'd be there on Monday. It wasn't a big deal, since we'd been invited for Christmas, which was Friday. Her parents lived in Ardmore, a small town about two hours from our apartment in Manhattan on the Upper West Side. We had a two-bedroom on the thirty-third floor of a building called the Montana, on Eighty-seventh and Broadway. If there is a piece of real estate in the world that should not be called Montana, it is that one.

Jen had told me a couple of weeks before that her parents were excited to meet me, that I was the first boyfriend she had ever brought home. As always, it was jarring to hear her call me a "boyfriend"; we seemed to be so much more than that. I think on some level that's why I bought a ring and planned to ask her to marry me the following week. If she accepted, and I anticipated that she would, I would instantly make the quantum leap from "boyfriend" to "fiancé."

In a matter of hours after first meeting Jen I had regressed from independent twenty-nine-year-old male, unwilling (or afraid, if some of my dates were to be believed) to make a commitment, to pathetic twenty-nine-year-old puppy, panicked that she wouldn't like me. My amazement that she did, that in fact she grew to love me, was not modesty, false or otherwise. The simple truth was that Jen could have had absolutely anyone she wanted, and she chose me. It was the kind of situation for which the word "hallelujah!" was coined.

Jen moved into my apartment four months after we met. We chose mine because it was bigger, and because I owned it, while she was just renting. In a matter of hours, the apartment went from a place completely devoid of personality to a real home. When Jen got finished with it, my impersonal group of rooms had become the kind of home the Waltons would beg to spend Thanksgiving in.

Jen even liked my friends, few in number as they were. Don't misunderstand, for the most part my friends are intelligent, successful people. They may have their faults, but there's not a terrorist in the bunch, and the world would be a better place if their level of goodness prevailed everywhere. But as a group, we have one flaw; we argue about everything. They are heated, sometimes stimulating, sometimes childish debates about a wide range of topics from sports to politics to people, and the truth is, most outsiders find it a little off-putting.

Since I had only arrived in town three months before meeting Jen, I had only had time to develop two close friendships. I had met both John Sucich and Willie Citrin playing basketball at the Y, and discovered we all had a love of politics, sports, and women. Not necessarily in that order.

Jen was an insider from day one, and one particular night was a perfect example as to why. We went out to the Legends Sports Bar to have dinner and watch the Knicks-76ers game. John and Willie brought along dates, who in my mind were named Somebody and Whoever. For both John and Willie, two dates was a long-term relationship, so I didn't spend too much time memorizing the women's names. I knew it was dehumanizing, but I figured that if they didn't want to be dehumanized, what the hell were they doing with John and Willie?

That night we were arguing about the death penalty, a frequent topic. John and Willie were for it; I am so strongly against it that I once wrote a series of articles advocating my position. As

6

always, they told me that if my sister were murdered I'd feel differently. I don't have a sister, but they'd probably killed her off fifty times. Jen was on their side; this was a woman who quite literally wouldn't harm a fly, but would apparently toast a convicted murderer or rapist without thinking twice.

I neither won nor lost the argument—in fact, the one common thread through all our arguments was that no one ever won or lost. Not a single time in my memory had anyone been convinced to change a position, no matter how stupid that position might be. But I could always tell when Willie and John were unhappy with how things were going, because they would say that they were fed up with my "Ivy League bullshit," as if my having gone to the University of Pennsylvania disqualified me from having a legitimate point of view.

Our second argument this night was about third basemen. It was and is my opinion that Mike Schmidt is the best all-around third baseman ever to play the game. John went with Brooks Robinson, while Willie picked Pie Traynor. Now, I'm sure Pie was great, but he was sucking dirt for about fifty years before Willie was born, so Willie's position was inherently uninformed. You could always tell the guy with the inherently uninformed position; he was the one who yelled the loudest.

Jen cast her vote for David Wright, a ridiculous choice so early in his career, but he was a Met and she always thought the Mets were the best. Somebody and Whoever were bored silly by the entire spectacle, though at one point Somebody said, "My brother likes sports."

Before long, Somebody and Whoever said their good-byes, while John and Willie stayed with Jen and me so we could keep the arguments going. When all the yelling was over, Jen announced, "Richard's spending Christmas at my parents' house."

"Whoa!" was John's response. "This is more serious than I thought."

"We're living together, idiot," I pointed out with my characteristic subtlety. "You didn't think that was serious?"

"Well, Richie, my boy, I'm afraid things are about to change."

"What are you talking about?" I asked.

John turned to Willie. "You tell him."

Willie sighed, as if he hated to have to break the bad news. "Rich," he said, "suppose you had a daughter who looked like that." He pointed at Jen. "Now suppose she brought home a guy who looked like that." He pointed at me. "You see where I'm going with this?"

"I'm afraid I do," I said.

Jen wouldn't hear of it. "They'll love him." She kissed me. "I love him."

A stupid grin on my face, I turned to John and Willie. "She loves me. Eat your heart out."

# Sunday brunch had become my favorite meal

of the week.

Jen and I would buy a *New York Times* and go down the street to Cassidy's Café. We'd order Bloody Mary mixes (I can't seem to get myself to say "Virgin Mary"), and then Jen always had an omelet, while I had French toast and bacon.

The only conversation that would take place was the ordering of food and the occasional "Please pass the sports section" and "Are you done with the News of the Week in Review?" We both viewed *New York Times* reading as a serious matter, and one that was not compatible with chitchat.

Unfortunately, on that day I hadn't even finished Maureen Dowd's column when I heard Jen's name called out. I looked up to see Sandy Thomas and her husband, Adam. Sandy had been Jen's best friend since she got to the city two years ago, and they were co-owners of a small art gallery in Soho. It's another of the things that Jen and I did not have in common; she was a terrific painter and a true connoisseur, while my favorite "art" was Garfunkel.

I knew Jen wanted us to be alone almost as much as I did, but she invited them to sit down, and they jumped at the offer. I wasn't pleased, but it wasn't that I didn't like them. Adam was a decent enough guy, although he mostly talked about how much money he had, and I liked Sandy quite a bit. It was more that this time with Jen and the *Times* was sacred, and only came along once a week.

But my charm soon asserted itself, as it was wont to do, and it was a quite pleasant couple of hours. Jen and Sandy had a discourse on artists, books, and music, while Adam and I grunted about sports. Of course, I had to call an early halt to the session, so that I would get home in time to see the game.

I have to admit I didn't think about Jen's parents during the Redskin-Giants game. Basically what I thought about were the Redskins and the Giants. It was a typical game, played on a cold December afternoon where the teams played ball control and fought over small pieces of real estate like it was Hamburger Hill. The outcome was in doubt until the final play of the game, but the Giants won, which meant they were going to the playoffs, and therefore all was right with the world.

In the morning, I dressed, packed, and went down for a newspaper. Jen dressed quickly, as always, but packing to her was something akin to what pyramid-building was to the ancient Egyptians. It was an agonizing, arduous process, with seemingly thousands of difficult decisions every step of the way. The end result was always the same; she packed virtually everything she owned.

When I returned there were four suitcases near the door, waiting for Richard the pack mule to take them downstairs.

"I assume you want me to take these to the car?" I asked.

She nodded. "Please. I'll get the ones in the bedroom."

"There are more?" I asked, but didn't wait for an answer. I reached down to pick up the first one, which was either nailed to the floor or weighed a thousand pounds. "What's in here, your rock collection?"

"Tell me about it," she said, and laughed, and within twenty minutes I managed to get all her stuff, plus my one bag, loaded into the car. It was a relatively warm day, in the high forties, and

Jen suggested that I open the top on my convertible. I declined, since I preferred not to listen to the sound of my teeth chattering all the way upstate. We did open the windows, though, and it felt good as we got farther and farther out into the country.

We stopped for lunch along the way, and then drove through Jen's hometown on the way to her parents' house. She lived there until she was eighteen, and she took pride in pointing out every landmark there was to point out. The town had clearly overdosed on quaint, but my big-city, cynical eye recognized it as a great place to have come from, even though I was quite pleased that I hadn't.

We actually stopped at a place called the General Store, and it was exactly as one would expect. I could picture Ben Cartwright coming in from the Ponderosa to shop there, or more likely Hoss, since there was an entire corner of the room devoted to a display of licorice.

It was almost four o'clock when we got to Jen's parents' house. They hugged Jen intensely, greeted me warmly, and told me to call them Janice and Ben, which I assumed were their names. All in all, it felt like a good start.

Their house was a Colonial, probably literally, though Janice informed me that it was "only" a hundred and fifty years old. In the city, when we talk about a prewar home, we're referring to World War II. In this town they meant the Revolutionary War. But it was a cool house, with a great fireplace and wood-burning stove in the large combination living room and den. I was starved, and the scent from dinner, as we entered the house, was so extraordinarily great it made me want to eat the air.

Jen and Janice went off to the kitchen, leaving Ben and me sitting on the two chairs near the fireplace. My sense was that he relished this first chance to get to know the man who might marry his little girl. If the roles were reversed and Jen were my daughter, I would be torturing him on a rack to learn the truth about him.

"She's quite a girl," he said.

I nodded. "Sure is."

"What am I talking about?" he asked himself. "She's a young lady."

I nodded again. "Sure is." I thought I was doing pretty well.

"Always had a mind of her own," he said.

A third nod from me, with a small chuckle thrown in for effect. "Still does."

The conversation went on pretty much that way for the next ten minutes. He mouthed a series of platitudes about his daughter, and I vigorously agreed. They all happened to be true, but I probably would have agreed with him if he said Jen was secretary general of the UN. When I arrived, I had checked my integrity at the door; my goal was to be liked.

Dinner was soon served, and though I'm sure I must have had food as good as that sometime in my life, I was at a loss to remember when. Janice made a meat loaf fit for the gods, should the gods happen to eat meat loaf. When surrounded by the mashed potatoes and gravy, it was so delicious that I simply could not stop eating it. If she could liquefy it, I would have taken it intravenously while I slept.

"Would you like some more, Richard?" asked Janice, for the fifteenth time. I had responded to the first fourteen either with yes or, if my mouth was too full to speak, an eager, drooling nod.

"I can't," I said, "unless you have a crane to carry me away from the table."

Janice thought for a moment. "I don't think we do, but Ben has a wheelbarrow in the garage."

I nodded and handed her my plate. "That'll work."

When it was time to go to sleep, I was amazed to discover that Jen and I were sharing a bedroom. I hadn't wanted to bring it up, and just assumed that her parents wouldn't be comfortable with it. Jen, bless her heart, had cleared it with her mother ahead of time. We didn't have sex, but the fact that I was able to hold her through the night was a substantial consolation.

And a wonderful memory.

**If I had any reservations about going there,** I couldn't remember why, as the next few days were totally pleasant. Nothing extraordinary, just eating and talking and looking at the four million pictures they had of Jen at various phases of her life. Unfortunately, it seemed like half of those pictures included one Jack Winston, Jen's high school sweetheart, who Ben informed me was by then a cop in town. As a teenager, Jack was muscular and good-looking, if you happen to like that type. I don't, but since I was the one sleeping with Jen, I could deal with a few pictures of Jack, who hopefully by that time was bald and fat.

The point was, I was quite comfortable with Janice and Ben, and Jen reported that they liked me as well. Mission accomplished. Victory was mine.

On Christmas Eve, after Janice and Ben had gone to sleep, Jen took me outside and gave me my favorite present. She led me out to a gazebo at the rear of the property, and we made love. Afterward, she started to laugh.

"What's so funny?" I asked.

"When I was a girl, maybe ten or eleven years old, my friends and I used to come back here and talk about the type of man we were going to marry. We used to describe our Mr. Wonderful down to the last detail."

"And you described me?"

"No." She smiled. "That's why I'm laughing."

"You do realize you'll never get me with that attitude?"

She looked at me and smiled her knowing smile. "Are you kidding? I've got you neatly wrapped with a bow."

I was going to hold off until New Year's, but that seemed like the perfect time. I reached into my pocket and took out the little box that had been burning a hole in it for two weeks. "Then you might as well have this."

She looked at the box and then at me, disbelieving. She opened the box, saw the ring, and started to cry. Then she hugged me, so hard that I thought I was going to break.

"I love you, Richard."

"So you're saying yes?"

She shrugged. "Might as well. I don't see Mr. Wonderful coming along anytime soon."

She dragged me back to the house, then woke up Janice and Ben to tell them the news. Much to my relief they seemed pleased, and things were all warm and cuddly, except for the part where Ben threatened to dismember me if I ever hurt his little girl.

Christmas morning dawned with the sun shining and temperatures expected to reach into the mid-fifties, unheard-of for December. Jen wanted me to take a ride with her, so after polishing off seven or eight of Janice's waffles, I rolled my fat, overstuffed self out to the car.

I was feeling so good that I agreed to Jen's request to open the convertible top. Our first stop was to see a high school friend of hers, Nancy Brunell, who had just gotten back into town to spend the holidays with her parents. They spent a half hour gushing over the ring and our engagement, then an equal amount of time rehashing what sounded like boring high school times, though they laughed hysterically at each recollection. Nancy even took out their yearbook, and they discussed the fate of virtually every one of their classmates since high school. Jen sensed that I was about to doze off, so she announced that we were off to see Kendrick Falls.

"Uh-oh," Nancy said to me. "You'd better watch yourself."

"Why is that?" I asked.

"Whenever Jen took a boy to Kendrick Falls, they didn't come back the same."

Jen laughed and, once we were back in the car, explained that Kendrick was a waterfall that served as the local make-out place in high school.

"Did you go there with Jack Winston?" I asked.

She nodded. "I believe that I did. Pretty much every night."

"He's probably bald and fat by now."

"Could be."

"You repelled his advances, right?"

She nodded again. "Almost every one." Then she sniffed the air. "I love the smell of jealousy in the morning," she said. "It smells like victory."

Before long we were out on a country road, heading for the falls. In a few minutes, what had been a beautiful day seemed to be turning somewhat cloudy, and the wind started to pick up. Somebody obviously reminded Mother Nature that it was December.

"You want me to stop and put the top up?" I asked.

"Not yet," she said. "It feels good. And the falls is just another couple of miles up the road."

Within a few moments, even Jen seemed to be regretting her decision. The wind picked up in intensity, and with ominous black clouds seemingly everywhere, I had to turn on my lights.

Jen's look was one of surprise and a little concern. "It looks like just before a summer thunderstorm," she shouted, so as to be heard above the wind.

I was yelling by then as well. "I'm going to pull over!"

"Be careful!"

With amazing speed, it had gotten totally dark out, pitch-black, and it seemed as if the lights were not working. I quickly pulled the switch in and out, then I was gripped by panic when I realized that they were working, but that somehow this was a darkness they could not pierce.

I quickly looked toward Jen, but I couldn't make her out in the blackness. "I can't see!" I screamed.

"Richard!" she yelled, the fear in her voice reflecting my own. We had driven into a nightmare.

I tried to slow down and pull over, but I really had no idea where the sides of the road were. The one thing I did know was that I had to stop that car. Suddenly the wheels on the right side started to give out, and I realized that I had moved too far over and that we were careening off the road.

"Richard! No!" Jen yelled again, but in the wind it sounded more muted, almost as if she were calling me from a distance.

We started to pitch to the right, and the ground seemed to disappear under us. The car was out of my control, but I would not have known where to take it anyway, as the darkness was complete.

It was as if an unseen hand had picked us up and rolled us over. I reached out to grab Jen, to protect her, but I came up with air. The car started to roll; it was probably just once or twice but it felt like a hundred times, as if it would never stop. Jen was no longer screaming; I couldn't tell if I was or not.

The car finally stopped moving, and had fortunately landed right side up. "Jen? Are you okay?"

She didn't answer, which sent a new shock of panic through me like a needle. "Jen? Answer me, please!"

Suddenly, as if someone were drawing a curtain, the clouds started to disperse. I have never seen anything like it, before or since, but within no more than five seconds the wind had abated, light had been restored, and the sun started to come through.

Jen was not in the car.

There was not a trace of her, and I instantly cursed my decision to leave the top open. Jen was no doubt thrown from the car, and might be somewhere out on the road, possibly in danger from oncoming traffic.

I scrambled out of the car and headed back toward the road. I felt fuzzy, light-headed, but I don't remember my head hitting anything. In any event, I figured I was okay, since I was running, but I didn't stop to check. I had to find Jen; she simply had to be all right.

It was only ten or so yards to the road, and drivers who saw my car slowed down and stopped to inquire about my condition. I didn't see Jen anywhere, which I took as semi-good news, since she must have landed in the softer shrubbery along the side of the road.

A man stopped his car and rushed over to me. "Are you okay?"

"My girlfriend . . . she was thrown from the car. Help me find her. Please."

"But are you okay?"

He was looking at my forehead, and when I put my hand to it, I realized that I was bleeding from a wound just above my left temple. It didn't hurt, and I had other things to worry about at the moment.

"I'm fine. We need to find her."

He nodded and yelled the message to others who were coming over, and we all started combing through the brush. I was in a total panic, screaming her name and desperately rushing around, but knowing in my gut that if she were all right, she would be answering me.

Three police cars arrived and I told one of the officers what had happened.

"How far back did you start to lose control of the car?" he asked.

"I don't know . . . it couldn't have been too far," I said. "The storm came up so fast . . ."

"What storm?"

I did not have time to discuss the weather with this man;

I needed to focus on finding Jen. "There was a storm. It got completely dark, and windy . . . I couldn't see, even with the lights on."

"We need to get a bandage on that wound," he said, referring to the blood coming from my head. It had mostly stopped, and was not something I was worried about. I told him to disregard it, and reluctantly he did.

The police helped to organize the search, going well back down the road in case Jen had been thrown out early in the incident. It didn't seem possible, since I had heard her scream just before we rolled over. But I didn't want to rule anything out, and they weren't listening to me anyway, so I continued looking.

Time passed; it seemed like hours but it was probably only minutes. It wasn't possible, but Jen just wasn't there. I was starting to face that fact when one of the officers came back to me and confirmed it.

"Your girlfriend is not here," he said.

I nodded, but none of it was making any sense.

"Have you had any alcoholic beverages, sir?"

"You think I'm drunk?" Was this guy kidding me?

"I didn't say that, sir. Please answer my question."

"It's eleven o'clock in the morning. . . . We went for a ride. . . . No, for God's sakes, I haven't had anything to drink."

He asked me to perform a few physical maneuvers . . . walking a straight line, touching my nose with my eyes closed . . . things like that. I was frustrated, but I did it so we could move on.

He was finally satisfied, and the talk turned back to the accident and Jen's disappearance.

"Maybe she was dazed," I said, though not really believing it. "Maybe she walked away."

He obviously didn't believe it either. "Where would she go?"

"Well, she was from around here, so . . . ," I said, and then I saw it. On his uniform shirt, the name WINSTON.

"Are you Jack Winston?"

He was surprised that I knew that. "Yes. How is it you know me?"

"The woman I was with is Jennifer Ryan."

There was no sign of recognition in his face, so I pressed on. "She was your girlfriend in high school. Jennifer Ryan."

Still no reaction. "I don't believe I know the name, sir."

How stupid was this man? "Her family lives up the road. Can we go there? Maybe somebody picked her up and drove her home."

"Without you?" he asked.

"I don't know . . . but she's got to be somewhere."

He agreed to take me to the house, and I led him there. When we pulled up, he said, with apparent skepticism, "Your girlfriend grew up here?"

"Yes."

As soon as the car stopped, I jumped out and ran to the front door. Somewhere in the back of my mind it registered that the house looked slightly different, perhaps more tattered and less well-cared-for. Effects of the storm?

Officer Winston came up behind me as I rang the bell and Janice answered. "Yes?" she asked in greeting.

I started to babble about the accident, but my attention was drawn to the interior of the house. It appeared different; it's hard to explain, but it looked as if somebody had gone over the place with a warmth remover.

Janice was confused and looked at Winston. "Jack? What's going on?"

I didn't hear his answer, as I was already moving past Janice and into the house. The differences were even more stark than I had first realized; the furniture was not the same, family pictures were gone from the walls. . . . I moved quickly toward the room that Jen and I had slept in.

I vaguely heard Winston yelling after me as I opened the door and received what felt like an electric jolt. It was no longer a bedroom; it was more like a den or office.

My mind couldn't seem to process what might be going on. I headed back to the living room and ran into Janice and Winston, who had been following me.

"What is going on here?" I demanded. "Why have you changed everything?"

"What are you talking about?" Janice asked.

"Where is Ben?"

Janice almost recoiled from my question. "My husband Ben?"

"Yes."

"He died almost twenty years ago."

I was starting to lose it, and I grabbed her arm. "Why the hell are you saying this? Why are you doing this?"

Officer Winston roughly pulled me away. "That's enough. We're out of here. Sorry, Mrs. Ryan."

I pulled back. "Wait. Janice . . . Mrs. Ryan . . . I stayed here the last four nights. With your daughter. Jen and I are going to be married, but we were in an accident."

Her reaction was immediate; she slapped me in the face and would probably have killed me if Winston would have let her. "Get out of my house," she said through clenched teeth. "Get out and never come back."

Winston led me outside, but I again pulled away and ran toward the rear of the house. I headed toward the gazebo where Jen and I had made love the night before, where we had committed to a life together, but it no longer existed. In its stead was an old pickup truck, out of service and up on blocks.

And that's when I went crazy.

**The next thing I can remember, a shrink was** asking me questions. If he told me his name, I don't recall it. He seemed to be assigned to this small-town medical clinic emergency room, so it probably wasn't Freud.

I was a little fuzzy-headed; they checked me out and bandaged my head, and I assume they gave me a sedative. I can't blame them; I had gone berserk to the point where I can't remember exactly what I had done. I regretted my actions, since they were counterproductive, and they left me lying in the hospital instead of out looking for Jen.

"This young woman who is missing . . . you can visualize her clearly?" he asked.

I nodded. "Of course. We are engaged. This is not somebody I met once on the street."

"Have you had many serious relationships with women?"

This guy had to be kidding me. "Look, am I being held here?" I asked. "Did I commit a crime?"

He smiled. "You committed no crime, so you are not under arrest. But I think you will admit that you are troubled, and—"

I stood up, adjusting myself so as not to lose my balance. "Troubled? You have no idea."

21

The doctor tried to persuade me to stay and talk to him some more, but that was obviously out of the question. I was already trying to formulate a plan in my mind. There was some kind of conspiracy going on, some effort being made to keep Jen away from me, maybe even to deny her very existence. But too many people knew the truth; not everyone could be in on this, and I planned to retrace our steps until I found people I could count on.

Once I left the hospital, I got my bearings, at least location-wise, and realized that I wasn't far from Nancy Brunell's house. I headed over there, understanding that she might well be a part of whatever was going on, but hoping that she wasn't.

I rang the doorbell and a young man answered it. For a brief moment I feared that there was no Nancy Brunell, that maybe she had disappeared as well. "Is Nancy home?" I asked.

"Sure," was his cheerful response, before calling out, "Hey, Nance! Somebody here to see you!"

Moments later Nancy appeared, and my relief was tangible. I was not crazy; I had met this woman the day before, I was in this very house, and my knowing that she lived here was proof of it. At least to me.

"Nancy," I said, "something really weird is going on. Jen and I were in an accident, and now she's gone."

Nancy's face reflected confusion and then a little fear, and I saw her tug on the young man's shirt as he started to leave, in effect asking him to stay. No doubt to protect her from the stranger saying these strange things. To protect her from me.

"Do I know you?" she asked.

I could hear my heart hit the floor. "I was here yesterday. With Jen."

"I'm sorry," she said. "But I don't think I've ever met you before, and I don't know any Jen."

"Not you too . . . ," was all I could say. "Not you too . . ."

The young man said, "Sorry, pal. You must have the wrong

house," and closed the door in my face. As I walked away from the door, almost staggering to the street, I saw Officer Winston sitting in his squad car, obviously keeping an eye on me. He was clearly waiting for some provocation to arrest me, to get me off the streets of his happy, cozy, stinking town.

I figured that maybe this was all a dream. That would be a good thing, because it would still be going on, and Jen would be there when I woke up. There could be no other explanation. I was not crazy. I simply was not crazy.

I knew I had to get out of that town. I walked down to a rental car place I had seen a few days before, when I was with Jen, when the world made sense. My car was badly damaged and I remembered Winston saying it was being repaired, but I couldn't stay there another day. I rented a car and had reached the outskirts of town when I saw the General Store, which Jen and I had stopped in on the way into town. I pulled into the parking lot, willing to give this insanity one more chance to end.

A woman stood behind the cash register, and I approached her.

"Excuse me, ma'am. Do you know someone named Jennifer Ryan?"

She thought for a moment. "Don't think so. She from around here?"

I nodded. "Do you know Janice Ryan?"

She brightened. "Sure do. Lives about two miles from here."

"Does she have a daughter?"

She hesitated for a moment. "No."

"Is Janice married?"

"Not anymore," she said.

"What happened to her husband?"

She seemed suspicious. "Why do you want to know all this?"

"I think I might know her."

She nodded, as if that were good enough. "Ben must be dead a good twenty, twenty-five years now."

"Can you tell me how he died?" I asked.

A wary nod. "Killed himself. Hung himself out in back where they used to have a gazebo."

"Do you know why he did that?"

She looked at me even more suspiciously. "After all this time . . . why are you asking these questions?"

"Please, I'm not trying to hurt anyone. It's just important that I know."

"Their little girl died . . . she was murdered. Ben just couldn't handle life after that."

# I had to get home.

Home was where I lived, where my friends were, where I prayed Jen was. I didn't feel like there was any chance of my getting to the bottom of this; at least not in that town. The unhappy truth seemed to be that there could be no real-world explanation. None of this was consistent with reality; it was either a dream or I was insane. Or both.

I would find out when I got home.

The drive was surreal. I kept looking over to the passenger seat, to Jen, to see her as she was when we'd made the drive out earlier in the week. The fact that she was not there didn't stop me from looking.

I drove down the West Side Highway and parked in the lot underneath my building. Our building. I realized with some embarrassment that I was not ready to go upstairs. It was as if our home were the last card I had to play, and I didn't want to use it quite yet.

I walked over to the Legends Sports Bar. It was college bowl season, so I could be pretty sure John and Willie would be there. I was feeling very mixed emotions; on the one hand I was craving being with someone I knew, friends who would acknowledge the

25

history we had together. On the other hand, I was afraid of what they would say about Jen. They had to know her, I was positive they knew her, but I was still scared shitless that they wouldn't. And for all I knew, maybe they didn't exist either.

I felt some relief when I saw them sitting at our usual table. There were three women with them, two of whom I recognized from the other night, which seemed decades ago. The third one I'd never seen before.

At least I didn't recall ever seeing her before. She was the first one to notice me walking toward the table. She brightened, an immediate look of recognition on her face, and stood up. She said, "You made it," with obvious pleasure, and kissed me. It was a light kiss, on the mouth, but it didn't feel like a first kiss.

Willie said, "We were about to put out a police report on you," and John added with apparent concern and relief, "Where the hell have you been?" He looked at my bandage. "What happened to your head?"

I decided to go straight for it. "I've been at Jen's house. Where she grew up."

The woman who kissed me put an exaggerated pout on her face and said, "Who's Jen?"

"It's his sister," John said.

"No, Jen's his grandmother," was Willie's response.

"His dog," John said. "Definitely his dog."

They were joking, trying to cover for me in front of this woman, who apparently had some right to be jealous. But the question was, did they really know Jen?

"I've got to talk to you guys."

I apparently said it with enough intensity that they realized that whatever was going on was not a joke.

"Okay . . . sure," John said.

"Can we take a walk?" I asked.

Within moments we had left the table, and I could hear the women talking among themselves about the weird way I was acting. I waited until we got outside to start.

"I've got to ask you guys something. I am not joking, so please give me straight answers."

They both nodded, worried but clueless about where this was going.

"Last weekend, was I here with you, at this bar, watching the Knicks play the 76ers?"

They both nodded, and John said, "Sure. What's going on, Rich?"

"Who were we with?"

Willie motioned back toward the inside of the bar. "Them."

"Those three?" I asked.

"Right," said Willie. "You okay, Rich?"

"Was one of them my date?"

John nodded again. "Lauren."

"She's the one who kissed me?" I asked.

Willie said, "Of course. Hey, Rich, you're weirding me out. What the hell is going on?"

Asking me what's going on would have been humorous if it wasn't so pathetic. "Do you guys know somebody named Jennifer? Jen?"

Willie shook his head no, and John said, "I dated a girl in college named Jen. I don't think you ever met her."

I sagged against a parked car. My nightmare was ongoing. They asked me again what was going on, and I told them everything, in excruciating detail. I kept hoping for some flash of recognition, some restored memory, but there was none. Nor was there any sign of deception, but I wouldn't have expected that. These were my friends; they wouldn't be a part of any conspiracy. And there couldn't be a conspiracy this wide.

When I was finished, John put his hand on my shoulder. "Rich, I don't know what to tell you. I would say it's some kind of amnesia deal, except then you'd be forgetting things that happened. What you're doing is remembering stuff that never happened. But if you were living with somebody, if you were going to get married, we'd know about it."

"I don't know much about this stuff," said Willie, with apparent embarrassment. "But I think you ought to talk to somebody. My sister went to this shrink, she says he's really good, and—"

I interrupted him. "Will you guys take a ride with me?"

They agreed, and John went back in to tell the women that we had to leave in order to deal with something. Willie took advantage of the time to say, "Hey, Rich, you're not bullshitting us, are you? I mean, this isn't some kind of weird joke, right? I mean, I hope it is, in a way, but if it is, you should tell me now."

"Willie, it's the furthest thing from a joke I've ever experienced."

We walked over to the parking lot and got in my car. On the way, I kept mentioning stories of things they had done with Jen and I, of times we had shared. I was desperate to get them to remember something, anything, but they kept drawing blanks. They thought I was crazy, and it was becoming pretty likely that they were right.

We drove down to the art gallery in Soho, the one that Jen was a partner in with Sandy Thomas. John and Willie had never been to the gallery, though they certainly should have known of its existence through Jen.

If Jen ever existed.

The gallery was instead a check cashing/Western Union place, with MoneyGram advertisements in the front window. I drove around the block, in case I had the wrong address, but I knew that I didn't. I had been there numerous times. To pick up Jen, not to send MoneyGrams.

I begged off going back to the bar and dropped Willie and John off there. I asked them to convey my regrets to Lauren, whom they informed me I had been dating on and off for almost six weeks.

As they were getting out of the car, John said, "You gonna be okay?"

"Probably not," I said.

"I'll get you the name of that shrink," said Willie. "Just in case you want to use it."

"Okay," I said, if only to get them out of the car.

It was time to go home.

I took a deep breath before I entered my apartment . . . our apartment. I turned on the lights and felt like I had been punched in the gut. It was nothing like I had left it, and exactly like it had been before Jen came into my life. No pictures on the walls, no throw rugs, no treadmill, none of the small touches that Jen had added to turn it into a home.

I moved through the apartment, almost in a daze, but coherent enough to realize that there was no trace of Jen there. I got to the bedroom and looked at the bed, still unmade, yet Jen had never left an unmade bed in her life.

I didn't feel my legs give out from under me, but somehow I found myself sitting on the floor.

And then I started to cry.

*The subject has returned to his environment.*

That was how the man known as Juice began his first official report. He knew that was the kind of language his superiors preferred, so he used it, even though he thought it was ridiculous. Were he to write in his normal style, it would have read, *Kilmer went back home.*

It was also their idea that he use a code name in all aspects of the operation, and though he found it a little dramatic, he would have suggested it had they not. These people put everything in writing, that was their style, and he didn't want his real name showing up anywhere.

Not with murder involved.

The name "Juice" was his own idea. It was taken from O. J. Simpson, a man he had no use for, but one he felt he could learn from. The real Juice had literally gotten away with murder, and was living what seemed to be a carefree life in Florida, playing golf and thumbing his nose at those who would have him in jail, or worse.

Then he tempted fate by doing that stupid thing in Vegas, and in the process gave the people who hated him another bite at the apple. They didn't waste it, and they put him away.

The lesson for the new Juice was that there is always time to screw things up, no matter how well everything is going. And when this job went well, his life would make Simpson's time in Florida seem like living in a dungeon.

The new Juice would never have to work again; he would buy some villa on a beach in the Caribbean and spend all his time sucking down drinks with those little umbrellas in them. Or better yet, he'd buy his own beach. Either way, doing something stupid simply wasn't his style.

For the time being, all Juice had to do was keep close tabs on Kilmer and chronicle every move he made. With the technological tools at Juice's disposal, that would be easy enough. Maybe even a little boring . . .

Kilmer was likely to be pretty pathetic, running around like a chicken without a head. But that wasn't Juice's problem; all he had to do was keep track of him and deal with any eventualities that came up.

And then, of course, when the time came, to put Kilmer well out of his misery.

# I slept for about an hour, just long enough

to dream about Jen. It was a bizarre dream, but certainly no more bizarre than my waking life. We're walking on the street, and she takes my arm. The look on her face is frightened, but when I ask what's wrong, she says that I know what's wrong, that I've always known.

Within moments, she starts to disappear . . . no, it's more like disperse, right in front of my eyes. Her body starts to somehow blend in with the air, until there is no distinguishing it and air is all that is left. The entire time, her grip on my arm is getting stronger, as if she is fighting this force, and she's saying my name, over and over.

Until finally she is gone.

Unlike most dreams, this one didn't fade when I woke up; every bit of it remained embedded in my mind, like frames in a movie. It was somehow comforting, though I'm not sure why. Maybe it was simply because in a way I had gotten to spend more time with Jen, when I no longer expected to.

I made myself coffee and tried to make some sense out of what had happened. I believed that Jen did, maybe does, exist. She was too real, my memories too vivid, for me to have made her up. I'm simply not that imaginative, nor do I consider myself that crazy. I say this knowing that if someone else told me this exact story, I would dismiss it as looney.

I did a fairly thorough search of my apartment, which confirmed my fear and expectation that there would be no trace of Jen. I was already realistic enough to doubt that I was going to find her anywhere, except perhaps in my mind, but I simply could not give up looking. I was not yet ready to go on with my life as if Jen had never happened.

I spent the next three days retracing our steps, talking to people who knew Jen, going to places we went together. I ran into one wall after another, and accomplished nothing other than convincing pretty much everybody that I was a lunatic. The jeweler who sold me Jen's ring claimed never to have met me, and I had no financial record of my ever having purchased it. Sandy Thomas said that I looked familiar, but she couldn't quite place the face. Et cetera, et cetera, et cetera.

I was not doing too well.

Willie's sister set up an appointment for me with her shrink, Matthew Rawlins, a kindly gentleman who specialized in art therapy. He would have his patients draw pictures, artistic talent didn't matter, as a way of opening up one's feelings about the subject and related matters. He had me draw Jen, and I spent about thirty minutes of the forty-five-minute session crying.

As we approached the end of the session, he said, "You're in terrible pain."

"That's not exactly a news flash," I said. "I've known that for a while."

Dr. Rawlins said that it was the pain that was important, more so than the credibility of the cause. He suggested long-term treatment, it was a hundred and fifty an hour and he supplied the crayons. I told him I'd think it over.

Lauren, the woman from the sports bar whom Willie and John told me I was dating, called to find out why I had stopped coming around. I apologized, but told her I had met someone else. She hung up on me, which was probably as smart a thing as she had ever done.

After a few more days, I set up a meeting with Scott Carroll, an editor I've worked with at *Manhattan* magazine, since even a raving, mourning lunatic needs money to live. We met at a small Italian restaurant called Spumoni's, on Second Avenue and Eighty third Street. Scott's also a friend, and he and his wife once had dinner at this place with Jen and me.

I didn't ask him about Jen, since I dreaded the reaction it would get. Scott is funny, incisive, and brutally honest, and there was a chance he would cut me to ribbons with his comments, once he heard my story. So instead I pitched him ideas for pieces I could write for the magazine, none of which I was really interested in or motivated to write. He didn't seem terribly impressed either.

"Don't take this the wrong way, Richard," he said, "but why don't you write about what you're going through?"

Since I hadn't mentioned to him anything about what I was going through, I wasn't sure what he was saying. "What are you talking about?"

"I'm talking about this woman you're looking for, Jennifer?"

"Did I speak to you about her?" I asked.

He shook his head. "No, but I'm the only person in America you haven't." He leaned forward. "Conservatively speaking, twenty people have told me about it."

"So I've become the laughingstock of the city?"

"Why are you limiting it to the city?" he asked, smiling to soften the blow. "Richard, you're screwed up, okay? Join the club. But at least you're screwed up in an interesting way. People would lap it up."

Was he serious? "You're suggesting I expose myself as a maniac in your magazine?"

He laughed. "You're already exposed. Why not get paid for it?"

"I'm having trouble seeing the humor in this, Scott."

"Sorry," he said, though I doubt that Scott has ever been sorry about anything he's said in his life. "But writing the piece is a good idea. A great idea, actually."

"I don't think so."

"That's because you're not opening your mind to the possibilities. Think of it as a chance to present your side of it. Or as a cathartic, cleansing experience. Or as an attempt to help others who might have the same delusion. Or as an opportunity to find Jennifer. Or as a way to sell magazines. Whatever works for you."

"No, thanks," I said, still a little miffed. However, by the end of the lunch he had turned me around. It really could be a way to broaden my search for Jen or, if she was simply a figment of my imagination, to help others with similar figments.

"When can you get it in the magazine?" I asked, by then enthused about the prospect.

"How fast can you write it?"

"I'll get started right away," I said. "As soon as I get home. I'm starting it in my mind right now."

"Great. And one more thing. The magazine will hire a portrait artist who will draw Jennifer to your specifications. Like the police artists do. Can you describe her?"

I nodded. "To the last detail."

"Good," he said. "I'll set it up."

I left him with his coffee and the check, and went home to get to work. I sat down at my computer and had the most intense writing experience of my life. I can usually remain detached from what I write, but this time I couldn't even come close.

I finished at four o'clock in the morning and read over what I'd written.

Jen had come back to life.

She was on every page, in every word. I had conveyed the real Jen, while at the same time openly admitting to the readers that I could not otherwise prove she ever existed. It was simultaneously and incongruously an acknowledgment of insanity and a piece of which I was very proud.

I read it again, and then walked over to the easy chair in the corner of the room. It was the chair Jen always loved to sit in while reading or listening to music. I leaned my head back, and was jolted once again. I felt like I could smell her scent, that incredible scent, in that chair. She was with me, at that moment, in that room, even as I knew she would never be with me again.

And at that moment I did not know how I was going to survive all of this.

**The article appeared four days later, and it** was all that I had hoped it wouldn't be. The primary reaction I received from friends and colleagues, the one they showed to my face, was a combination of pity and incredulousness. I'm sure it cemented my position as the laughingstock of the city, but the stock himself is usually the only person who doesn't actually hear the laughter.

The only positive that initially came out of it was that Jen's picture was out in the media. Under my direction, the sketch artist had done an eerily good job; it looked exactly like her. Since the article was bizarre enough to be picked up by the wire services and online outlets, hopefully anybody who might have known Jen would be able to identify her.

What I did not expect, but should have, were the number of cranks that came out of the woodwork. I got letters and e-mails from every nut in America, all of whom I probably shared a kinship with. They claimed to know Jen, claimed to be Jen, or claimed to be in contact with Jen on the "other side."

The worst part was the phone calls. My phone was listed, and a good many cranks were resourceful enough to look it up. One such person was Lydia Teretzky. I had been pretty much hanging up on everybody, but she sounded older and somehow kindly. She said she could help with my problem, and I said something really dumb. I said, "How?"

It turned out that Lydia Teretzky was a self-described psychic genius, and that wasn't all. By her own admission, she was the world's leading folliclist, which meant she could tell the future by reading hair.

She asked if I had a strand of Jen's hair, but didn't seem overly deterred when I didn't. She professed to understand Jen's plight, babbling on about windows between life and death, and crossing from one side to another.

"There's something else you should know," she said.

"And what is that?" I asked, half expecting her to tell me that Jen was Princess Diana in a previous life.

"Your Jen was dead the entire time that you knew her."

At that very moment I hung up on Lydia Teretzky, world's leading folliclist, psychic to all but the baldest among us. But the calls kept coming, and I starting getting invited on weird local cable TV shows. I declined them all, as my humiliation quotient had already been reached and exceeded.

I'd been having the dream pretty much every night, which, despite how it sounds, felt like a good thing. Simply put, it continued to allow me to spend time with Jen, to reexperience her. It was no wonder that John and Willie kept telling me I needed to get a life.

One night as I was getting into bed my phone rang. It was almost eleven o'clock, and while I had until this point accepted the crank calls with resignation and tolerance, this time I was pissed.

I picked up the phone. "Hello?" It was more of a snarl than a greeting.

I heard a female voice, very tentative. "Mr. Kilmer?"

Something about her tone lessened my anger, but didn't increase my willingness to be bothered at that hour.

"Look, I don't want to be called at my home," I said. "So—"

She interrupted, so I guess I overestimated her tentativeness. "It's about your article, the one in *Manhattan* magazine."

"I'm sure it is, but I don't remember printing my phone number."

"Please, I'm sorry, I know what you're going through. I know everything about what you're going through. I can't tell you how sorry I am."

"Thank you. Good night."

I was about to hang up when she said, "Mr. Kilmer, please hear me out. I think I know who Jennifer is, and I believe I can prove it."

Something about the way she said it, maybe even her lack of certainty, caused my arm to freeze in midair and not hang up. "I'm listening. Who is she?"

"My sister."

"You said you could prove that."

"Yes, I believe I can. Will you give me your e-mail address?"

I gave her the one that I use for readers to write to me to comment on my columns.

"I'll send you an e-mail when we get off the phone," she said. "Hopefully it will prove that I'm right about this. If not, I'm truly sorry to have bothered you."

"Okay," I said, "I'll check it out in the morning."

"Thank you. If it's okay, I'll call you back tomorrow."

"Fine."

We hung up, and I tried to fall asleep, with absolutely no success. After about a half hour, I got up and went to the computer. I opened my e-mail account, and saw that she had sent one. I clicked on it.

I have a cable modem, which is incredibly fast, so within a couple of seconds I was looking at the picture she'd sent.

It was Jen.

My Jen.

"The sister called him," Juice said. That was a piece of information he wanted to convey immediately, which was why he was doing it by phone, rather than by written report.

The voice on the other end was calm and dispassionate, as always. In the little time he had known him, Juice had dubbed him "the Stone" because of his apparent total lack of emotion. "What was the nature of their conversation?"

"What the hell do you think it was? You think they chatted about the weather?"

The Stone was undeterred. "What was the nature of their conversation?"

"She said that her sister and Jen were the same person; she could tell from the sketch in the newspaper. And she sent him an e-mail to prove it; I would assume there was a photo attached. He said he'd look at it in the morning."

"So you have not seen the e-mail?"

"No."

"Why is that?" The Stone's voice was measured, not showing any significant feeling at all.

"I told you," Juice said. "He left his computer in Hick-land. This is a borrowed computer that we haven't penetrated."

"Perhaps you should."

"I will, but it takes time. What do you want me to do?"

"Continue monitoring and recording his actions and communications, and report the results to me. As always."

"You want me to deal with the sister?" He was asking if the Stone wanted her dead, but he wasn't the kind of guy you used the words "kill" or "murder" with. You had to beat around the bush.

"I want you to continue monitoring and recording his actions and communications, and report the results to me. As always."

"Will do."

Click.

**The e-mailed picture looked so much like** Jen that it had to be her. Every feature was exactly the same, down to the minutest detail. In the photograph she was smiling, and it completely captured her personality, the gleam in her eye. It left me stunned, because it meant that there was a Jen. She existed outside of my mind. She was real.

Once I gained control of my emotions, I mentally berated myself for not getting the caller's phone number, or even her name. The call had come through on the caller ID as "Private," so there was no way for me to contact her.

So for now I had nothing but the e-mail. The sender's e-mail address was tallison@gmail.com. At some point, if I had to, I could probably do some tracing using that, but at midnight, sitting at home, it did me little good.

I replied to the e-mail, asking her to call me back immediately, at any hour. I said that it was important, but did not say that the photograph was an exact duplicate of Jen. I wanted to say that to her when I could hear her reaction; it was probably a reflection that I was not feeling very trustful of anyone.

I didn't get an answer. Hopefully all that meant was that she was asleep, and that she would contact me in the morning.

I hoped it would be early in the morning, because I wouldn't be doing much sleeping.

No matter how intently I stared at it, my phone didn't ring until a quarter to ten, and it wasn't Jen's sister. It was Craig Langel, a private investigator I've used a number of times to help me research stories, mostly about big business.

Whatever publication I happened to be writing for at the time usually picked up the tab, which was just as well, since Craig can be expensive. But he's worth the money; he can find out anything there is to find out about anything or anyone, especially in the corporate world.

I don't think Craig ever wasted a word in his life; he came right to the point and always let you know exactly where he stood. He had what I consider a healthy disregard for everything and everyone, and CEOs were singled out for special scorn.

"You okay?" he asked. We hadn't talked since Jen's disappearance.

"I'm getting there. Things haven't gone quite as well as I would have liked lately."

"Yeah," he said, meaning that he had heard about my situation. Everybody on the planet was aware of my situation. "Can I help?"

"I don't think so, but thanks."

"Anything new on your story?" he asked.

I was immediately put off by his referring to my life upheaval as my "story." "What story is that?"

"You don't remember?" he asked, sounding more than a little surprised.

"I don't know what you mean."

"You called me about three weeks ago, said you were working on something major, and that you'd be needing me."

I had no idea what he was talking about. "Craig, I'm sorry, I just don't remember that conversation. Did I get any more specific?"

"You said you couldn't talk more about it yet, but that it had the potential to be Pulitzer territory."

Craig was not prone to hyperbole or inaccuracy. We must have had the conversation exactly as he was describing it, yet as momentous as it sounded, I had no recollection of it at all.

"Shit. I just don't remember."

"Richard, I'm here if you need me. For anything. No charge; not for you personally." The concern was evident in his voice.

"Thanks, I appreciate that. Craig, you can track an e-mail address, right? You can find out whose it is, and where they live?"

"Sure. You got it now?"

I debated with myself for a moment, but then decided to wait. "Maybe tomorrow," I said, and got off the phone, even more worried than I had been before. I was remembering things that everyone else said had never happened, and I was completely forgetting that which clearly did happen. For me to fail to recall something that I thought could win me a Pulitzer was incomprehensible, yet I obviously had.

Was I losing my mind?

# I watched and listened to the phone not

ring until three P.M.

At that point I had to get out of the apartment, even for a couple of minutes, so I went down and got the mail.

When I first got back from the nightmare in Ardmore, checking the mail was something I looked forward to, in the vain hope that I would receive something that would yield some clue about Jen, some proof of her existence.

Once the magazine article ran, getting the mail became a form of torture, as I received literally thousands of letters either wishing me well, mocking me, or providing some form of unproductive tip or piece of information about Jen's whereabouts. I forced myself to read each one, though most of them I discarded before finishing the first couple of sentences.

The number of such letters had started to trail off, but this time there were still at least thirty, intermingled with bills and catalogs. It would give me something to do while praying for Jen's sister to call.

As I opened the door to my apartment, I heard the phone. I dropped the mail on the floor and ran to answer it. I got it on the third ring, or at least the third ring that I heard. I don't know how many rings there were before I entered the apartment, but I was in a state of panic that I might be too late.

"Hello?"

"Mr. Kilmer, my name is Allison Tynes. I called you last night, and sent you the e-mail, and . . ."

"Yes . . . Allison . . . thank you for calling. The photograph is Jen; I'm sure of it."

I could hear the relief in her voice. "Oh, that's wonderful. I was so afraid I was wrong. I was hoping that's what your e-mail meant, but I put off calling you today because I was scared of what you might say."

"Where is she?"

"She's missing. She moved out to California, but disappeared on the way. The police have it as a missing persons case, but haven't come up with anything."

"I have so many questions; can we meet and talk?"

"Of course. When?" she asked.

"When? Soon. Now. Right now."

"That won't be possible," she said. "I'm in Wisconsin. That's where I live. That's where Julie was from."

"Julie?"

"Yes. That's her real name. That's your Jennifer's real name."

It took a moment for me to digest this, before I told her I would fly out to see her the next morning.

"No," she said. "I'll come to New York. I already have my ticket. I was hoping to have a reason to use it."

I told her I would pick her up at the airport, and she agreed, and gave me her flight number.

"Mr. Kilmer . . . ," she said hesitantly, nervously.

"Call me Richard, please."

"Richard, I just wanted to tell you something, for when you see me. Just so you won't be surprised."

"What is it?"

"Julie and I . . . we're twins. Identical twins."

I thanked her for alerting me to this, and when we got off

46

the phone I started mentally bracing myself for the moment when I'd see her. In the back of my mind, actually in the front of my mind, was the very obvious possibility that this might be much ado about nothing, that this woman and her sister might only look very much like Jen, or at least my mental image of her.

Making the situation more interesting, though, was the fact that her sister was missing. If this was not somehow connected to Jen, then it increased the amount of coincidence involved, and I am not a big believer in coincidences.

I picked the mail up off the floor and dumped it on my desk. I couldn't focus on it then; I couldn't focus on anything except meeting Allison Tynes at the airport, and hearing what she had to say.

And seeing what she looked like.

# I waited for her at baggage claim.

I got to JFK an hour early, and the plane was an hour late, so altogether it felt like I stood there for two weeks. I didn't think to hold a sign with her name on it; if she was an identical twin to Jen, I wouldn't need it.

The moment I saw her coming down on the escalator is something I will never forget. It was Jen, gliding down toward me, eyes scanning the room for me. I'm sure that I would have cried, if I were able to breathe. It turns out that breathing is crucial to crying, so I involuntarily was able to fake composure.

She recognized me, I guess from my picture in the magazine, and she waved, a little tentatively. When she got off the escalator, she came over to me and shook my hand. "Richard, it's so nice to meet you. Thank you for picking me up."

I didn't say a word, I couldn't say a word. I just stood there and stared like an idiot.

"Your Jen looked like me?" she asked.

"My Jen is you," I said.

This seemed to make her uncomfortable, as it certainly should have, and she reminded me that she needed to go to the carousel and wait for her bag. Amazingly, it came off quickly, and before long we were in my car heading back to the city.

I found myself reluctant to ask questions, even though I desperately wanted to hear the answer. I was afraid she would say something that would make me realize her sister was not Jen after all and this was all an incredible mistake.

She told me that they lived in Fort Atkinson, Wisconsin, a couple of hours from Milwaukee, and that she and Jen ran an Internet business, selling and shipping individually designed gift baskets.

"So who takes care of the business while you're here?" I asked, glancing over at her. I was doing a lot of glancing; it was something I couldn't control.

"Oh, that's not a problem. We've got some employees who can handle it. The business is doing very well, and besides, there's nothing more important than finding Julie."

I nodded. "Do you have a place to stay while you're here, Allison?"

She nodded. "Everybody calls me Allie. I've got a reservation at the Parker Meridien Hotel. I think it's on Fifty-sixth Street."

"I know where it is. I have a guest bedroom at my place. You're welcome to stay there."

"No, I don't think so. This will be fine."

"Okay," I said. "How about if we drop your things off there, and then grab some lunch, so we can talk?"

She smiled Jen's smile. "Sounds good."

I parked at the hotel, and we walked over to the Capital Grille on Fifty-first. We got a booth, which would provide privacy when we talked. I sensed that she was at least as nervous as I was, and we waited until we ordered before getting down to it.

"Why don't you tell me about Julie's disappearance?" I asked.

She took a deep breath and nodded. "Julie was getting restless last spring. She had always taken acting classes, and had done some modeling, and she was afraid she was going to be stuck in small-town Wisconsin her whole life. She said her "occupational clock" was ticking. So in September she decided she was going to go out to L.A. and try her luck. She promised to be back within three months if she wasn't making progress."

"So when did she go?" I asked.

"May fourtcenth."

I took a deep breath of my own; the timing was right.

"When did you meet Jen?" she asked.

"June."

She nodded her own relief. "Anyway, she promised to stay in touch, though the promise wasn't necessary. I can't remember a day when we didn't talk, no matter where we might be. In fact, she called me a few hours after she left, just to say hello. That was the last time I heard from her."

"So what did you do?"

"We, my parents and I, started to worry after the first day. We couldn't reach her cell phone; it just immediately went to voice mail. By the third day we were going crazy, and we went to our local police chief, Tony Brus."

"What did he say?" I asked.

"That it was really too soon for police action, that an adult on the road who hasn't checked in for that short a time was not worrisome or unusual enough. But we know him, and he's a great guy, so he did some things to try and ease our minds."

"Like what?" I asked.

"He ran traces on her credit cards and cell phone, to see whether she used them. She hadn't made or received any calls except the one to me, and she only used her credit card once, at a gas station about six hours from home."

"So did he pursue it further?"

She nodded. "Yes. He put her information into a national database, which notifies law enforcement agencies everywhere. After a few more days, when we still heard nothing, he notified the FBI."

"So they're on it?"

"Technically, yes. But I don't think they've actively pursued it. I don't think this is high-profile enough. And local police aren't doing much, because no one has any idea where she disappeared."

"What about your police chief?"

"He's doing what he can. He interviewed all of Julie's friends, but there was really nothing to learn. Nobody from Fort Atkinson hurt her; everybody there loves her," she said, starting to choke up and dab at her eyes with her napkin.

"So nothing happened after that, in all this time?"

"Nothing until you," she said.

"I wish me entering the picture was a positive for you," I said. "But at this point I don't see it. None of it fits."

"What do you mean?"

"I'm afraid it raises more questions than it answers. For instance, is Jen . . . Julie . . . the kind of person who would tell you she was going to California, but instead come to New York and never contact you?"

She shook her head. "No."

"But let's assume she did just that. When she got here, why would she completely take on a new identity?"

Allie didn't answer; she obviously couldn't explain it any better than I could.

"Was she afraid of anyone?" I asked. "Was anyone after her? Threatening her for some reason?"

"No. She would have told me if that were the case. I was with her every day. I was with her when she left. Julie was not running away. She was going towards something."

"So all we have is a resemblance," I said, then corrected myself. "No, it's even more than a resemblance. It's uncanny."

"We have more than that," she said. "Both of the people we're talking about, Julie and Jen, they disappeared without a trace. And around the same time Julie left, Jen appeared. That's way more than a coincidence."

"That's true, but it doesn't explain nearly enough." I found that I was forcing myself to be negative, because negative in this case was the same as realistic, and Allie deserved the truth. "There's so much more to this. I lived with her; we were going to be married. She was part of my life. But nobody remembers her; everybody I know and trust tells me that she never existed, that I imagined everything. There can't be a conspiracy this wide."

Again she had nothing to say to this, no way to refute it, so she stayed silent.

"So absolutely none of this makes sense," I said.

"Tell me about it."

I looked up suddenly, surprising her. "What is it?" she asked.

"What you just said . . . 'tell me about it.' Jen said that all the time."

Allie took a deep breath. "Julie and I have been saying that since we were kids. It was a running joke in our family because it drove my mother crazy. She would say something to us, and we would say, 'Tell me about it,' and my mother would say, 'I just did!' "

"So here we have another coincidence," I said.

She smiled. "Tell me about it."

"We have to figure out what to do with this," I said.

"Yes, we do."

"How long are you going to be in town?"

"As long as it takes."

"You're so much like Jen," I said. "Not just how you look, but how you talk. Your mannerisms."

"I'm also just like my sister."

# I walked Allie back to her hotel.

Even saying good-bye to her was awkward; she looked so much like Jen that it would have seemed natural to kiss her. I knew I needed to get that under control. She was not Jen, and in all likelihood her sister wasn't either. In all likelihood there was no Jen.

Allie said that she was going to stay in New York for a while, that she had her computer and could do her work from anywhere. We agreed we would talk the next day and try to plan out our actions. I feared it was going to be a short talk, since I couldn't think of any more actions to take. I had already tried everything I could think of, and had gotten nowhere. If Allie's arrival on the scene presented me with new avenues to pursue, I couldn't quite see them yet.

I also needed to get back to work. I had some money put away, some of it from an inheritance when my father died last year, but if nothing was coming in, it would disappear fast. It was just so hard to focus; all I had thought about for weeks was Jen.

I got the mail before going upstairs, and when I entered my apartment I added it to the mail I hadn't opened the day before.

I made myself a frozen pizza, even though I wasn't hungry, basically because I couldn't think of anything else to do.

I tried to plan my next step, some concerted effort that Allie and I could take to find the person missing from our lives, though we didn't really know if her sister and my Jen were the same person. That lasted about a half hour, during which time I came up with absolutely nothing.

I wasn't too disappointed; coming up with nothing was something I was getting used to.

I finally decided that if I couldn't concentrate, I might as well not concentrate while going through the mail, so I sat down to do so. There were at least sixty pieces, maybe forty of which were more responses from readers to my piece about Jen.

I had become proficient at judging the quality of a letter just by looking at the handwriting on the address. The percentage of nutcases was about twenty, down from a high of maybe forty when the piece was first published. The others were well-intentioned letters of sympathy or understanding, or tips to Jenny's whereabouts. I read at least part of all of them, on the theory that you never know.

The remainder were bills, junk mail, and the like. I'm pretty good about paying my bills, always have been, so I was surprised to see one from my cell phone company. You can always tell the notices that are notifying you of an overdue bill, they're ominously thin. It's as if they don't want to waste a lot of paper on a deadbeat.

This notice said that I owed a hundred and forty-nine dollars, and that my account was fifteen days overdue. I checked my records, which were not in the best shape since Jenny's disappearance, and I had no record of having made a payment. But I also didn't remember seeing a bill.

I called the company and, after at least ten computer prompts, got through to a human being. I explained that I had received the notice but had not gotten a bill.

"Can I put you on hold?" she asked.

It didn't seem like I had a choice, so I consented, while wondering if anyone had ever successfully refused. She surprised me by coming back on the line within twenty seconds.

"Mr. Kilmer?"

"Yes?"

"You can disregard the notice; that bill has been paid. Perhaps the notice and payment got crossed in the mail."

"When did you receive it?"

She told me a date, which was just ten days previous, meaning it was since I had gotten home from Ardmore. "Are you sure about this?" I asked. "I have no record of sending it."

"I'm quite certain, sir. Your account shows a zero balance."

This was confusing; there was no way I had paid that bill in the last couple of weeks. "Can you send me a copy of the check?" I asked.

"I'm afraid I don't have access to that. Perhaps the billing department can help you with that."

"What about the bill that was paid? Can you send me a copy of that?"

"I can certainly do that, sir. But you can also access it online if you'd prefer. It would be faster."

Accessing things online is not my strong point, though I have become better at it over time. She told me exactly what to do, and I dutifully wrote the directions down. It involved creating an online ID and password, not my favorite thing to do, but it seemed worth it to avoid having to wait for the copy of the bill in the mail.

Once I had navigated the Web site, I printed out a copy of the bill that they said I had paid. It listed 171 calls I had made the previous month. I recognized many of the numbers, but there were also a lot that were unfamiliar to me. This was not surprising, since I always made so many calls for work, researching stories, etc.

The positive to all this was that I now had something to do, which was check into the unfamiliar numbers. Craig wouldn't have lied about my Pulitzer story comment, which meant I'd said it to him. And I would not have said it if I hadn't believed it to be true. Hopefully these numbers could reconnect me to that story, or even to something having to do with Jen.

Since it was seven o'clock and businesses would be closed, I resolved to get going on the list of phone numbers the next day. Tonight I would watch televised basketball and attempt to use it as an escape from thinking about the train wreck that had become my life.

The phone rang and it was Willie, telling me that he and John were at Legends preparing to watch the game. It was a call that one of them had made pretty much every day since I'd been home, and I had declined every time.

"If I come down there, are all you guys going to do is drink beer, watch sports, leer at women, and act stupid?" I asked.

"That pretty much sums it up," he said. "Except we're also going to suck down some burgers and wings."

"Okay. I'll be there in a few minutes." I'm not sure why I decided to go that time; maybe it was a glimmer of mental health.

"Really?" he asked, obviously surprised. "I was sure you'd say no, so I only got a table for two."

"Good," I said. "Then it can be just me and John."

"I'll get a bigger table."

He did, and by the time I got down there it was covered with plates and beer bottles. The Knicks game had already started, so we didn't do much talking until halftime, such was and is sports bar etiquette. It felt good to be there, doing what for me felt normal.

Conversations I'd had with John and Willie since I got back had been awkward; they obviously didn't know whether or not to ask me about Jen, and didn't know whether I had recovered from my obvious lunacy. So they basically limited our talks to sports, which actually wasn't that different from "pre-Jen" days.

At the half, ESPN cut to a brief SportsCenter segment, and included in it was a piece about the upcoming Super Bowl. I had been so preoccupied with my chaotic life that I was completely out of touch, and wasn't even aware that the game was between the Colts and the Packers. But, of course, I couldn't come out and say that; it would expose me to ridicule. I'd had my fill of that.

Willie had come to the firm conclusion that the Packers would win the game, which meant that John was positive the Colts would blow them out.

"If they could handle the Redskins as easy as they did, they'll shut the Colts down. Colts are too one-dimensional," Willie said.

"How can you be 'too one-dimensional'?" John countered. "You're either one-dimensional or you're not."

"Bullshit. There are varying degrees of one-dimensional." The argument had reached a typical intellectual valley. "But either way they'll shut them down."

"Nobody shuts the Colts down, moron."

I was only half listening, so it took maybe twenty seconds before it clicked in. By that time they were on to other disputes.

"Did you say the Packers handled the Redskins?" I asked, and they both looked at me, as if surprised I was there.

"Yeah," Willie said. "Why?"

"What about the Giants?"

"What about them?"

It was no longer a time to mask my ignorance; it was time to reveal it. "The Giants beat the Redskins to get into the playoffs, so why did the Redskins play the Packers?"

Willie and John made eye contact with each other; they weren't reflecting their confusion, but rather their concern and pity.

For me.

Willie spoke slowly and patiently, as if to a child. "Rich, the Redskins beat the Giants to get in the playoffs. It was one of the most bizarre endings to a game in NFL history. You're not familiar with this?"

"I saw the game," I said, not mentioning that I saw it with Jen. "The Giants won that game. It was close, but I don't remember anything special about the ending." They were looking incredulous, so I added, "I can't be wrong about this."

Willie turned to John, as if to give him the floor, and John spoke in that same patient tone. "The last play of the game, the Giants stopped them on the fourth down when the Washington receiver caught the ball with his foot on the out-of-bounds line in the back of the end zone. They reviewed the call, and it took like ten minutes, and the teams were just standing around waiting to hear who would go to the playoffs."

I remembered the last play, but not the fact that it was reviewed.

John continued. "They ruled in Washington's favor, and the Redskins won the game. Then later in the day somebody in the stands, a fan, showed a videotape he made of the play, and it was a different angle. It showed the guy was out of bounds, and the Giants should have won, but it was too late to change the call."

"You don't remember that game?" Willie asked.

The truth was I did remember the game; I remembered it well. When I described a lot of it, Willie and John said that I was exactly right. Yet I thought the Giants won; until that moment I had thought they won.

But they lost.

How was that possible?

**"I'm going to try and re-create my life, or at** least the part I forget."

I was talking to Allie at the Carnegie Deli, which I chose for lunch because it was as non-small-town-Wisconsin a place as I could think of. If it turned out she was going to be in New York for only a short time, I figured I should give her a taste of it. And in this case, I meant "taste" in a literal sense.

The inside of the place was as it always was, barely controlled chaos. Customers are shuttled to large tables, where they sit adjacent to strangers. It's not a problem, because everybody is focused on the food. It's delicious, and the aroma it causes throughout the room is so thick that you feel you could chew on the air.

The waiters and waitresses, if not rude, are at the least brusque. They never write down an order; they could be serving a table for twenty and they would just nod dismissively as each request was given. But if they've ever made a mistake, I've never been witness to it. It is pure New York.

Allie seemed mesmerized by it all, and let me order for her. I got her a baked salmon and whitefish platter, because Jen loved it. She used to call it "Jewish fish," and bemoaned the fact that it was not available to her growing up in Ardmore.

"Re-create your life?" Allie asked. "What does that mean?"

"Well, obviously there are many things that I remember that don't seem to have happened. But there are also things, a key one in particular, that happened which I don't remember."

"Like what?" she asked.

"I told someone that I was working on a story that could get me the Pulitzer prize."

"You have no recollection of that?"

"None. But I must have said it. And if I said it, it had to have been a story I was working on intensely. It would have been my sole focus. My career has not been a series of ongoing Pulitzer contentions."

"Wouldn't you have been writing it for a particular publication? Wouldn't they know what you were doing?"

I shook my head. "No. My investigative stuff I do on my own, and when it's ready I sell it to the place I think is right."

"Why do you do it that way?" she asked.

"Because stories change the more I dig, and I dig a lot. I ask so many questions it drives people crazy. They talk to me just so I'll stop bugging them. But depending on where the story goes, the publication best suited to them can change."

"I'm sorry that I'm asking so many questions myself; I hope I'm not bugging you," Allie said. "If I had answers I would be more than happy to offer them. But do you have any idea what the story was about?"

"None. But if it happened in 'real life,' should there be such a thing, then there's got to be a record of it. I would have done research, gone places, talked to people, taken notes . . . I'm a compulsive note-taker . . . there would have to be something tangible that I can follow. I just have to re-create it."

"Let me help you," she said.

"I have no reason to believe it has anything to do with Julie, or even with Jen."

She nodded. "I understand that. But maybe it does. And at this point, I don't have a lot of other clues to follow, or things to do. I can oversee the gift basket business from here, so I'm going to stay awhile."

I didn't have the heart to say no, nor did I have the inclination to. I enjoyed being around Allie, though I was aware it was because it almost felt like being with Jen. I knew that wasn't particularly healthy, and that at some point I'd have to sort it out, but I had a list of things to sort that were ahead of it in line.

"Where do we start?" she asked.

"I have a cell phone bill which was paid, but which I have no record of paying. There are quite a few numbers I'm not familiar with; maybe some of them have to do with the story I was chasing."

She smiled. "I'm great on the phone."

I returned the smile. "My place or yours?"

"Yours. There's only one phone line in my hotel room."

"Then you'll have to excuse me; I haven't exactly been a tidy housekeeper lately. The place is a mess; it's been a mess since—" I caught myself before I said *Jen left*, but Allie knew what I was going to say, and she smiled her understanding.

"Then I'll tell you what," she said. "I'll have another platter of Jewish fish while you go home and clean up."

"Really?'

She laughed. "Of course not. Let's go."

**There is no such thing as a private conversa-**tion. Anyone who thinks there is such a thing is wrong. Juice knew that better than anyone.

Anything someone says can be heard by anyone who wants to hear it. All it takes is money and technical savvy, and the Stone obviously had plenty of both.

Juice sat in his car on Fifty-third Street and Seventh Avenue, in front of a Starbucks, the motor running and the hazard lights on. The car's presence there was certainly something that was not unusual in New York, and not likely to attract attention. Nor would anyone have paid any attention to the small device on the open window, pointing toward the Carnegie Deli.

The device was sending an invisible laser to the window of the Carnegie. Juice didn't know that much about how it worked, but he knew that it "blanketed" the window on impact, and maintained the effect as long as it was turned on.

The data that the device recorded was sent back directly to the Stone and his people for analysis, and it would be remarkably detailed. It would reveal every single conversation that was taking place within the restaurant, and each one could be isolated. As long as the eavesdropper had a record of the timbre and pitch of the targeted voices, their conversations could be listened to as easily as if he or she were at their table with them. And certainly they had the data about Richard's voice, and by now Allison's as well.

Amazingly, the device could even paint a visual picture of the inside of the room, based on the sound waves. If the Stone wanted, he could learn exactly where everybody was sitting, and where all the furniture, etc., was positioned. It was not something that would be of any interest to him, but it would be there if he wanted it.

With nothing better to do than sit in the car and wait for Kilmer and the sister to leave, Juice had time to reflect on the potential a device like this inherently possessed. If it were used to target an expensive restaurant during a busy lunch or dinnertime, the possibilities were limitless. In private conversations, businesspeople would be discussing lucrative secrets, and personal indiscretions would be revealed in abundance.

The potential for profit by capitalizing on the business secrets or stock tips was great, as was the opportunity to use what was gleaned in the personal conversations for blackmail. Of course, Juice was thinking about this in the abstract, since money was never going to be a problem for him again.

Back to the matter at hand. Juice did not expect that the information garnered from this particular effort would be terribly enlightening. Since Richard's apartment and phone were bugged, Juice already knew that he had uncovered the phone bill, and was now going to check the numbers. That was most likely what they were discussing now.

Dealing with the phone bill had been tricky, and Juice had handled it in the best way possible. But it hadn't worked; Kilmer was both smart and lucky and had discovered the bill's existence. Now he might use it to uncover the recent past, and like always, Juice would have to be the one to clean up the mess.

It would be a hassle that he didn't need, and it would likely result in more people dying.

Juice actually shrugged at the thought, and the word that came to mind was the one his niece used when she tried to feign disinterest.

"Whatever."

**It was the call Susan Donovan dreaded, but** the one she knew would come. Frank had told her otherwise, that he was free and clear, and that they would never come to him. But her fear was about to be realized, and she somehow knew it as soon as she heard the phone ring.

At first she considered not answering, especially with Frank not at home. If it was who she thought, she didn't want to make a mistake, and with the pressure she was feeling it was likely that she would do so. But the thought of not knowing for sure was terrible, so she picked it up on the third ring.

"Hello?"

"Hi, my name is Allison Tynes," said the woman's voice, and the relief that Susan felt was tangible. It was not who she expected; she was wrong to be afraid. "Can you please tell me who I'm speaking with?"

"Susan Donovan. If you're selling something—"

Allie interrupted. "Oh, no, I'm not selling anything. I'm actually calling for Richard Kilmer. . . ."

Susan was gripped by panic, so much so that she didn't hear the next few words that Allie said. She tried to focus, and heard,

". . . had called this number a while back, and we are retracing his steps, trying to figure out why."

"We don't know Mr. Kilmer," Susan said.

"We?"

Susan immediately realized her mistake, but didn't know how to compensate for it. "Yes."

"Who are you referring to besides yourself?"

"My . . . my husband and I."

"Is your husband there?" Allie asked. "Might I speak to him?"

"No . . . he's not here."

"But you know he doesn't know Richard Kilmer?"

"I really can't speak to you now; I have to go. I'm in the middle of something."

"Can you ask your husband to call me when he returns?"

"Yes. Now I really have to go."

Click.

As soon as she hung up the phone, she picked it back up and dialed her husband. Her hand was shaking so much that she pressed an incorrect button, and had to hang up again. She took a deep breath to calm herself, realized there weren't enough deep breaths in the world to accomplish the task, and dialed again.

Frank answered on the second ring. "Donovan."

"Frank, he called."

"Kilmer?" He asked the question, although the sound of her voice made the answer a foregone conclusion.

"Yes. It wasn't actually Kilmer, but someone calling for him. A woman. I don't remember her name."

"What did she say?"

"She wanted to know if we knew Richard Kilmer. I said we didn't."

"That's all?"

"Yes, I think so," she said, trying to recall the details. "She asked if you would call her when you got home."

"What did you say?"

"I'm not sure; I might have said you would. But I didn't get her number."

Frank tried to do the calculations in his head. This could end here; the woman might have believed Susan and moved on. It wasn't likely, though. If Susan sounded this nervous when talking to him, he doubted that she would have sounded otherwise to the woman calling about Kilmer.

"What are we going to do, Frank?"

"We're going to wait; there's nothing else we can do right now."

"We can leave," she said. "We can pick up right now and leave. We should have done so already; I knew this was going to happen. I told you it was going to happen."

"Susan, they can find us wherever we go," he said.

"Kilmer? Kilmer will find us?"

"Kilmer is not our problem."

**"I think we might have something,"** Allie said, as soon as she hung up the phone.

I was starting to dial another number in what had been appearing to be a series of dead ends, so I put the phone down immediately. "Tell me."

"A woman named Susan Donovan said she didn't know you as soon as I asked. And she said her husband didn't know you either."

"Doesn't sound like much of a breakthrough," I pointed out.

"She volunteered the part about her husband, even though I didn't ask about him. I had no way of knowing she even had a husband, and he wasn't home at the time."

"That's it?" I asked, sounding more negative than I intended.

Allie shook her head. "No, she sounded strange."

"Strange how?"

"Richard, the woman was afraid. I heard it in her voice as soon as I said I was calling for you."

"Do we know anything else about her, or her husband?"

She shook her head. "Not yet; let me scout around online. See what I can find out."

It didn't make sense to me that some woman I didn't know

would have a reason to fear a phone call from me, but Allie seemed to have a strong instinct about it, so I was fine with her following up on it.

Certainly I wasn't doing any better; all of the calls I was making were benign and seemed to have nothing to do with either a story I might be working on or Jen's disappearance.

For example, I apparently had called a wine shop on Madison Avenue in Manhattan, though I am much more of a beer drinker. And I had placed two calls to Jefferson Auto Parts, a dealership near Damariscotta, Maine. They didn't have any record of me buying anything from them, and didn't seem to care much one way or the other. Not exactly suspicious stuff.

Allie came over, having finished with her own calls, and watched me make the rest of mine. As I always did, I took meticulous notes as I did so.

"What are you writing?" she asked, trying to read them over my shoulder. My handwriting is indecipherable to anyone but me, so she didn't have a chance.

"Nothing important, I'm afraid."

"So why the notes?"

"I'm a journalist. That's what we do; we write everything down, and then we write about what we wrote."

My last call was to a 212 area code, which meant it was located in Manhattan. An answering machine picked up.

"This is Dr. Philip Garber. If you are calling between the hours of nine A.M. and five P.M., I am likely in session and unable to come to the phone."

The message then went on to list numbers to call if it was an emergency, and then an invitation to leave a message for a return call. I left my name and number, and hung up.

I didn't have that much to base it on, but based on the tone of voice, the reference to a possible emergency, and the use of the word "session," I had a hunch that I had reached a psychotherapist's phone, which was intriguing.

All I had to do was Google Dr. Garber's name to know that

I was right. Not only was he a shrink, but he was apparently a shrink of some stature: the head of a psychoanalytic institute. There were also a bunch of articles about him being the keynote speaker at some international conference of shrinkdom.

By this point it came as no surprise to me that I had no recollection of ever talking to, or even hearing of, Dr. Garber. It had already become crystal clear that I only remembered those things that did not happen, while completely blocking out everything that did.

Nothing else eventful came out of the phone numbers, which was a disappointment to me. I guess I was hoping to reach a number where a receptionist would answer with the perky message, *Welcome to the Explanation Institute. Please hold for a counselor who will explain all the insanely bizarre things that have been happening to you.*

Allie had a decidedly different point of view about the day's events. "I really feel like we're getting somewhere," she said.

It was good for me to have someone with that level of irrationality around. Ever since Jen disappeared, I'd been the lunatic in whichever room I've been in. Comments like Allie's gave me the opportunity to play the cynical realist, which certainly helped me widen my range.

"Where might we be getting?" I asked.

"If Julie was with you all that time, then you're the key. We need to know what happened to you. And now I think we've got some leads."

"We do?"

She nodded vigorously. "Susan Donovan and that shrink, Garber."

"You realize that they could have nothing to do with this?"

She looked at me like I was nuts; it's a look I'd come to recognize. "What good does it do for us to spend time and energy thinking like that?"

I didn't have a good answer for that, so I didn't offer one. Instead, I asked, "Do you need help checking into Susan Donovan?"

She shook her head. "Not right now. I'll get started looking online right away. I'm really good on a computer."

"Okay; find out why Susan Donovan is afraid of me. You want to grab an early dinner?"

"You don't have to babysit me, Richard. I'm not here to take over your life."

"Is that a no?"

She smiled. "Of course not. I just don't want to become a burden."

"That doesn't seem to be a clear and present danger."

"Good," she said. "So where's all this great Italian food I hear New York has?"

I took her to Peppino's, a terrific Italian restaurant down on Hudson Street in the West Village. It is one of hundreds, if not thousands, of New York restaurants that are simultaneously popular and undiscovered. By that I mean that most New Yorkers have never heard of them, yet they're always crowded.

We arrived without a reservation at five-thirty, a time when no self-respecting New Yorker would be having dinner. That's why we were able to get in, though we were told that there was a reservation for our table at seven-thirty, so we had to be out by then.

The waiter came over to the table to tell us the specials. It turned out to be a five-minute recitation of at least fifteen dishes, mentioning every ingredient in each dish. His memorization of it was fairly amazing; I kept looking around to see if there was a hidden teleprompter.

We decided when we sat down that we would try to talk about something other than the person missing from our lives, but that vow lasted less time than it took to recite the specials. Neither of us could think about anything else, so it was only natural that we talk about it.

We didn't figure anything out, of course, but it was still the most pleasant evening I had spent in a while. Allie was fun to be with, upbeat but not venturing into the dreaded "perky-land,"

and whip-smart. She reminded me so much of Jen, yet surprisingly being with her didn't increase my pain.

After dinner, we took a cab back uptown and I dropped her off at her hotel before heading home. On the way, she looked out the window at the busy streets and endless lights and said, "Someday I'm going to love this city."

I knew exactly what she meant. Now was not the time that she was free to love anything, not with the constant pain and emptiness we were both feeling.

When I got back to my apartment, the message light on my phone was flashing 3, but the first one was the only one I cared about.

"Richard, this is Philip Garber. I'm very glad you called. Please call me back at any hour, or if you prefer, I have an opening tomorrow at eleven A.M., so I could see you in my office. I hope you're well."

I played the message back four times, taking in every nuance. He called me Richard, which indicated to me that he knew me from more than my phone call. He referred to himself as "Philip" rather than "Mr." or "Dr." Garber, which felt like another sign of familiarity.

More importantly, he seemed very pleased to hear from me and anxious to speak with me, which certainly came as a surprise. The fact that he was leaving time open to see me also felt significant, as was the fact that he didn't bother to give his office address.

Maybe I'd been there before, even though I didn't know it. Maybe he'd been my shrink for twenty years. Maybe he was my cousin or brother.

Maybe Philip Garber would know what was going on with my life.

# The Lexington Institute for Psychoanalytic

Training was located in a four-story brownstone on East Sixty-eighth Street, not surprisingly just off Lexington Avenue. It was the kind of building that very, very rich people might call home, and was probably worth many millions, even in a down market. Training shrinks must be profitable.

I did have a vague feeling that the building was familiar to me, though I had no recollection of ever being there. I considered it possible that there was a memory that was repressed but near the surface. Maybe I could get in touch with it.

Or maybe not.

The receptionist told me that Dr. Garber's office was on the third floor, and that I could either take the spiral staircase or the elevator. The elevator was so small that I figured I couldn't inhale on the ride up, so I took the stairs. Another receptionist-type person was waiting for me at the top of the stairs, and she brought me directly to Garber's office.

Philip Garber was younger than I expected, probably no older than forty. He greeted me with a handshake and a smile that seemed meant to be soothing. "Richard, thanks for coming in.

Nice to see you again," said the man I had never seen before in my life.

In the hallway right near his office was a coffee machine, and he walked toward it. "Still black with one sugar?" he asked, and I nodded. He definitely knew me.

I hadn't really thought about how honest to be with him, but in the moment I decided to lay it all out there. I mean, the guy was a shrink, so he was used to interacting with psychos. Besides, he obviously already had an idea what he was dealing with, from some previous meeting we apparently had.

"I've got to be honest with you, Dr. Garber. I have no recollection of ever meeting you before. Or drinking your coffee. Or being in this building."

If he was shocked to hear this, his face didn't show it. "I see," was all he said. "That must be very disconcerting for you."

"I can think of stronger words," I said, and he smiled. "Was I here?"

He nodded. "Yes, you were. Three times. For one hour each time."

He said it with no particular affect, yet it felt like I was punched in the face. "Three times," I repeated, because at the moment I couldn't think of anything else to say.

"Why don't you sit down?" He pointed to a chair I had probably been in three times before; it was probably my favorite chair, and I sat in it.

I was a little nervous about what I was going to hear, so I opted for a pathetic attempt at small talk. There was a picture on Garber's desk of him in the cockpit of a small plane, waving to the camera, so I said, "You fly?"

He smiled. "It's a passion of mine which I indulge far too often. But let's focus on you. Please start at the beginning." He then opened a notepad and held a pen at the ready, and took a few notes during our talk.

"This is the beginning for me. So if you don't mind, please tell me what we talked about when we met. Was I here as a patient?"

"You were, and we talked about some things you were feeling."

I felt a quick flash of anger; my life was down the tubes and he was using bland shrink-talk on me. "Any chance you could be more specific? Did I talk about a woman named Jen?"

"Yes. And I should tell you that I read your article in the magazine. I considered contacting you, but decided that if you wanted to talk, you would reach out."

"What did I say about her when I was here?"

Garber paused for a few moments, as if measuring what he should say. It made me realize that as unique as this experience was for me, it was not an everyday occurrence for him either. "You were having fantasies about her, and it was frightening you."

"What kind of fantasies?" I asked, dreading the answer.

"You were having moments, extended moments, when you believed that she was real."

"Was she real?"

He shook his head sadly, as if in sympathy. "No, Richard, she was not real, or at least I saw no evidence that she was. You knew that then, and that's what you told me. You were frightened by your fantasies about her."

His words were devastating to me, and I'm sure he could see it. "Why don't you tell me everything?" he said. "Perhaps I can help you."

I wasn't looking for help; it was too late for that. I was looking for truth. "I'm insane; is that what you're saying?"

He shook his head. "You're not insane, Richard. You're troubled, and you're in pain, but there's a way back from this. So let's get started, shall we? How did you come to call me, if you have no recollection of having met me?"

I told him about the cell phone bill, and then I told him all about Jennifer, starting at the beginning. I was able to give him an abbreviated version, since he had read the magazine piece, but I went on to talk at length about Allie and her missing sister. He listened without saying a word.

When I finished, he asked me a few questions, mostly about how I was dealing with all this.

"Look," I said, "I'm sure this is standard procedure. The patient talks, and you listen, and you make observations. I'm sure that's how it went in the three sessions that I don't remember. But that's not why I'm here, not today. I'm here for information."

He nodded. "If I have it, it's yours."

"Did I talk to you about a story I was working on?"

He thought for a while, trying to remember, then started skimming through his notepad. "Yes, though not in much detail. It was in the context of your saying that these fantasies were getting in the way of a story you were pursuing, affecting your concentration."

"Did I say what the story was?"

He was reading from the pad now; none of this was from memory. "You mentioned a man named Lassiter. At least I had the sense it was a man; I'm not sure if you actually said that. You made a comment about returning to your journalistic roots, but you didn't explain what you meant."

I knew exactly what I would have meant by that. Sean Lassiter was the indirect subject of the first major story I ever worked on, though it was left to other writers to really bring it to fruition. My piece was an intimate study of a young woman who had taken a prescription medication for a kidney infection.

Within three weeks she was paralyzed, and she and her family were positive that the drug was at fault, though they did not have the resources to fully explore their legal options. We had a friend in common, so when I heard about her I wrote about her plight, and I thought that would be that.

That wasn't that. It created a mini-stir, and set other, more experienced reporters on to the story. A scandal was uncovered, and bribery was alleged between the small, very successful biochemical company that developed the drug, and the FDA. Nothing was ever proven, but high-level people at the FDA resigned from their jobs, and the biochemical company shut down.

The head of that company was Sean Lassiter, and he came after me, both in the press and through intermediaries. I was actually told that Lassiter was going to "get" me; it wasn't a physical threat so much as an inference that he would use his substantial resources to destroy my career.

That revenge never happened, and by all indications, Lassiter had landed comfortably on his feet. He managed to stay out of jail, and apparently to put away enough money to live very comfortably for a very long time.

I couldn't imagine why I would be chasing another story about Sean Lassiter, and Garber could not provide any further help.

"Why did I come here?" I asked. "I mean, why you? How did I come to you?"

"You said it was by reputation. And a motivating factor was the work I have done in the field of memory. Apparently you had researched it and read some of my papers in the field."

"I was worried about my memory?" I asked.

"You were floundering, Richard. You were forgetting things that had just happened, and remembering things that hadn't. You were having increasing difficulty distinguishing between what was real and what was fantasy. It scared you, and you were looking for help. That was understandable and nothing to be ashamed of. It was actually a healthy reaction."

"So it's possible that eventually the fantasy took over, and the reality was wiped from my mind?"

He nodded. "If your mind needed to do that to protect itself, then it might certainly do exactly that."

"Protect itself from what?" I asked.

"That is what we would work to find out."

That was an invitation to become his patient on a regular basis, so we could explore the depths of my feelings . . . blah, blah, blah. I wasn't having any of it. "Jen was . . . is . . . real."

"The mind creates its own reality."

I shook my head. "No, I mean actually real. Flesh-and-blood real."

"I think on some level you know better than that," he said. "Just the fact that no one else in your life has any recollection of her proves that to you on a conscious level. Unfortunately, the conscious level is not enough."

"What about Allie and her sister?"

"Richard, I'm going to say something to you, to ask you a question, that you will not like hearing."

"I have quite a bit of experience with that lately," I said. "Pile it on."

He nodded. "Have you considered the possibility that Allie is a creation of your mind as well?"

# I didn't want to tell Allie what Garber said.

I'm not sure why, but it was probably because if Garber was right it tended to prove that Jen was not real, and that therefore she was not Julie. According to Garber, there had once been a time that I knew Jen was a fantasy, and I had been trying to claw my way back to the reality-based world.

Allie would be crushed by this news, and I didn't want to be the one to do the crushing. There was also a chance that she would go to Garber's office and punch his lights out; she was not exactly the shy, retiring type. But either way she deserved to be told, and I did so when we went out to dinner that night.

She wound up dismissing it out of hand. "I'm sorry, Richard, I'm not buying it."

"You think Garber is lying?"

"No, but that doesn't mean he's right. Look, none of this has made sense from day one, and if I was only thinking logically, I'd be back home, curled up in the fetal position, whimpering. But that doesn't get me anywhere; it doesn't get us anywhere. So I'm going on instinct, and I'm going to continue doing so until I can't anymore. You can join me or not."

"He also questioned whether you are real."

Hearing that actually reduced the tension, and she smiled at the ridiculousness of it. "Just what we need: psychobabble bullshit. Now let's get serious, okay?"

I could have argued, but I didn't. She was willing her energy level to be so high, and her focus to be so complete, that I was fine being dragged along by it. I felt a kind of relief that I didn't have to be the driving force, that I was no longer alone in my search. "Good. What's our next step?"

"I'm going to see Susan Donovan; I found out where she lives."

"Where?"

"Up near Monticello, in the Catskills."

"It's not very far from Ardmore."

She smiled. "Exactly. But I don't want to call her again; I want to surprise her by showing up. I'll get a better sense of how she reacts that way."

"I'll go with you."

She shook her head. "No, if she sees you, she might panic."

"You realize she could easily have nothing to do with this."

"She was scared on the phone," she said.

"Maybe she thought you were a bill collector."

"Richard, let's be a little more positive, shall we?"

I smiled. "Sorry; I'll try."

We ordered dinner, and tried to talk about something else. I excused myself to go to the bathroom, passing near the front of the restaurant on the way. It was then that I noticed the car across the street, with the device sitting on the window.

I went back to the table and sat down. "There's a car across the street, with a man sitting in it, and something on the window."

"So?"

"So I think the same car was across from the Carnegie Deli when we were having breakfast yesterday."

"How can you tell?"

"The thing on the window; when I saw it the first time I thought it might be a siren, and that it might be a police car. It caught my eye, that's all."

"Did you see the driver?"

I nodded. "Yes, and it looks like the same guy, although I can't be sure. He's staring at the restaurant, just like he was doing last time."

"Do you think he might have anything to do with you?"

I shook my head. "I can't imagine what. It just struck me as an odd coincidence."

"Are you sure about this?" she asked.

"I'm a reporter, Allie. I notice things."

"So let's find out what he's up to," she said.

"How?"

"Confront him; see how he reacts."

Once again Allie was advocating the direct approach, but I thought I had a better idea.

"When we're done eating, if he's still there, I'll leave alone. You stay behind and see if he follows me. Go to your hotel, and I'll meet you in the lobby."

"Perfect," she said.

We didn't focus too much on the man outside, and managed to have a pleasant dinner. But when we finished, he was still there, so I left alone. I grabbed a cab and went to the hotel.

About fifteen minutes after I arrived, Allie showed up. The excitement on her face was evident. "He followed you. As soon as your cab left, he pulled the device back inside the car, and then pulled out after you."

"Is he outside now?"

"I didn't see him, but he certainly could be. Either way, he left because you did. It was obvious."

"Who the hell could that be, and why would he be following me?"

She smiled. "We're getting somewhere, Richard. I can feel it."

I let that be the final word, because I wanted to believe it. When I left, I walked twice around the block, looking for the man in the car and trying to figure out if anyone was following me.

I didn't see him or anyone suspicious, though picking out suspicious people was never really a talent I cultivated. I finally hailed a cab and went home.

When I got into my apartment, the one that did not feel like Jen was ever there, I tried to focus on Allie's proclamation that we were getting somewhere.

Damned if I could see it.

"They are aware that you are following them," the Stone said.

Juice was no amateur; there was no way they could have made him. "That's not possible."

"This is not conjecture. I've just finished listening to their conversation at the restaurant last night." He proceeded to recount it in some detail, ending with the fact that Kilmer left first to determine if he was being followed.

Juice was annoyed with himself and embarrassed. He had underestimated Kilmer and gotten burned. That would be the last time it would happen.

"He won't see me again."

"You are losing control of the situation," the Stone said.

"No, I'm not. What else was on the tape?"

"Tape?" the Stone asked, making no effort to conceal his amusement. "Welcome to the digital age."

"You know what I mean," he said. The Stone had not been making a joke or poking fun. That wasn't his style; Juice had come to realize the Stone made Osama bin Laden look like Don Rickles. Instead he was subtly asserting his superiority, and Juice knew it. "What else do I need to know about their conversation?"

"A transcript is being sent to you electronically, as always. You're going to be a busy man."

"What does that mean? I'm already a busy man."

"Read the transcript and you'll understand. I shouldn't have to remind you of this, but this is a tightly controlled experiment. Its value is entirely dependent on that."

"When are you going to make your deal?" Juice asked.

"That doesn't concern you. But let me put it this way: My end is going considerably better than yours."

An hour later Juice had read the transcripts of Kilmer's conversation in the restaurant. He was angry, not at Kilmer, but at himself. To have been detected by an amateur like Kilmer was inexcusable. The Stone was right about that.

The Stone was right about one other thing as well. Juice was going to be a busy man.

**Monticello, New York, is what passes in the** Catskill Mountains as the big city. That hasn't changed over the years, even though everything else about the Catskills has.

The Catskills, back in the fifties and sixties, was where it was happening, at least if you lived in the New York metropolitan area. And if you were Jewish. And if you liked to eat a lot.

It was home to literally hundreds of hotels, the most prominent being the Concord, Kutsher's, and Grossinger's, and far more bungalow colonies. Big-name entertainment—Alan King, Zero Mostel, Milton Berle, Buddy Hackett, Red Buttons—headlined in the showrooms. The facilities were remarkable: hotels featured indoor and outdoor pools, bowling alleys, ice-skating rinks, pro-style golf courses, and even skiing. The restaurants served thousands, and part of the lure was that one could order as many appetizers, entrées, and desserts as he or she wanted, for no extra charge.

Since the clientele tended to be old, the food didn't contain that much seasoning, and walkers were sometimes lined up outside the showroom.

But it's almost all gone by now. As the years go by, old people have a tendency to die, and in this case there weren't young people to take their place. Part of this was because of the advancements in travel; it became almost as easy to take a flight to Vegas or Miami as it was to drive up to the Catskills. And Florida and then Arizona became the retirement destinations of choice.

Part of the decline came from a decades-long failure to bring in casino gambling. Local businesspeople saw it as the panacea, the miracle cure to save their way of life. Atlantic City residents might not agree at this point with that theory, but it never got tested in the Catskills. They're still trying.

But Monticello was and is the hub. That is probably because of the presence of Monticello Raceway, which is still hanging on despite the economic tidal wave. Ironically, the racing is buttressed by slot machines and video poker, leaving table games as the last vestige of banned immorality in New York.

Of course, "hub" and "big city" are words that should be taken in context, since Monticello has barely six thousand residents. Two of those residents were Frank and Susan Donovan. Frank did well as a plumber, and in fact had two offices, in Monticello and Ellenville, and two other plumbers working for him. They worked mostly for companies, with some residential jobs to fill in when times were slow.

Frank was in his mid-fifties, and Susan was just three years younger. He talked about retiring; thirty-five years of twelve-hour days had been getting to him for a while. They considered moving to Florida or Arizona, though the irony that people moving to those places had killed the Catskills was not lost on them.

Juice arrived at their house just outside of town at a little before ten P.M. The back door was unlocked, so he easily slipped in unnoticed. Frank and Susan were upstairs, asleep in bed, so that's where he headed. He entered their room, flicked on the light, and shot Frank through the head before he had time to lift it off the pillow.

Then came the part that Juice dreaded. He took Susan down to the living room and raped her, not because he had any desire to, but because he wanted it to look like a home-invasion robbery. Then he shot her as well, and proceeded to ransack the house. He took some cash and jewelry, not even enough to justify the drive up there, but again simply for appearance's sake.

Juice was finished by ten-thirty, and deliberately left the front door ajar when he left. He was back in the city by midnight, and in bed by twelve-thirty. It was a decidedly unpleasant way to spend an evening, but it was necessary, and Juice knew it was his own fault. He should have killed the Donovans way back when the initial report about them was filed.

Allie finished the two-hour drive to the house at ten o'clock the next morning, guided flawlessly by the miracle known as GPS. She parked across the street and headed for the front door. It would be very annoying if they weren't home, but she was still glad that she hadn't called first.

When she got on the porch she saw that the door was partially open. After ringing the bell and getting no response, she opened it slightly more and peeked in. With Susan Donovan's shattered body deliberately placed within her sight line, it was left to Allie to discover the horror that took place in the house the night before.

Once she did, she ran across the street, not so much out of fear, more from a desire to put a distance between her and the nightmare scene she had witnessed. Once she caught her breath, she called 911, and then Richard Kilmer.

Then she waited.

"Richard, Susan Donovan has been mur-dered," she said, in place of "hello."

She sounded shaken, and I had a thousand questions to ask her, but I only got in three before she told me that the police had shown up and that she had to get off the phone. Fortunately, she had time to tell me exactly where she was, and I was in the car and on the way up to Monticello within five minutes.

I didn't need my GPS to tell me which house on the street was the Donovans'. There were at least half a dozen police cars there, along with a coroner's van and two other official-looking vehicles. In the center of them, and parked directly in front of the house, was Allie's rented car.

A bunch of neighbors had gathered and were watching from a distance, blocked from the scene by officers there for just that purpose. I went up to one and said that I was a friend of Allie's and wanted to see her.

He was not impressed. "She's busy now," he said.

"I know that. She called me. Can you at least tell her that I'm here? My name's Richard Kilmer."

"No," he said, ever helpful.

I dialed Allie's number and when she answered, told her I

was outside. I heard her ask if I could come in, and I assumed she was in the house. She was told that I could not, and was not given a good answer when she asked how long they would need her. "Sorry," she said. "They're not in a compromising mood."

"I'll be here," I told her. "Look for me across the street when you come out."

I was still there two hours later when she appeared, with three guys I figured were detectives. She did not seem to be in any kind of custody, and she walked over to me. "They're both dead, Richard. Susan Donovan and her husband."

I saw that a couple of the neighbors were trying to listen in, so I said, "Let's go grab a cup of coffee and talk about it."

We got in our cars, and she followed me to a diner I had passed, down the block from Monticello Raceway. We asked for a booth that was off in the corner, with the one on each side of it unoccupied. As I was starting to do from habit, I looked out the window to see if I could spot the man with the device in his car window. I did not.

Once we sat down, Allie described everything that had happened to her, from the moment she had arrived at the Donovans'. She spoke in a clinical way, strangely devoid of emotion, as if she were trying to keep herself under complete control.

"You okay?" I asked.

She shook her head slightly. "Not so far, but I'm working on it."

"You want to stop talking about this for a while?"

Another shake of the head. "No. We need to deal with this."

"Do the cops have any idea who might have done it?"

"I don't know," she said. "They seemed to want me to do all the talking, and didn't say much when I was around. But I did overhear a couple of things. Susan Donovan was raped before she was killed, and the house was ransacked. It looked like a robbery that turned deadly."

"Maybe to them. But I think we know better," I said. "Soon after she seemed afraid of you over the phone, she and her husband were murdered. That's pushing the coincidence scale way too far."

She nodded. "I agree completely," she said, and then, "I feel like we killed them."

Even though intellectually I knew better, I was feeling the same thing. But there was nothing to be gained from dwelling on it, and I told her so.

It didn't work, and she started to cry. "Richard, it's like I broke into their lives and killed them myself. One minute they're planning their retirement, or getting ready to go see their grand-children or something, and then I call them, and their lives come to an end."

I let us both sit with it for a while. I could have pointed out that there was a real murderer out there, and he wasn't us, but intellectually she already knew that. For the moment, it wasn't her intellect that was in control.

Finally, I asked, "What did you tell the police . . . I'm sure they asked why you were there?"

"I said a friend's phone bill had shown their number on it and he didn't know why." She managed a small smile. "I said that my friend was having memory issues, and that I was trying to piece his life together. They didn't seem particularly interested in any of that."

We debated the logic of going to law enforcement and trying to enlist them in our search. It seemed to both of us that it would be a dead end, we had nothing concrete to go on. The things that interested us—that Julie and Jen were both missing and looked so much alike, and that Susan Donovan had seemed afraid on the phone the day before her murder—were unlikely to interest the police.

Especially since no one other than the two current occu-pants of our diner booth even believed that Jen ever existed.

As if we needed anything else to hang over our conversation, I was hoping she wasn't thinking what I was, that if in fact the people we were dealing with committed this brutal crime, the chance that Jen was alive was very low.

The coincidences were piling up, and I really had come to believe there could be a conspiracy that had targeted both Jen and me. I still couldn't begin to understand how it included everybody I knew, and how all evidence of Jen could have been so completely wiped out, but I felt I just had to keep pushing until I had the answers.

Of course, resolving to keep pushing is easy; the tough part is in knowing where to push. "I think we're looking in the wrong place," I said.

"Where's the right place?"

"Julie didn't disappear in Fort Atkinson, so you had no reason to look for her there. And the same thing is true of Jen and Manhattan."

Allie nodded. "Jen disappeared in Ardmore."

"Which is only about twenty minutes from here. That's where we should be looking."

"Are you up for going back?" she asked. "It won't be an easy thing for you to do."

"I'll handle it."

She nodded, and I could see her resolve and determination returning. "When do we go?"

"As soon as we figure out a strategy for when we get there. Right now the people in that town think I'm a total nutcase who tied their police department up for an entire afternoon. They won't be welcoming me back with open arms."

"In the meantime, we have to figure out where the Donovans fit into this," she said.

"I think I've got an idea how to do that."

## "Do I want you to write a follow-up?" Scott

asked. "Come on, is that a serious question?"

"It's a serious question," I confirmed.

"Just to be clear, we're talking about a follow-up to the piece about Jennifer?"

"We are."

"Richard, I've been asking you to write a follow-up since ten minutes after the first piece hit the street. That edition broke every sales record we've ever had, and we got by far the most reader reaction ever."

"Is that a yes?"

"Is it a yes? How's this: I'll clear out up to twelve pages for you, and I'll refuse advertising if you need more than that. And if a nuclear war breaks out before we go to press, you still get the cover."

"My deal is you won't edit it," I said.

His mood changed instantly. "Won't edit it? I'm an editor; it says so right on my door."

"You didn't change a word the last time."

"But the point is I could have. It was brilliant, so I didn't touch it. Retaining that option makes us editors feel secure."

"Not this piece. It runs the way I write it. Word for word. And I'm going to need Craig Langel to do legwork on it, on the magazine's dime."

"Then I'm going to need some information, some hint of what the hell is going on."

So I told him what was going on, starting with Allie and the missing Julie, then the phone bill, the shrink, the guy who'd been following me, ending with the brutal murder of the Donovans.

He listened until I was finished without asking a single question, then said, "Richard, the first time around this was goofy, you know? A little nuts. Now it's serious, and downright weird."

"So you don't want to run it? I'm coming to you first, Richard, but we both know I can take it elsewhere."

"Don't want to run it? Have you lost your mind?" He realized what he'd just said, so added, "Sorry, bad choice of words."

"And you'll pay for Craig?" I asked.

"Can't you find someone cheaper? The son of a bitch charges a fortune."

I shook my head. "It's got to be Craig. I trust him."

"You haven't really learned the art of compromise, have you?"

I shook my head. "Maybe next semester."

"Okay, use Craig. But don't overdo it. When should I expect the piece?"

"I have no idea," I said.

"That's helpful. Let me ask you this, Richard. What are you hoping to accomplish with it?"

It was a good question, and one I couldn't yet completely answer. I decided to be as honest as I could be. "Well, for one thing, it gets Craig working on this, which can only be a positive. And the truth is that my ability to reach the public is one of the only weapons I have, so I have to figure out a way to use it. But most importantly—"

He finished my thought for me. "It might help you find Jen."

I nodded. "It might help me find Jen."

As soon as I got home, I called Craig and told him he was officially on the payroll. "I would have done it for nothing, Richard. I told you that."

"But money's better, right?"

"Money's always better."

I told Craig that we would meet in a day or two and I'd bring him completely up to speed on the situation, but for the moment I told him all I knew about the Donovans, which wasn't much.

"What do they have to do with your missing girlfriend, except for the fact that the wife sounded scared on the phone?"

"I don't know, but the more you can find out about them, the better chance we have of making the connection."

"Okay, I'll get right on it," he said, and as well as I knew Craig, I understood that he meant it literally. He would start working on it the moment he hung up the phone.

With nothing specific to do for the rest of the night, I called Allie and asked her if she wanted to have dinner. I could have gone to Legends and hooked up with Willie and John, but I chose Allie instead, as I had pretty much been doing every night.

I told myself that it was because we were working on this together, and the more we talked about it, the better the chance that we would hit on the answer. And I reminded myself that she was alone in a strange city, and I needed to watch out for her. But no matter how many times I told myself that stuff, I knew that there was more to it.

I enjoyed being with her, and I was attracted to her. I wasn't sure why, and that was disconcerting. Of course, I recognized the obvious fact that it was likely because she looked and acted exactly like Jen. This added a healthy dose of guilt to the mix; I felt like I was betraying Jen by being with Allie, even though nothing romantic had transpired.

Or was ever going to.

I was starting to think that Allie was having the same kind of feelings, and was equally uncomfortable with them. But she hadn't said anything, and I sure as hell wasn't going to.

The bottom line was that I couldn't explain my feelings, even to myself, but I really didn't have time to figure it out. And I wasn't prepared to stop spending time with her. I enjoyed it too much.

So Allie and I went to Dock's, a restaurant on Broadway in the Eighties, and did our best not to talk about anything other than what our next steps should be. It made for a less-than-scintillating conversation, since neither of us had a clue.

My idea to go back to Ardmore still seemed like a good one, especially because the Donovans lived not far from there. I knew that town, I had been there, I'd met and talked with some of the people, and all of that was because Jen brought me there.

It was the only place where it made sense to look.

"When are you going to write the magazine article?" Allie asked.

"As soon as I can figure out what I want to say. But very soon."

"Am I going to be in it? Is Julie?"

It was a measure of my self-absorption that I hadn't even thought that she might have the right to privacy in all this. "I'm sorry," I said. "I should have asked you."

"So you do want to write about my part in this?"

I nodded. "Yes. I think it can be a positive. But it's completely your call."

She thought for a moment, then said, "Whatever it takes."

We left the restaurant and walked all the way back to her hotel. It was about a three-mile walk and felt great. I kept looking for the man who had been following us, but he was nowhere to be seen.

I mentioned that to Allie, and she said, "I guess we scared him off."

We walked another half block before the significance of that statement hit me. "How did we do that?" I asked.

"What?"

"Think about what happened that night. We spotted him,

and I went back to the hotel, and you followed later. We never confronted him or gave any indication that we knew he was there. Or that we suspected he had anything to do with us. How the hell could that have scared him off?"

"Maybe it didn't. Maybe he just decided he had seen enough. Or maybe we were wrong about him in the first place."

"You believe that?" I asked.

"No way."

**"Donovan was a plumber,"** Craig said, as we walked in Central Park.

"I already told you that," I said.

"I know, but the point is that's all he was. He wasn't a spy pretending to be a plumber, or a dope-dealing plumber, or a serial killer plumber. The guy was a plumber, Richard. That's all. At least that's all I could find."

"You have a list of his clients?"

He nodded. "Right here." He stopped walking and took some papers out of a plastic bag that he used instead of a briefcase. "What do you want to know?"

"Did he have any clients in Ardmore, New York?"

He scanned the papers. "Four of them that he saw in the last six months."

"Any of them named Ryan?"

He looked again. "Two were companies, the other two residential. No Ryan."

"I've got some other things I want you to do," I said.

"Can we sit down somewhere? It's easier for me to take notes. And my hands are already frozen."

"Sure. How about that bench?"

"What's with this meeting-in-the-park stuff?" he asked. "You going romantic on me? It's cold as hell out here."

We walked over to the bench and sat down, and then I waited for a young couple to pass before I answered him.

"I think my apartment might be bugged; maybe my phones as well."

"Why do you think that?"

I told him about the guy following me, and the fact that he seemed to have either stopped doing so, or taken greater pains to hide himself. "I talked about him with Allie in my apartment, and on the phone."

"Richard, you okay?" he asked.

"I'm getting by. Why?"

"You see a guy on the street and decide he's following you. Then you don't see him anymore, so you decide he's bugging you. Your friend talks to somebody and that person gets murdered, and you think it's all about you. You see where I'm going with this?"

"Craig, I know it sounds bizarre, but humor me."

He looked like he was about to argue, but then shrugged. "Okay. You want me to bring in somebody to check your apartment and phones?"

"Thanks, but I'm going to get that done," I said.

He looked skeptical. "How?"

"I did an article last year on espionage in business, and I interviewed a guy who's an expert in this stuff. I'm going to call him."

"You sure?" he asked. "Because I can take care of it."

I shook my head. "I'm sure. I'll have plenty of other things for you."

On the chance that my cell phone calls were being monitored, I stopped at a pay phone on the way home and called Mark Cook, the electronics guy I'd mentioned to Craig. He remembered me and agreed to come check out my place, and even said he wouldn't charge me. Chances are he had read my article about Jen and, like everyone else in America, felt sorry for me.

I went back to my apartment to write the magazine piece. I wasn't smart enough to figure a way to draw out the people I was searching for, if they existed at all, so I went with the straightforward approach. I essentially wrote part two of what might become an ongoing series, which started with my previous article about Jen's disappearance.

So I told the truth, or at least as much of it as I thought necessary. I wrote about Allie and Julie, and I included Julie's picture. I wrote about the Donovans, and I also wrote about the guy following me, describing him and his car as best I could.

I didn't mention anything about my apparently having been working on a major story that had been wiped from my mind, nor did I mention Dr. Garber and his comment that I had said the story was about Sean Lassiter. I still had to follow up on the Lassiter connection and see if it led me anywhere, but there were just so many hours in the day.

I really didn't care that the majority of people who read the story would think I was descending further into a paranoid insanity. If sunlight was the best disinfectant, I was doing the best I could to flush out the germs.

The more I could bring everything out in the open, the better chance I had of finding out what the hell was going on.

Before I submitted it, I gave it to Allie to read over dinner. "It's powerful," she said, but didn't say so with much enthusiasm.

"What's wrong?" I asked.

"I don't think you'll scare them with this, Richard. You're pulling your punches."

"I'm drawing attention to what's going on."

She nodded. "Until some family pretends to send a kid up in a hot-air balloon, or another athlete or politician gets caught with his pants down. I think you should try to do more with this. I think you should try and scare the people we're chasing."

"Why?"

"So that maybe they'll make a mistake," she said.

"They might try to rectify that mistake by coming after us," I pointed out.

She nodded again. "They might."

"We don't really have anything to scare them with. All I could do would be to put in the piece that we have leads I can't talk about, but that are bringing us closer to the answer."

"I think you should include that," she said. "Make it sound like we're hot on their tail, and that we're about to go to law enforcement with what we know."

"Good idea," I said. "You know, I told Scott that he couldn't edit the piece, and now you're doing it."

She smiled. "Somebody had to."

# The Stone made the presentation six times
to eleven people.

At no time did he make it to more than two people at once. It was a game that had to be played; even though each of the people knew very well who they were competing with, there was no way they would ever get in the same room.

Stone was surprised that the repetitive process did not bore him. Such was the power of the presentation, and the recipients were so clearly impressed that he enjoyed it each and every time.

It was a multimedia show, starring Richard Kilmer, and broken into two parts, with an intermission so that questions could be asked. The dividing line was that day in Ardmore, with the post-car-crash material primarily a collection of the amazing video and audio surveillance that had followed Kilmer wherever he went.

The object was to show the great stress that Kilmer was under, and the fact that it was having no effect on the ultimate accomplishment. But the Stone didn't hype anything; he just let the material speak for itself.

The Stone had long ago decided that using Kilmer was the smartest move he had ever made, and he had made a lot of smart moves. Kilmer had gone public, as the Stone had hoped he would, giving the project the kind of credibility that all the presentations in the world could never fully accomplish.

These people were smart enough to comprehend what they were looking at, and they had long ago understood how it could benefit them. Most of them weren't the ultimate decision makers, but their recommendations would have great influence on those who were.

But the Stone was not looking to make the sale yet; it would not be in his best interest to do so. That would come when the demonstration was concluded, after Kilmer starred in the grand finale.

Then the final bidding would begin, and the winning bid would be more than ten billion dollars. The Stone had already decided on that minimum amount, and he knew he could get it. It was at least twenty times more than he figured he could get if he had acted legally. And then he would first have had to share that with his cocreators, before dealing with all the other vultures who would come looking to piggyback onto his success.

But the difference in money, while compelling, was not his only reason for going this route. He was determined that this country was not going to reap the benefits of his genius. The powers that be had long ago decided he was beneath them and was not to be respected or trusted. They would pay dearly for the way they treated him.

Based on the faces of the people watching his presentation, respect was there in abundance. They were in awe of his work, and prepared to pay a fortune to acquire it.

Which was fine with him.

**"Did you see this?"** Hank Miller walked into the room without knocking and laid the open magazine on the desk of his ex-brother-in-law, Lieutenant George Kentris of the Ellenville Police Department. Ellenville is a town about twenty minutes from Monticello. It's similar in size, though slightly smaller.

Kentris looked up and frowned. "If I worked as hard as you, I'd have time to read magazines," Kentris said.

"Then it's lucky I stopped by. Read it."

Kentris picked it up and scanned through Richard's latest article, reading more carefully as he realized why Hank had brought it to him.

Kentris had been on station duty about eight months before when a man had been reported trying to enter a home in an upscale residential Ellenville neighborhood, and two officers had gone to get him. They brought him back to the station, which was how the guy became Lieutenant Kentris's problem.

What made the situation unusual was that the guy, who seemed to be in his early forties, claimed to be the owner of the house he was trying to enter. And it wasn't that he was breaking the door down or climbing through a window; he had knocked on the door because he said he had misplaced his key.

The man said his name was Daniel Richardson, but had no identification to prove or disprove it. He said he lived at that home with his wife, Cynthia, and their eight-year-old son, Andrew. He was employed as a science teacher at the local high school, and had been there for ten years.

Kentris had done some checking, and absolutely nothing the man said was true. He had never lived in the house, was not a teacher at the school, and there was absolutely no evidence that he or his family ever lived in Ellenville, or anywhere else, for that matter. Kentris let him call his wife, but the number he dialed was out of service, which he couldn't explain and which seemed to both puzzle and worry him.

But the man sounded completely credible and earnest, and claimed to be confused by what was going on. There had to be some mistake, he proclaimed, because everything he was saying was true. What would he have to gain by lying?

He also didn't seem like the typical vagrant. He was reasonably well dressed, clean and freshly shaven, and spoke clearly and articulately. He did not seem in any way impaired, no alcohol on his breath or needle marks on his arms, and passed a field sobriety test that Kentris administered, even though they were not in the field.

So he was either lying through his teeth or completely delusional.

It was late in the day, and Kentris would have to start the process of identifying the guy in the morning, but he wasn't sure where to keep him that night. The jail was a possibility but somehow didn't seem right. Kentris liked the guy, felt sorry for him, and wanted to help. And the guy hadn't tried to break into the house; all he had done was knock on the door.

So Kentris had called Hank, who owned a motel out near the highway, and asked if he could put the guy up in a room.

"No problem," Hank said. "As long as the department is paying."

"I was hoping you wouldn't charge for the one night."

"I was hoping the bank wouldn't ask for my mortgage payment this month. And I was hoping your sister would send back my alimony check," he said. "Hope is for suckers."

"Okay, you cheap son of a bitch. The department will pay," Kentris said. "Can you lock his room from the outside?"

"Sure, but there's an additional locking fee for that."

"You're an asshole, Hank. My sister was smart to dump you."

"No argument there," he said cheerfully.

Kentris dropped off the mysterious guy on the way home and stayed while Hank put him in a room. He'd pick the guy up in the morning on the way in, and either solve the mystery or turn him over to Social Services. Or maybe the guy would have a true story to tell by then.

"You stay here, and we'll get started on finding out what's going on in the morning," Kentris said. "You all right with that?"

"Sure," the guy said. "I'm really tired."

Kentris left after Hank locked the door from the outside. "What if he gets hungry?" he asked.

Hank shrugged. "Hopefully he has some Tic Tacs with him. Room service is closed."

"When did it close?"

"I think during the Carter administration."

As it turned out, the man had no need to call room service, because he was dead within an hour of his entering the motel room. Kentris discovered him in bed the next morning. He had placed a .22-caliber gun to his temple and pulled the trigger. His fingerprints were on the gun, and gunpowder traces were on his hand. The coroner ruled it a suicide; it was not a difficult call for him to make.

Both the arresting officers and Kentris had previously determined that he was not armed, and the door to the motel room had remained locked from the outside. No one had reported hearing a gunshot. After an investigation by the state police, the officers and Kentris were all given reprimands for their lax handling of the matter.

It was and remained the most upsetting incident of Kentris's career, and not because of the reprimand. A man had died on his watch, and it was a death that could have been prevented. Having said that, Kentris did not understand how the weapon could have been concealed.

Two weeks after the body was found, it was learned that Daniel Richardson was really Larry Collins, from Norman, Oklahoma. He was an associate professor of mathematics at the University of Oklahoma, and had disappeared from his home three weeks before. His family and the local police could not provide any reason why.

When Kentris finished reading Richard's article, Hank asked, "Sound a little familiar?"

"Worth checking into, that's for sure," Kentris said. The article had referred to a previous article written on the same subject, and Kentris had vaguely heard about it. But he never really paid attention, because until now he never knew it had any connection to anything he was involved with. But the Donovans were murdered less than ten miles from Kentris's office, so now the connection was there.

"So if this turns out to be anything, can you deputize me?" Hank asked. "Maybe give me a commendation, or the key to the city, or something?"

"Why don't you go back to the motel?" Kentris asked, looking at his watch. "The after-lunch, one-hour-quickie crowd should be showing up around now."

**"Who do you work for, the KGB?"** The question was asked by Mark Cook, who was in my house waiting for me when I got home from dinner with Allie. He had just spent the last three hours checking to see if my place was being bugged.

"What does that mean?"

"Somebody has heard every word you said in this house, and seen every move you've made. Somebody who knew exactly what he was doing, and had an unlimited supply of money to help him do it."

"The place was bugged," I said. It wasn't a question, but a statement. I was trying to let my mind process the implications.

"About twenty-five years ago the U.S. government built a huge new embassy building in Moscow. While it was being built, the Russians put bugging devices everywhere, even in the foundation. The Americans discovered it and never moved in, but if they hadn't, nothing they ever did or said would have been private."

"So?"

"So, compared to this, that embassy was clean," Cook said.

"Should we be talking about this outside?" I asked.

Cook shook his head. "Doesn't matter; it's all been disabled. Took a while."

"So they know we know."

Cook shrugged. "They knew the moment I started looking. They watched me do it. I even gave them the finger."

I couldn't even think of anything to say, so Cook went on. "This is serious stuff," he said, "and you are dealing with serious people. Some of the devices were so state-of-the-art that I had to call some friends to check them out. Half of them are classified."

He handed me what looked like a golf tee, only maybe a tenth the size. At the end of it was glass; it couldn't have been more than an eighth of an inch wide. "What is it?" I asked.

"A video camera. Set to turn on by heat. Body temperature. There were eleven of them in your house. Each one cost about six grand."

"And we have no idea who received the pictures that they were transmitting? Is there any way to determine that?"

He shook his head. "No way at all. And if there was, these people would be smart enough to send us on a wild-goose chase."

All of this was completely stunning to me, but the shock was starting to give way to anger. Having said that, it was also mingled with some relief. I was not crazy. Some outside, diabolical force was behind Jen's disappearance from the very beginning. I don't know how they completely wiped all traces of her from my life, and all memories of her from everybody we knew, but I would figure it out.

No matter what it took, I would figure it out.

When Cook left, I called Craig Langel and told him what I had just learned. "Jesus Christ," he said, whistling softly to emphasize his surprise. "You trust this guy to be telling you the straight scoop?"

"Totally. He had nothing to gain. He didn't even charge me."

"And you have no idea who's doing this?" he asked.

I responded by telling Craig that I had reason to think the story I had mentioned to him was about Sean Lassiter, and asked him to investigate what Lassiter was currently doing, and who he was doing it to. "Maybe Lassiter is somehow involved in this," I said.

"That wouldn't surprise me," he said. He had done some work on the original Lassiter story. "I'll check it out."

Allie operated on a higher emotional level than me; she felt the same things I felt, she just was more intense about it. So when I told her about the bugging of the house, she was even more outraged than I was, and at the same time so relieved that she seemed thrilled.

"This confirms everything," she said. "The guy following you, the Donovans' murder being connected to all this . . . everything. We have a real enemy to defeat now. There's no question about it."

Once again she didn't seem to want to focus on the fact that the enemy had demonstrated a capacity for cold-blooded murder, probably because of what it would say about the chances for Jen to be alive. I didn't bring it up because I wanted to push it as far back in my mind as I could.

"We need to get to Ardmore," I said.

She nodded. "Tell me about it." Every time she used that expression that Jen always used, I found it jarring.

"We'll go tomorrow."

"Have we decided what we're going to do when we get there?"

"We'll visit all of Donovan's clients; I've got the list from Craig. We'll talk to all the people we know he saw there."

"And then?"

"Then we go see the people that I met while I was there. Including Jen's mother."

I could see Allie react to this, but she didn't say anything. She was of the belief that Jen's mother and hers were one and the same, and that the woman in question was in Wisconsin.

"I'm sorry . . . you know what I mean," I said.

She nodded. "Yes. I understand."

"I think we have to turn over as many rocks as we can, try to stir things up as much as possible. Then see what happens."

"Let's do it," she said.

**The drive out to Ardmore was excruciating;** I was literally going back to the scene of my worst nightmare. I had never imagined I would ever go near the place again, unless it was to bring Jen home. And that certainly was not going to happen, at least not this time.

Allie was sensitive enough to leave me alone with my thoughts, and we drove in relative silence for almost the entire trip. I'm sure she was grappling with her own emotions as well; this was possibly even tougher on her than on me. At least I knew I was searching for Jen; for all her confidence, Allie couldn't be sure her sister had any connection to this other than an amazing resemblance.

When we passed the WELCOME TO ARDMORE sign, Allie put her hand on mine, which happened to be on the steering wheel at the time. "Good things happen starting now," she said.

I smiled. "It's definitely time."

The first thing we came upon was the general store at the edge of town, where Jen and I had stopped the first time, and where I had stopped on the way out to question the clerk. I pulled into the parking lot, and Allie said, "You've been in here?"

"Yes. Twice." Then I smiled. "Or more. Or never. Or this place is a figment of our imaginations."

We went inside; it looked exactly like it had the previous time, and the same woman that I had spoken to was working the register. When I walked over to her, she looked up at me, and her face brightened.

"Well, look who's here." She opened the door leading to the back room and yelled, "Cassie, come on out here!"

Within seconds a teenage girl came out from the back, and did a double-take when she saw me. "I don't believe it."

"What are you two talking about?"

"You're the guy that wrote the articles in that magazine, aren't you? You stopped in here and asked about Janice Ryan."

"Yes."

She turned to Cassie. "I told you. He was in here then just like he is now."

"Look, I—"

She cut me off. "Mister, you sure turned this town upside down. Can I get a picture of you with Cassie?"

Before I agreed to the picture, and after I exchanged amazed eye contact with Allie, I questioned them to find out exactly what the hell they were talking about. It turns out that my original article on Jen had actually attracted tourists to the place, according to the clerk by the thousands.

She even showed me what was literally an entire wall of T-shirts and trinkets that she had on sale, with Jen's picture on them and the words LAST SEEN IN ARDMORE? I had actually never thought about whether or not my article had penetrated this town, and I was very surprised to hear about the effect it had and the reaction it provoked.

Surprised and annoyed.

Jen was not a gimmick, a curiosity, or something to attract tourists and cash, but that was what had happened. And I had no one to blame but myself.

Allie stepped near me and said, "Are these people getting on your nerves as much as they're getting on mine?" She said it just loud enough for them to hear her, and the surprise registered on their faces.

Allie and I left, and outside there were at least a dozen people standing there watching us. Somehow word had leaked out—maybe from one of the other customers—that we were inside, and curiosity-seekers had already started to come out.

We disregarded them and got in our car. "These people have got to be kidding," Allie said, obviously annoyed. Then she called out to them, "Anybody here considering getting a life?"

She didn't wait for an answer, and got into the car. I said, "I expected them to throw rocks at me, not treat me like a rock star."

I decided to take Allie out to where Jen had disappeared before making any other stops, so we headed out toward Kendrick Falls, which we never reached last time. It was likely going to be the toughest part of the day for me emotionally, and I wanted to get it over with.

It was a beautiful day, nothing whatsoever like the last time, when the ominous clouds formed and essentially forced us off the road. It took us less than fifteen minutes to reach our destination.

"Here's where the storm started to build," I said, trying to maintain my composure. "And here's where we rolled over into the ditch."

I pulled over and stopped the car. I kept gripping the wheel tightly; it was my best shot at keeping my hands from shaking.

"Let's get out," Allie said, and she proceeded to do so before I could object. I got out as well.

"So where did the car wind up?" she asked.

"What's the difference?" I responded, feeling very uncomfortable to be there at all. "Why is that important?"

"I don't know. I just want to understand what happened, to see it for myself. Bear with me, Richard. Okay?"

"Okay." I looked around, trying to get my bearings, and walked over to the tree that the car had lodged against. I knew I had the right one, and it was confirmed by the slight damage that had been done to the tree. I hadn't crashed into the tree; the car's momentum had already mostly stopped when it arrived there.

"We landed here," I said. "Then I ran up to the road, stopped some cars, and we all looked alongside the road on both sides for Jen."

"Come on," Allie said, and started retracing the steps up to the road. I didn't follow her, because I was looking at something else. I was looking at the area behind us.

When Allie realized I wasn't with her, she turned and said, "Is something wrong?"

I didn't answer; I just stood there, and then slowly walked in the direction I was staring.

"Richard, what is it?" she asked, and came back toward me to see for herself.

"Allie, we were probably going sixty miles an hour when the storm hit. It came up so fast that we didn't have much time to slow down. So we would have been going at least forty, forty-five when we went off the road."

"So?"

"So we would have been still moving forward after we left the road. We would have gone through all of this shrubbery before we wound up at that tree."

Allie looked and realized what I was talking about. The shrubbery seemed undamaged, the small trees untouched. "So it didn't happen that way at all," she said. "At least some of those trees would have been knocked down if it had."

"I was there, Allie. I experienced it."

"Then maybe you have the spot wrong. Maybe it happened farther up the road."

I shook my head. "No. It was here. It just didn't happen the way I lived it. Nothing happened the way I lived it."

I could see Janice Ryan looking out the window as we pulled up. I was reacting emotionally to everything I was reexperiencing in Ardmore, but I would have to really gird myself for this one. This house was where I stayed with Jen those last few days. It was where we made love, where I asked her to marry me.

Where she said yes.

Janice came out on to the porch, and I saw it as a positive that she wasn't carrying a shotgun. The last time I saw her she had smacked me in the face; this time I expected worse. I had no idea if she would talk to us, but I took it as a bad sign that she wasn't wearing one of the FIND JEN tourist T-shirts.

We got out of the car and I approached the porch, with Allie walking a few steps behind me. "Mrs. Ryan, I know that you were upset by what happened, and I—"

She didn't let me finish. "Come in. Please."

I introduced Allie, and they exchanged pleasantries. Janice had no particular reaction to Allie, certainly not the way she would have reacted if Allie looked exactly like her missing daughter. We went inside, and the interior of the house still bore little resemblance to how it looked when Jen and I stayed there, but that was what I expected.

Janice offered us coffee and we accepted, and we all sat down in the den to drink it and talk. "Thanks for inviting us in," I said. "I'm sorry for the way I acted the last time I was here."

She shook her head. "No, I'm the one who should apologize. There is no excuse for the way I behaved."

"It was understandable," I said.

"You mentioned my daughter, Jennifer. She was my baby. She died when she was two years old. Nothing was ever the same after that."

I had known she had a daughter who died very young, but I did not know her name was Jennifer. I should have checked. "I'm sorry," I said. "I can understand why what I said upset you so much."

"I read your magazine articles," she said, then smiled. "Pretty much everybody around here has. I just want you to know that I was not here with you or Jennifer, and Ben, my husband, died twenty years ago. I know you think it all happened the way you wrote it, but it did not."

"We're trying to figure out what did happen," Allie said.

Janice looked at her and nodded. "So am I."

Her comment surprised me. "What do you mean?"

She stood up. "I'll show you."

We followed her to the bedroom where Jen and I had slept, which was furnished as a den. As in every other room in the house, the rooms were filled with things . . . trinkets, paintings, photographs . . . the tables and walls were pretty much loaded to capacity.

"I was on vacation. . . . I went to see my brother in South Carolina for a week . . . just before you were in Ardmore."

She walked over to the wall and touched a few of the pictures, straightening them slightly. They were of a happier time in her life, and most included her with a particular man, who I assumed was her late husband. He was not the man I remembered, not the father who bragged about his daughter.

"When I came back, things were different. Small things, but enough for me to notice."

"What kind of things?" I asked.

"Some of this was out of place. A few of the pictures were mixed up, things on the tables were out of order."

"Out of order?" Allie asked.

"Yes. When you don't have people, family, around you anymore, you live with things. They represent my memories. I know exactly where they are; I could close my eyes and describe everything that was in every one of these rooms."

"And it changed when you were away?"

She nodded. "I could give you at least five examples. I couldn't understand it; I didn't know what to make of it. The doors were still locked, and the alarm had not gone off. If it had, the police would have been called. And nothing was missing; there was no robbery. I thought I must have been wrong, but I knew I wasn't."

I believed her, and I could tell that Allie did as well. But like everything else, it made little sense. She'd been already back from vacation when I was there with Jen, and the house had looked nothing at all like this.

We talked for a while longer; Janice seemed eager for the company. But we made no progress in understanding what had happened in this house. I knew I was here, with Jen, for those four days, and she knew for certain that I was not.

The facts were on her side.

As we got ready to leave, Allie said to her, "We're so sorry you had to go through all this," and they hugged.

Janice teared up noticeably, and stepped back, as if to look at Allie. "My Jen would have been just about your age," she said, and then hugged Allie again.

We finally left, and it was too late to track down anyone else. We weren't terribly in the mood to do so anyway, both of us were feeling a little drained by what we had already been through.

"Doesn't make much sense to drive back to the city tonight, only to come back up here tomorrow," I said.

She nodded her agreement. "There was a motel near the exit where we got off the highway; it looked okay."

I had seen it; it was a Hampton Inn and certainly seemed fine for the night. We went back there and checked in to two rooms, then went into the restaurant/bar off the lobby for dinner.

Neither of us wanted to talk much about our search; we had been blanketed by it for so long that we shared a desire to be rid of it, if only for a short time. So we talked about everything else, about how we grew up, about politics, about sports, about how we liked to spend time when we weren't searching for missing loved ones.

I continued to be amazed at how at ease I felt with Allie, and I could tell she felt the same about being with me. Maybe it was our shared loss, or our shared goal, but we just clicked in a way I rarely have with anyone. Even the silences were fine, a sure indicator in my book that two people are in sync.

We didn't just talk; we also drank. More than we should have, but we didn't get blasted. Just drunk enough to feel good, a feeling that neither of us had experienced for a very long time.

We closed the place down, which was not exactly a sign of decadence in Ardmore, since closing time was eleven P.M. Our rooms were next to each other on the third floor, so we rode up on the elevator together and then walked together down the hall to the rooms.

What happened next I don't think was because we were drunk, but I'm not really clear on any of it, and I'm not sure I ever will be. Allie opened the door to her room, and then turned back to me, maybe to say good night. I kissed her, or maybe she kissed me. She pulled me into her room, or maybe I pushed her.

Within moments we were on the bed making love, and I was not inclined to ponder who was the instigator or whether it was the right thing to do.

It sure as hell felt right in the moment.

# I woke up at seven A.M. and discovered that

Allie was already showered and dressed. I wasn't sure how I was going to deal with the awkwardness left over from what had happened between us, but Allie solved it for me.

"It happened, Richard. There's no going back, and there's no undoing it. But it's yesterday, and we need to focus on today and tomorrow."

"So no guilt?" I asked.

She smiled, reached out, and lightly touched my face. "We don't have time. Maybe later."

We had breakfast downstairs and checked out. I had a list of the four clients that Frank Donovan had serviced in Ardmore, and we set out to visit each of them.

The first was a residential house on the outskirts of town. It was small and fairly run-down, and the people who lived there had no apparent desire to be helpful. They did tell us that they'd bought the place just three weeks before, and that they thought the previous owners had moved to somewhere in the Midwest. It would have been those people who hired Frank, so if we were being told the truth, there was nothing to be learned there.

The second client was also residential. Rita and Donald

Church lived only three blocks from the Ryan house. They reacted to us much like they might have if Brad Pitt and Angelina Jolie had shown up; I was a full-fledged celebrity in their minds.

Rita invited us in for some coffee and apple pie, which was about all we got out of the visit. They remembered calling Frank for plumbing services because a pipe had broken under their shower and their basement was flooding.

Ralph replaced the pipe and charged them what they felt was an exorbitant amount. The Churches were in their late sixties and retired, and if there was anything about them that would connect to the murders, neither Allie nor I could find it.

Our third stop was Ardmore General Hospital, where Frank had made three visits in the past two months. According to Craig, his company was on a retainer with the hospital, being paid a flat fee for handling whatever plumbing work needed to be done.

It was a much larger facility than I would have expected, and far bigger than the tiny place where I had been taken after the accident on the day Jen disappeared. There were three quite large two-story buildings, and a smaller annex building in the back, spread out over a tranquil, campus-type environment. The receptionist at the desk told us it was the only decent-sized hospital in the area, and people who lived as far as twenty-five miles away considered it their home hospital.

She also told us that the director of the hospital was Dr. Harold Gates, and we asked to see him. I told her I was from *Manhattan* magazine, and she said, "I thought you looked familiar. You're that guy, right?"

I nodded. "I'm that guy."

Allie walked back toward the hospital entrance as the receptionist picked up the phone and dialed a number, then talked softly so that I couldn't hear. I assumed she was telling Gates, or his assistant, that "that guy" was here, and wasn't that a big deal. It must have been, because within three minutes Allie and I were granted an audience with him.

Dr. Gates was surprisingly young, no more than forty. He

had a smooth way about him, polished, as if he would be better at selling medical supplies than using them. Perhaps political savvy was necessary to work one's way up the Ardmore General Hospital totem pole, and it seemed likely that Gates had it in significant quantity.

"Nice of you to see us without an appointment," I said.

He smiled. "You're a celebrity around here. If I turned you away, my staff would have revolted. So what can I do for you?"

"You had a plumbing company working for you run by Frank Donovan."

His expression revealed nothing, if there was anything to reveal. "Okay, if you say so."

"Mr. Donovan and his wife were recently murdered."

Again no change in expression. "I'm certainly sorry to hear that. What does it have to do with the hospital? Assuming, of course, that you're right about him doing work here."

"We have reason to believe that he saw something here in Ardmore, very possibly at this hospital, that made him a danger to someone . . . that resulted in his death."

"I can assure you that I have no knowledge of this whatsoever."

"Who would have been Mr. Donovan's contact here?"

"Probably someone in our engineering department. Why are you asking me these questions instead of the police?"

"I'm sure they will be," I lied. With the unsubstantiated suspicions we had about the Donovans being related to Jen's disappearance, there would be no chance we could get the police to back us up.

Allie, who hadn't spoken a word since hello, held up a flyer she had gone back to take off the bulletin board near the lobby entrance. "You run drug trials here?"

He nodded. "Yes, a great many of them."

"How does that work?" she asked.

"Pharmaceutical companies that have new drugs approved by the FDA for trial come to us. We carefully screen for people whose medical conditions fit the profile, and we conduct trials according to the specifications we are given. It is a specialty of ours. That flyer is for the purpose of recruiting volunteers."

"Why do you do it?" Allie asked.

"It is worthwhile work, and it enables us to provide traditional medical services to our patients at reasonable cost. That's not an easy thing for a hospital to do in this day and age. Now, if you don't mind my asking, what does all this have to do with Mr. Donovan?"

I knew where Allie was going with this, so I jumped in. "Have you done work for Sean Lassiter?"

Finally, Gates changed his facial expression from painted smile to a mixture of annoyance and concern. "We don't discuss our clients. That is privileged."

"So Lassiter is a client?"

"I didn't say that."

"I know," I said. "That's why I asked."

"I really have nothing to say about that."

The conversation took a downhill turn from there, and Gates became noticeably less forthcoming. Within ten minutes we were ushered out; apparently my celebrity status had its limitations.

"You struck a nerve when you mentioned Lassiter," Allie said when we got into the car. "I'd bet anything he and Lassiter are connected somehow."

"I thought so too. If Donovan worked here, and Lassiter has a connection to the place as well, then you could be right."

"About what?"

I smiled. "We could be getting somewhere."

Our last stop was at a diner in the center of town, where Donovan had been summoned when the drains were clogged about six weeks prior. It seemed innocent enough, and both Allie and I had the same reaction, that it was not in any way connected to Donovan's murder.

We drove back to the city, talking the whole way about our

search for Jen and what progress we might have made in Ardmore. I dropped her off at her hotel and then went home.

When I walked into my apartment, I saw that the answering machine light was blinking. I walked over and pressed "play."

"Richard, are you there? Richard, please be there . . . please. . . ."

Then there was a clicking sound, and that was the last I heard of the voice.

Jen's voice.

**Juice had no one to blame but himself.** Getting careless and letting the amateurs make him, so that they knew he was following them, was making his job much more difficult. He could still track them; that was no problem. But getting Kilmer on tape, on camera, had become much more difficult. And that was his main job.

Fortunately, he had technology on his side, and his access to and knowledge of state-of-the-art devices was a huge help. Also helpful was the fact that Kilmer was absolutely predictable in what he would do and where he would go. Juice thought he actually could have gone ahead of Kilmer and waited for him to arrive; that's how obvious his moves were.

But there was one surprise, one Kilmer move that Juice had not expected. That was his nailing the sister in her motel room; he didn't think Kilmer would have the balls for that. Juice counted himself smart, and a little lucky, that he had chosen to plant bugs in both rooms and not just Kilmer's, because it was her room that they had shacked up in.

Juice had also recorded every word spoken in the Ryan house as well as in Gates's office at the hospital. Even without hearing it himself, he knew that the Stone would find it all very interesting.

Except for the mistake made in revealing himself to Kilmer, Juice took comfort in the fact that up to that point he had done everything right. He hoped that the Stone was having similar success, because Juice was getting tired of this assignment. And since it was the last one he would have to undertake, he was impatient to get on with the more satisfying part of his life. That would really be living.

The irony wasn't lost on Juice that his life would begin when Kilmer's ended.

Allie started sobbing softly as soon as she heard the voice. That told me all I needed to know; as positive as I was that it was Jen, she was just as sure it was her sister Julie. It was further evidence that Jen and Julie were one and the same, and very strong evidence, at that.

"She sounded so scared," Allie said, once she had composed herself.

I nodded. "I know. But the most important thing is that she sounded alive. We need to hold on to that."

"Who are these people?" she asked, as her pained expression started to give way to rage. "Who are these goddamn people?"

She laid her head on my chest, and I held her as she started crying again. "We'll get them," I said. "We'll get them."

"We need to go to the police. There's a limit to how much we can do by ourselves."

I had thought about that, but shook my head at the suggestion. "We don't have anything that we can use. Think about it; they won't even believe that Jen existed. And there's nothing to tie Julie in to it. We have no proof of anything; it's as if they've designed it that way."

"What do you mean?"

126

"It feels like we're being played; like whoever's doing this is moving us around like pieces on a chessboard. But they're always one step ahead."

"Do you think that the call from Julie . . . Jen . . . was part of that?" she asked. "Could they have let her make the call because they wanted us to know she's alive?"

"It's possible. But we won't know until we know."

The phone rang and startled both Allie and me. I looked at the caller ID, which had been blocked on the phone call from Jen. It read *Ellenville Police Department*.

"Kilmer."

"Mr. Kilmer, this is Lieutenant Kentris of the Ellenville Police Department. I would like to speak to you about the articles you have written."

"What about them?"

"I believe that in some way they may relate to an open case we have up here."

"I'm listening," I said.

"I think it's better that we talk in person. Would you be able to come up here? We're about an hour and a half from the city, not too far from Monticello."

"I know where you are," I said. "Hold on for a second, please."

I put my hand over the phone and told Allie the substance of the conversation so far. I wasn't halfway through when she was already nodding eagerly and looking for my car keys.

"Would this afternoon work, Lieutenant?"

"That would work well, thank you. How about three o'clock in my office?"

I agreed, and Allie and I set off for Ellenville, with time to stop for lunch along the way. I brought along the answering machine with Jen's voice on it, though I didn't believe there would be a reason to play it for Kentris.

We arrived at the Ellenville PD at about two-thirty, but we were quickly brought in to see Kentris without having to wait.

After the introductions, he said, "Sorry to bring you all this way; it may turn out to be unrelated to your situation."

"Why don't you tell us what you have?" I said.

He told us a story about a man who was found in Ellenville, trying to enter a house that he swore was his, and that he lived in with his wife and child. As it turned out, everything the man had said was completely untrue, and that night he committed suicide.

After his death it was learned that he was a professor at the University of Oklahoma, and that his family had no idea how he got to Ellenville, why he would have made up a new life story, or why he would commit suicide. They described him as a completely stable person, in no way prone to eccentric or unpredictable behavior.

"They thought it had to be murder," Kentris said, "but the coroner said otherwise."

"What did you think?" I asked.

"That it was murder. But the door was locked from the outside, so I don't know how the killer got inside."

"I keep my apartment locked at all times, but they managed to bug every square inch of the place. It was like I had an open-door policy. I can't believe a motel room lock could have come close to stopping them."

Kentris's story was very interesting to me, because in many ways it mirrored mine, and because it took place so close to Ardmore and Monticello.

"Do you have a picture of this guy that we could look at?" I asked.

Kentris nodded. "I do. We got it from his wife in Oklahoma."

He took it from the file on his desk and handed it to Allie, who was closest to him. She looked at it, but didn't seem to have any reaction, and then handed it to me.

"I don't recall ever seeing him before," I said.

Kentris nodded and handed us a picture of a second man. "What about him?"

Again, neither Allie nor I recognized him, and we said so.

Kentris handed us a picture of a third man, whom Allie didn't recognize. But as soon as I saw it, I had no doubt.

"It's Jen's father," I said. I was looking at Ben Ryan, the man I had spent four days with, the man who bragged about his daughter and subtly questioned my intentions. I then went on to explain what I meant, since Kentris had no idea what I was talking about.

"Are you sure about this?" he asked.

"Positive. No doubt in my mind. Is he the guy you were telling us about, the one who died in his motel room?"

Kentris nodded. "That's the one."

"Who were the other two men?"

"Nobody related to this case."

"You were testing me?" I asked.

He shrugged. "I'm a cop; think of it as a lineup." Then he asked me to tell him what we knew or suspected. He had read my articles, so he knew a lot of it already, but I filled in the blanks, including the connections to Lassiter. He seemed to believe me, which was incredibly gratifying; nobody in a position of authority had ever taken any of this seriously.

Kentris said that he was intrigued enough that he would question Gates at Ardmore General about the dealings he had with Lassiter. "I don't have jurisdiction up there, but I know the chief. He'll send someone with me."

"He told us any dealings he may have had with Lassiter are confidential," Allie said.

Kentris smiled. "Unless he's Lassiter's lawyer or priest, that ain't going to fly."

**On the way back to the city, I asked Allie to** move in with me. Not in those words, of course. We were pulling up at her hotel, and I said, "This place has got to be costing you a fortune."

She smiled. "In Wisconsin, I could have bought a medium-sized hotel for the money I've spent already. Plus season tickets to the Packers."

"You're a football fan?"

She smiled. "I had a drawerful of Brett Favre shirts. Which, of course, I have since burned."

"Allie, this has nothing to do with what happened the other night. In fact, it's in spite of what happened. But I think you should stay in my apartment. You'll have your own room, your own bathroom, and the rates are ridiculously cheap."

"You don't think it will be awkward?" she asked.

"It probably will be a little, at least at first, but we'll deal with it. Everything has changed since that phone message. We know Jen is real, and alive. And we know she and Julie are the same person."

She still hesitated, so I said, "And we're spending so much

time together, it would just be more convenient if we're in the same place."

"Okay. Thank you. That would be nice."

"Can you cook?" I asked.

"I think I'm really good at it, but I've never actually met someone who shared that opinion."

We went up to her room and I waited while she packed and checked out. Then we drove to my apartment, and while she unpacked I went downstairs and picked up a pizza.

When I got back, she was straightening up the apartment. "What are you doing?" I asked.

"Attempting to make the place livable; it's going to be an uphill struggle."

"It was by definition already livable," I said. "I know that because I've been living in it."

"But now I'm going to be here, so we need to set the bar a little higher."

I couldn't help myself. "That's what Jen said."

Allie started to say something but then caught herself. Finally, "And she'll say it again when she comes back."

We had dinner and some wine and talked about the effect Kentris might have on our situation. "He's got to help," I said. "He's part of law enforcement; he can get access to things that we can't."

"And he seemed to believe us," she said. "That's a pleasant switch from everybody else in the world."

"We need to keep him motivated. It's an old case for him, and new cases must come in every day."

We decided to watch a movie, and chose *The Freshman*, with Marlon Brando and Matthew Broderick. It turned out that it had been a favorite of both of ours, and we both felt like seeing something familiar and funny.

There was no doubt that I was attracted to Allie. Actually, it was more than that, but that was as much as I would admit to at the time.

When the movie was over we were both ready for bed—separate beds, to be exact. There was no serious thought of anything else, and there was not going to be.

I went to the closet to get a blanket, sheets, and a pillow for Allie to use. I had offered her my room rather than the adjacent guest room, since it was larger and more comfortable, but she declined. There was a door connecting the two rooms, but I decided not to mention it, or, for that matter, ever open it.

I woke up at what my alarm clock said was 1:27 in the morning, and I realized it was the sound of a cell phone ringing that got me up. At first I started to grope for my cell phone, but quickly realized from the faintness of the sound that it was Allie's phone.

Middle-of-the-night calls are jarring, even when they're not to me. In this case it was even more jarring than usual because of all that had gone on. I had no real reason to think that the call had anything to do with me, but I couldn't eliminate the possibility either.

I got up and stood near the connecting door, hoping I would hear something, and feeling guilty about trying. I didn't put my ear to the door; that felt like it would be too drastic an invasion of privacy. But I certainly considered it.

I could barely hear Allie talking, and I certainly couldn't make out what she was saying. But then I heard her let out a small scream, followed by what I thought was crying.

I called through the door, "Allie, are you all right?"

She didn't answer me, which tended to confirm my belief that she wasn't quite all right.

"Allie?"

Again no answer; privacy or not, there was no way I was going to sleep anymore without knowing that she was okay, or what was going on.

I knocked on the connecting door, then waited a few seconds and opened it. For a moment it seemed like the darkened room was empty, but it couldn't have been, because I heard soft sobbing.

I finally saw Allie, sitting in the corner on the floor, shaking and crying. I went over to her.

"Allie, what is it?"

"She's dead, Richard. Julie is dead."

# The next morning I wanted to go with Allie

to Des Moines.

At that point all she knew was that Julie's car and body were found in a ravine near Atlantic, Iowa, and that test results proved it was Julie.

The phone call had come from Allie's mother, who was distraught. Add in Allie's own shock and grief, and it's not surprising that she did not get many of the details.

Allie and I had stayed up all night, and for most of that time she either sobbed quietly or yelled angrily. By morning she was starting to allow her mind to doubt the devastating news. Nothing else throughout this roller-coaster ride had proven to be what it seemed; why should this be any different?

. I, of course, had my own special point of view, which I did not share with Allie. I certainly wanted it to be a false alarm or a misidentification, and not be Julie's body that was found. But if it was her, then I desperately wanted her not to be Jen.

I wanted to get on the plane with Allie, to be there and comfort her, but she wouldn't hear of it. "I appreciate it, but no," she said. "You have things to do; you have someone to find. If this is really Julie, then my search is over."

I went along with her wishes, and drove her to the airport. I don't think Allie said three words the entire trip, and I couldn't blame her. She was dreading what she was going to see, dreading the potential finality of it.

We hugged at the curb; it wasn't a five-minute epic, but it was a long one.

And it made me really sad. I was getting tired of losing people I cared about.

Allie called me that night. She said that Julie's car had gone down a ravine, and was mostly concealed by the dense vegetation. She had asked to see the body, but was told that she couldn't, that the accident had happened six months ago, and that the body was decomposed. A 911 call had been made by the person who finally spotted it, but he hadn't hung around to talk to police.

"You were so sure that was Julie's voice on the machine the other night," I said.

"Yes, I was. But maybe I just wanted it to be. I don't know, Richard. I want to continue to hope, but they said the chance that the DNA is wrong is one in six billion. Even I can't hang on to odds like that."

The news was stunning to me, but if Julie died six months ago, and Jen just called me, then she and Julie were obviously different people.

Allie said that the police had very few questions for her. It was obvious they saw it as an accident, and it was in their best interest to do so. At this point, it was not like they were going to solve it if they called it a murder.

They gave Julie's possessions to Allie, but she hadn't yet gotten the strength to look through them. She was going to her mother's in the morning, and perhaps she'd do so then.

She was tired, so she got off the phone. She said she'd be calling me again, but I didn't know if she really would.

Or if she really should.

**After I'd hung up the phone, I started to** consider what I had learned.

There was a great deal, but none of it really fit together. One thing that was completely obvious was that there was some kind of conspiracy at work against me. The bugging, being followed, the Donovan murders, and much more certainly proved that to me.

But the thing that remained separate and apart from the events of the last few weeks was the circumstances of Jen's disappearance. It was simply impossible that everyone that Jen and I had ever met was part of the conspiracy. No matter what forces were for some reason arrayed against me now, and no matter why I was their target, the total erasure of Jen's existence did not make any sense.

I was going to miss Allie; there was no question about that. I had become very attached to her, perhaps too much so, but losing her so suddenly was already starting to hurt. It was also simply amazing to me that Julie had turned out not to be Jen.

Not having Allie around was also going to deprive me of something that I'd not had much recent experience with . . . someone who believed me. The only other person who came close to filling that bill was Lieutenant Kentris, and I was planning to rely on him as much as he would allow.

One thing I was starting to believe more and more was that Sean Lassiter was somehow involved. There were too many coincidences for that not to be the case. In addition to his stated desire to "get" me, I had mentioned him to Dr. Garber as part of the story I was working on, and I was pretty sure he was involved with Gates at the hospital in Ardmore. Sealing the deal was that the Ardmore hospital was a client of Frank Donovan.

Lassiter had to be in the middle of this.

When I got back from lunch, I had a voice mail from Craig Langel asking that I contact him. He was calling to update me on what he'd learned about Sean Lassiter's recent life.

"He's been running a company called Biodyne for the last two years," he said. "It's a small start-up with private funding, the source of which could be Lassiter himself."

"Where is it located?"

"Mahwah."

I was hoping it would be upstate New York, not this New Jersey town, and I mentioned that to Craig.

"There have been seventy-one phone calls from Biodyne to the hospital in Ardmore in the last six weeks."

"You have their phone bill?" Craig's contacts and ability to get things he shouldn't have never ceased to amaze me.

He laughed. "Nothing is secret, Richard. How many times have I told you that? And you of all people should know that by now."

"So he's doing business in Ardmore; I knew Gates was hiding something. Has he got a new drug they're testing up there?"

"I don't know yet. I'll keep you posted."

We got off the phone and I put in a call to Lieutenant Kentris, to tell him what I learned. He wasn't in, but called me back in twenty minutes.

"I've confirmed that Lassiter has been doing business with Gates at the hospital," I said.

"Is that right?" he asked.

"There were seventy-one calls back and forth between them in the last six weeks," I said.

"How is it you know that?"

"I'm telephonically psychic, but you can trust me on it. Have you spoken to him yet?"

"He's out of town. Back next week."

I brought Kentris up to date on Julie's death, and he said, "I guess that wasn't her on the answering machine."

"Right."

"You still think Jennifer is alive?"

I laughed a short laugh. "Thank you; your question means I'm making progress."

"What does that mean?" he asked.

"Until now the question was whether she existed. Now it's whether she's alive."

"Leaps and bounds," he said. "So what do you think?"

"She called me. She's alive," I said.

When we got off the phone I made myself a frozen dinner, then decided to call Allie. I told myself it was to see how she was doing, but that was really a secondary reason. The truth was that I missed her, and I missed having a partner in all of this to talk with.

That realization made me embarrassed by my selfishness and changed my decision to call her. It took me twenty minutes to get over that embarrassment, realize I was acting like a high school kid, and make the call after all.

"How are you?" I asked.

"I've been better," she said, sounding distant. "There's this big empty hole where my sister used to be."

"How's your mother?"

"Hard to tell. She's trying to be strong for me, and I'm trying to be strong for her. We're both full of shit . . . business as usual." She changed the subject. "What's going on there?"

I told her what I had learned about Lassiter and his involvement with Gates at Ardmore Hospital.

She perked up. "I knew it. Gates is neck-deep in this."

"In what? In making Jen disappear and then getting everyone she ever met to deny knowing her?"

"Don't be negative, Richard. You really are getting somewhere."

"You've mentioned that before. Any chance you can tell me where I'm getting?"

"You'll know when you get there. And Lassiter will be in the center of it all."

In an effort to avoid being negative, I changed the subject to Julie's funeral, which was the next day. That's me . . . Mr. Positive.

"It's just another step in the process," she said. "My mother has had to live with the uncertainty for a long time, now she's living with the loss. Six of one, half a dozen of the other." I could hear the bitterness in her voice, and every bit of it was justified.

"So are you, Allie. You have the same loss."

"It's different for a parent. It's beyond unbearable for a parent. A neighbor told her today that it's good she finally can get closure; if my mother had a baseball bat she would have hit the poor woman over the head. Closure doesn't exist when you lose a child."

"I should be there," I said. I wanted to tell her how much I missed her, but that would only have made her feel guilty.

"No, you have things you have to do."

"I know that."

"And just what are you going to do next?"

I decided in the moment. "I'm going to see Lassiter."

# I didn't think for a second that Sean Lassiter

would be willing to see me.

There was no upside in it for him, at least none that I could see. I had tried to do follow-up interviews with him back when the first scandal broke, and he never responded. And this time I didn't want to approach him in the traditional way, because I didn't want to alert him to the fact that I suspected him. And since I didn't have the slightest idea what I suspected him of, I was already at something of a disadvantage.

Craig gave me the listed address for Lassiter's company, which was in Mahwah. He also offered to go with me, but I declined. I didn't consider Lassiter a physical threat, that wasn't his style, and I instinctively thought I might get more from him if there were no witnesses to our conversation.

What Craig neglected to tell me, possibly because he didn't know, was that Lassiter's business address was also his home. And based on that home, Lassiter had not exactly suffered in the years since we tangled. It was a magnificent old Colonial, the kind that George Washington would have lived in if he had higher-paying jobs than general and president.

There was at least a five-hundred-yard circular driveway lead-

140

ing up to it, and there wasn't a neighbor close enough to hear if a bomb went off in Lassiter's living room. If I approached it, Lassiter would have plenty of time to know I was coming.

I decided to wait down the road, from where I could not be seen. If he went into town, there was only one way for him to drive, so I felt confident that I would see him. Of course, he might be out. Or in bed with the flu. Or on vacation.

But there was nothing else I could think of to do, so I waited. I felt stupid doing it, but the upside was that there was no one to see me. In two hours only three cars went by; this neighborhood was so exclusive that there were almost no people living in it.

Amazingly, the fourth car that went by contained Lassiter in the driver's seat. I did a double-take to make sure, but he never looked my way. I waited for him to drive down the road before I circled in behind him at a distance. Tailing was not exactly a specialty of mine, but on these roads it would be impossible to lose someone.

I followed him into the center of town, where he parked in the municipal lot. I parked on the street nearby, and got out of my car when he left the parking lot on foot. He never looked around, and acted as if he didn't have a care in the world.

And the son of a bitch probably didn't.

I needed to decide when to approach him, a decision made more difficult by the fact that I didn't know where he was going or how long he'd be there. His first stop was a bank, which I didn't think was the right place to make my move. I looked inside and saw that he was using the cash machine, and within three minutes he was back outside.

Next was a men's clothing store, and he was inside for almost a half hour. After twenty minutes, I regretted not going in, but still waited outside. My tailing skills definitely needed some work.

His next stop was an Italian restaurant, and I looked through the window as he stopped at the reception desk and then was led to a table. The table was large enough for four, but I had no way of knowing if anyone else was coming. Except me.

I was nervous about walking in. It was certainly not that I was afraid of Lassiter, it was more that I had no idea what I was doing and was afraid to do something that I would later regret. But if Lassiter was actually somehow a link to Jen, doing nothing was not an option.

I walked to the desk and said, "I'm meeting Mr. Lassiter."

I heard him say, "Very good, sir," but I didn't stop to chat with him. Instead, I just walked straight to Lassiter's table and sat down before he even realized that I was there.

I had to hand it to the guy; he seemed no more surprised to see me than if I had been a waiter there to tell him the specials. "Well, this is unexpected," he said.

"Is that right?"

"Of course, though it gives me an opportunity to thank you. You've been a source of much amusement for me with your recent magazine articles and your obvious mental deterioration."

"I'm about to be a source of aggravation for you."

"Those days are behind us," he said. "Now, it's been a real treat seeing you again, but it's time for you to go."

"I've got investigators going through your life," I said. "You're connected to Jen's disappearance, and I'm going to prove it. And then I'm going to put you away."

"Ah, your nonexistent girlfriend. Perhaps you also think I murdered Santa Claus?"

I nodded. "And you buried his body at Ardmore General."

For the first time, I saw a flash of concern on Lassiter's face, even though it was quickly erased. I thought I had gotten through to him; there was something about Ardmore General Hospital that worried him.

"Good-bye, Kilmer."

"And it's not just me, Lassiter. I'm working with a cop who's after you and Gates; it's only a matter of time."

He picked up his menu and looked at it, a not-so-subtle way of telling me that I was dismissed.

"It's only a matter of time," I repeated, and left. The drama of my last line and departure was diminished somewhat by the fact that I didn't exactly throw down my napkin and storm out. Instead, I stopped a waiter and asked where the restroom was.

It was in the back of the restaurant, and after finishing up, I saw that there was an exit back there. I used it, both because it was convenient and because it meant I wouldn't have to see Lassiter again. I'd had as much of him as I could stand for one day.

Of course, I had to walk around the block to get to my car, which was near the front of the restaurant. I did so, and as I turned the corner, I saw a car that looked very much like the one that had been tailing us. It wasn't parked directly across the street from the restaurant, and had I left through the front and walked to my car, I wouldn't have seen it.

As I got a little closer, I could see the device in the window, though it was back farther into the car than before, probably to escape detection.

I stepped into a drugstore, so that I couldn't be seen by the driver if he turned around. It was unlikely he would, since he was obviously expecting me to come out the front of the restaurant, but I didn't want to take any chances.

And I needed time to think. A week might not have been enough, but I knew I'd only have a few minutes.

I had just come from a confrontation that I initiated that had accomplished very little; if I was going to do anything now, it had to be productive. I wasn't worried about him knowing I was on to him; he had likely known that for a while.

I decided that the best I could do would be to get a picture of him, and hope to use that to identify him. My cell phone had a camera on it, but I had never used it, and didn't think I could figure it out in the moment.

I bought one of those disposable cameras from the drugstore I was in, turned it on, and walked out of the store. I hadn't been having lucky breaks for what seemed like a century, but I caught one when I noticed a police officer across the street, giving a ticket to a car that was illegally parked. If anything went wrong, I knew which way to turn.

The first thing I did from my vantage point behind the car was to snap a shot of the license plate. I wasn't sure how clear it would come out from that distance, but I figured it could always be enlarged.

I walked up to the car on the passenger's side, to reduce the chance that he would see me in the mirror. When I came close to the car, I took a deep breath and walked back into the street to the driver's side. He hadn't seen me yet.

"Smile," I said, and when he turned toward the sound, I snapped his picture. I then quickly took another picture of the device in the window.

The surprise was evident in his face, but he recovered smoothly and smiled. "Give me the camera," he said.

"No chance. Why are you following me?"

He started to open the door and get out, so I turned and called, "Officer! Help!"

The man saw the officer, seemed to consider his options, and then got back in the car. "You're a dead man," he said, and then drove away.

# Sean Lassiter had no knowledge of the con-
frontation across from the restaurant.

He had chosen to stay and finish his lunch. He thought that Kilmer might have waited outside, to see if the conversation had gotten him to cut the lunch short. He didn't want Kilmer to think their meeting had upset him.

But it had. It upset him a lot.

Kilmer had started Lassiter's downfall back when he was on top, but that was nothing compared to the stakes now. It could not be allowed to happen again. Because what Kilmer didn't know, what no one knew, was that Lassiter had been having very difficult financial times for a long while now. He was living well above his means, and his dealings with Gates were his last chance to dig his way out.

Of course, it would do more than just dig himself out. It would give him means that no one could live beyond.

When he got home he called Gates. "We've got a problem. I had a visitor at lunch today. Richard Kilmer. He's a magazine writer, and—"

Gates cut him off. "I know who he is. What did he want?"

"Information," Lassiter said. "He thinks I know where his girlfriend is."

"Do you?" Gates asked, though he already knew the answer.

"Of course not. But that's not important. What is important is that he's already connected me to you."

"That's nothing to worry about; even the FDA knows we're working together. There's no way he can know what we're doing. Our tracks have been covered."

"He'll figure it out," Lassiter said. "He's done it to me before."

"Maybe eventually, but it would be way too late. And he could never prove it anyway. That's the beauty of it."

Lassiter was not convinced, and said so. "We need to remove him from the picture."

Gates almost laughed into the phone, but caught himself. "You mean kill him?" He considered Lassiter's reaction to this pathetic.

"I mean whatever it takes," Lassiter said. "In the last month he's written two articles that have told the world he's lost a woman who does not exist. Which means he's announced that he's both grief-stricken and probably insane."

"So?"

"So he's a textbook suicide waiting to happen. He just needs a little help."

Gates remained amused but also a little concerned. If Lassiter were to take matters into his own hands, it would be a disaster. "Just relax," he said. "Let's not do anything that draws attention to what we're doing. We have time to deal with Kilmer if he gets close. Right now he doesn't know anything. He couldn't."

Lassiter finally calmed down and agreed with that assessment, but when Gates got off the phone he immediately called the Stone and told him what had transpired.

The Stone was not amused, and his mood was already bad from the call he had just gotten from Juice, reporting on the confrontation at the car.

The Stone had always prided himself on being a good judge

of people; he had spent his life perfecting the art. But the people he had chosen were not performing well. They would eventually die for their weaknesses, but right now that was small consolation.

As he always did when a setback, however slight, occurred, he reassessed everything to see if any changes in the plan were warranted. This time he decided that the plan should survive intact, but that increased speed was necessary.

He was so close.

**I spent the next twenty-four hours assessing** the situation.

I did this partially because a lot had happened, and I needed to figure out exactly what it all meant. But the main reason for my lengthy reflection was that I couldn't think of what to do next.

I wasn't happy about the results of my encounter with Lassiter. I'm not really sure what I had hoped to accomplish, but whatever it was, I didn't succeed. I learned nothing except an instinctive confirmation that Lassiter was doing business at Ardmore General, business that he wanted kept secret. But I really had already known that, based on the number of calls that Craig reported between Lassiter and the hospital.

Also on the downside, if Lassiter wasn't aware I was after him before, I had certainly tipped him off and helped him prepare. Kentris questioning Gates would have likely done so anyway, so that didn't bother me too much.

If I was trying to rattle Lassiter's cage, I probably shook it gently instead. It wasn't satisfying; what I really wanted was to put the son of a bitch in a cage for the rest of his life.

I was more pleased with how things went in confronting the

guy tailing me. I had gotten pictures of him, his license plate, and the device he was using. My plan was to give it all to Kentris; he would hopefully have the ability to use it to find out the guy's identity.

I didn't want to send Kentris the camera itself, because I wanted to keep the pictures for myself. I brought the camera to the drugstore and asked them to develop five copies of each, hoping their promise of "one-hour photo" was legitimate. I also asked them to put the pictures on two CDs.

The clerk seemed to know what she was doing, and I mentioned that these were very important pictures to me. If they screwed it up, bringing it there would have ranked as the stupidest thing anyone had ever done, and I regretted it the moment that I dropped the camera off.

But the pictures came out crisp and clear, and I e-mailed them to Kentris, in addition to overnighting him two sets. I called him to explain what had happened and what he was receiving, but I had to leave a message when I couldn't reach him.

I also called Mark Cook, and asked him to examine the picture of the device that always seemed to be pointed toward wherever I was. I e-mailed it to him, and he called back within two minutes of receiving it.

"It's a laser," he said. "State-of-the-art. Probably cost two hundred grand."

"What's it used for?"

"To overhear conversations," he said. "You said you were in a restaurant at the time?"

"Yes."

"This device blanketed the window and absorbed every single conversation, every single sound, in that restaurant. You didn't say a word that they didn't hear."

"How can they distinguish one conversation from another?" I asked. "There must have been at least twenty-five people talking in there."

"Richard, I can give you an hour-long technical explanation, or you can just accept what I tell you. Whoever is reading the data from this machine knows every word you said."

"And let me guess . . . we can't trace it back to anyone."

"Right."

"Where do they get it?" I asked.

"Where do they get what? The device?"

"Yes. I assume you don't walk into Walmart and pick one of these things up," I said. "Maybe we can find them that way; trace it back from where they purchased it."

"You're not understanding me, Richard. You're trying to find out *who* you're dealing with, when the problem is you have no idea *what* you're dealing with. This is how countries spy on each other; you piss off any countries lately?"

"Can you do anything about this? I need to be able to conduct private conversations. At least in my apartment."

"The only way is white noise."

"What about it?"

"If we attach white-noise devices to the panes themselves, then when they are forced to strip it out, they'll lose your voices in the process. I can take care of it right away; it'll be in by tomorrow."

"Is it expensive?"

"Depending on how many windows you have facing the street, maybe a couple of hundred bucks. That's the thing with these scientific advances; once you know how to defeat them, it's easy and usually cheap to do so."

Cook hung up to get the white-noise machines, and I called Craig Langel to see if he'd come up with anything. "I was just going to call you," he said.

"What about?"

"It isn't easy to penetrate what's going on at Ardmore Hospital; it's a small place and Gates has it locked down pretty well."

"That's what you were going to call me about?" I asked.

"No, that's my way of setting you up to be impressed with the information I have gotten."

"Let's hear it, and please make it be good news."

"Well, it's certainly interesting news. Gates is definitely conducting a drug study for Lassiter's company. It's an Alzheimer's drug."

The news was somewhere between intriguing and stunning. Lassiter was involved with a memory drug, and everybody around me had forgotten Jen. It could be a coincidence, but that didn't help me to think about it that way.

"Do you know anything else about it?" I asked.

"I thought that was pretty good, for a start. It's a stage-two trial, which is a very significant step if they get to move forward to stage three."

"Good. Now get me more information."

"I will. But Richard, there's something else I need to say. As a friend."

"Okay," I said, girding myself. I'd found that very often things people say "as a friend" don't sound too friendly.

"There's nothing that I've learned so far, absolutely nothing, that has anything to do with your girlfriend. No hint at all that she existed."

"I understand."

"I didn't say that to make you feel bad; it's just that I know that's your goal here, and you need to know the truth. But that's not the only reason I'm saying that."

"What's the other reason?"

"You've been, we've been, investigating this stuff as a way to search for her. But there's something major going on here, and it likely has nothing to do with her."

"So what does it have to do with?"

"I don't know yet. But I'll bet it's about that story you were working on, the one that was going to get you the Pulitzer. All I'm saying is that we might be better off going at this as a news story, rather than a missing persons case."

He was probably right, but I didn't want to admit it. "Fine, so let's uncover what's going on and get me the Pulitzer. Then it'll get a lot of publicity, Jen will read about it, and she'll come home." I was joking . . . sort of.

"You're a pain in the ass," he said.

"That's how you talk to a Pulitzer prize winner?"

"This is Richard Kilmer. I trust that by now you are quite familiar with him."

The Stone noticed his audience smile, an easy thing to notice, since the entire audience consisted of one person. This person would not have been there if his lower-level colleagues had not given a glowing and detailed assessment of the Stone's progress.

And nothing proved that progress more completely than the case of Richard Kilmer.

This was the first of three second-tier presentations the Stone would make. The competition was down to three finalists, and this was the next-to-last time that the Stone would have to address them before they made their final bids.

What followed next was a two-hour video and audio presentation in which Kilmer was the star performer. The Stone limited his comments to the rare times when he felt some explanation was necessary, but otherwise the presentation basically spoke for itself.

At the one-hour mark, the Stone always offered each audience a break, to have a drink or to go to the bathroom. The offer was always declined, a reflection of how riveting the presentation was.

When it was over, the Stone said, "As you can see, the stress that Mr. Kilmer has been under has been extraordinarily intense. Much of this has been by design, but much he has brought on himself in the process of conducting his amateur investigation."

The question the man asked of the Stone was the expected one. "He seems to be making progress in that investigation. How are you planning to deal with that?"

The Stone smiled knowingly. "Good question. Much of that progress has been, shall we say, allowed to happen. The more stress, the more knowledge, the more conflicting the emotions, and the more the perfection of our system becomes obvious. Our intent is to show that nothing can break through; that the effect of our process is permanent."

The Stone hesitated, to let it sink in. Then, "Nothing Kilmer can learn, or fear, or deal with, can change what for him is an immutable truth. He knew this woman, he loved her, he slept with her, he was going to marry her. That is the reality that he has lived."

"And the publicity he is generating?"

The Stone believed in being candid, and this was certainly the time for that. "That is exactly why he was chosen, along with the fact that he was beginning to interfere with the secrecy of our work. His ability to reach the public was a way for us to demonstrate to you . . . and other potential buyers . . . the power of what we possess, in a way that is completely credible."

"I have no doubt it is credible, and you may be assured that we remain very interested. However, you understand that as important as it is to us to re-create the past, it is at least as important to influence future behavior."

The Stone smiled. "That is why the process continues and bids are not yet being solicited. Mr. Kilmer is going to behave exactly as we dictate."

"Can you be more specific?"

"Certainly. He is a nonviolent man; to the best of our knowl-

154

edge he has never even been in a fistfight. Additionally, he has often written of his disdain for capital punishment, calling it 'barbaric and not consistent with enlightened society.'"

"What are you saying?"

The Stone smiled again. "I am saying that Richard Kilmer is going to commit murder."

# When I answered the door at nine A.M., Jen

was standing there.

Suddenly there was no air in my lungs and no support for my legs. I let out a noise somewhere between a gasp and a moan, not too loud and certainly not voluntary. I caught myself when I realized that it wasn't Jen at all.

It was Allie.

"I'm sorry," she said, instantly realizing what had happened. "I should have warned you."

I was going to try and deny that I had thought she was Jen, but there would have been no way to convince her. "It's okay," I said. "I'm glad to see you." And the truth was I was very glad to see her.

She hugged me, longer than I might have expected, but not as long as I would have liked. "Can I come in?" she asked.

"Actually, I'm enjoying myself out here."

She laughed, and we went inside. "Coffee," she said. "Urgent. Coffee."

I poured cups for both of us. "I didn't expect to see you," I said. "I've missed you."

"I should have called, but I was afraid you'd talk me out of it. I flew in last night, but got in late."

"How is your mother?"

"Even after all this time that Julie's been gone, she's still in denial. I don't think a parent can ever be the same, not after something like this."

"What made you come?"

"Besides you?"

I didn't know how to answer that, so I took the easy way out. "Yes."

Allie reached into her handbag and took out something I never would have expected, a pair of woman's shoes. "These."

"How did you know my size?"

I thought it was a pretty funny line, but she didn't smile. Her answer told me why. "Julie was wearing these when they found her body."

"And?"

"And all of the clothes she was wearing when they found her were not the clothes she was wearing when she left the house that day."

I knew what she was saying immediately. Julie had left in the morning, and only driven six hours before her car went off the road. Why would she have stopped to change clothes?

"There could be a million reasons for that, Allie."

"Name one."

"She could have stopped for lunch, spilled something on herself, gone into the restroom, and changed."

"No. None of that can be the explanation."

"Why not?"

Allie held up the shoes. "Because of these. They're called flats. When Julie was eighteen, she got in a car accident. She sped up when she should have stopped, and hit a tree. Broke her arm and cut her chin. She said it was because she was wearing flats like this, and the shoe got caught on the gas pedal. She never wore them again when she drove. Never. She would sooner have driven barefoot."

"So what's your theory?" I asked.

"I don't have one, except I know it didn't happen the way they said it did."

"But it was definitely her body?'

She nodded. "The DNA matched."

"Are they sure they are matching it to the right sample? Would they have had a sample from Julie?"

"They used hair from her brush, but to be sure, I made them repeat the process using my DNA. Identical twins have the same DNA. It matched again."

"What does this have to do with what I'm doing?" I asked. "Jen couldn't have been with me if she was in that car. It's great to see you, Allie, but why are you here?"

She held up the shoes. "Because these don't make any sense, Richard. So I brought them to the 'no sense' capital of the world."

I smiled. "Kilmerville. Population one nut-job."

"Two."

"I think it might be better for you if it stayed at one."

"Why?" she asked.

"Because you're not going to find Julie here. And on some level you're still looking for her. It can't end well."

She pretended to be sniffing the air in the room. "Do you smell psychobabble?"

"I'm serious, Allie. I love having you here, and I've missed you terribly, but you need to think about yourself and what's best for you."

"Which is?"

"Dealing with your loss. Not with mine."

"Richard, I want to help you find Jen. Maybe it's because I see her as a surrogate for Julie, maybe it's because I care about you, or maybe I just want to see justice done against the assholes that took her. But the point is that I don't really care why; I know when I want something, and I go after it."

"Allie . . ."

"If that's not good enough for you, then throw me out of here. Otherwise, bring me up to date on what's happened since I left."

"It's good enough for me," I said. "It's easily good enough for me."

I told Allie about my encounters with Lassiter and the guy following me, and what Mark Cook said about the device he was using.

"So right now he could be listening to what we're saying?" she asked, then cupped her hands around her mouth and yelled out, as if into a megaphone, "You're a piece of garbage!"

I laughed. "They can't hear you, at least not according to Mark. He installed white-noise machines, which for some reason defeat lasers. It's a rock-paper-scissors deal."

Allie went into the kitchen and attempted to make us breakfast, although she had hinted that cooking was not her strong suit. But it was great having her back.

I followed her in. "Craig Langel said that what's happening to me might have nothing to do with Jen at all; that it might be about the story I was working on."

"Meaning Lassiter?" she asked.

"I guess so. Maybe I was getting too close to derailing whatever he was doing."

She shook her head. "Chalk up another one for the doesn't-make-sense list."

"Why?"

"Because if I were Lassiter, and you were getting close to destroying something that was very important to me, I wouldn't go to the trouble of creating this whole bizarre situation." She smiled her sweetest innocent smile. "I'd just shoot you in the head."

I returned the smile. "That's because you are a delicate flower."

**Philip Garber said he had a full schedule, be-** tween patients and classes he was teaching.

But that didn't stop him from calling me back during a break and agreeing to meet me for a drink at six o'clock.

The fact that he would see me so quickly, and in a setting like that, away from his office, told me two things. One, that he didn't consider me a patient, and two, that he thought I was such a world-class nutcase that he wanted to be a key part of future historical descriptions of my lunacy.

We met at a club on East Seventy-first Street, between Park and Lexington. I was able to identify it only by the address; there was no sign on the building and no hint that it contained a bar inside. The door was locked, as Garber had said it would be, but my knock was answered promptly, and the mention of Garber's name got me admitted without question.

The bar itself was dark, both in the amount of light and the wood the entire room seemed to be carved of. Everything about it said "rich," and there was no doubt that the trees used came from the right side of the tree tracks.

Dr. Garber himself seemed a little embarrassed by the surroundings. "Not exactly the singles scene," he said, smiling after we shook hands. "But it's quiet, a good place to talk."

We ordered drinks, and he suggested I try a 'dark and stormy,' a New England–based combination of Gosling's rum and ginger beer. It was terrific.

"Is this a private club?" I asked. "Because if not, a sign on the door might be called for. Neon or otherwise."

He nodded. "It was originally started seventy years ago by wealthy members of a college fraternity. Since then, membership has been limited to descendants of those founders."

"You're one of the descendants?"

"My grandfather was president of the fraternity. Every year I say I'm going to stop being a member, but then I feel disloyal to my heritage."

"Maybe you can deal with that in therapy."

He smiled again. "Perhaps so."

"Will you show me the secret handshake?"

He smiled. "Don't get your hopes up. But what else can I do for you?"

"I've been checking into Sean Lassiter." He knew who I was talking about, since he had said I had spoken about Lassiter during our sessions, none of which I remembered. "I found out something interesting, something I need your point of view on."

He didn't say anything, instead just waited for me to continue. Once a shrink, always a shrink, even when sucking down a dark and stormy in a dark bar with no sign on the door.

"I have information that he, or his company, is conducting some kind of a drug study, a trial. On an Alzheimer's drug."

"Where?"

"At a hospital in Ardmore, New York."

"Where you lost your Jennifer," he said. He spoke about Jen as if she were real, and I was grateful for that.

"Exactly. I assume you're not aware of the study?"

"Why would I be?"

"I know you're an expert on memory."

He shook his head. "No one is an expert on memory; it's a process we are just beginning to understand. But my specialty is repressed memory, which clearly has nothing to do with Alzheimer's. Further, even if this drug were directly related to something I was doing, I might not be aware of it. Such studies are rarely publicized in their early stages, which I assume is where this one is. I'm sorry."

"Now that you know about it, is there any chance you could learn the details?"

He started to answer, but then stopped himself. The length of the hesitation became uncomfortable, so I said, "If you don't want to . . ."

"To use a term from your profession, I would say that I have a reluctance to become part of the story. It's an instinct we psychiatrists have."

"I understand," I said. "But I'm not your patient, even if I once was."

"If you could be specific about what it is you want to know . . ."

"Everyone but me has forgotten Jen. I think Lassiter is a crook, and I was obviously investigating him. He hates me, and right now he's involved with something regarding memory. The connections and coincidences are too much for me to disregard."

He shook his head slightly, as if saddened to have to enlighten me. "Memory drugs, no matter how advanced, don't change homes or apartments. They can't erase all physical traces of a person."

I asked the question that was most worrisome to me. "Can they create memories?"

He knew what I was talking about. "No. Not to the degree you are experiencing them. Not even close. Memories can be false. You can be positive that something happened, even remember details of it, yet it may never have happened at all. But it's a trick that only your mind can play on itself, and never voluntarily."

He was closing doors one after the other, but finally opened one a crack. "I'll make some discreet inquiries," he said.

"Thank you for that."

I ordered another dark and stormy, and we drank to it.

## Dr. Harold Gates surprised Kentris.

That in itself was highly unusual; Kentris could count on one hand the number of times he was surprised in the last five years. And each of them involved either sports or women.

It had taken a while to arrange the meeting, and Kentris had believed that Gates was avoiding him. He expected to have a difficult time getting information, and thought he would have to get a court-ordered warrant.

That wasn't the way it turned out at all, though it took a little prodding. "I'm interested in the business you're doing with a company called Biodyne, run by Sean Lassiter."

"That seems to be going around lately," Gates said. "A journalist named Kilmer was here with the same goal."

"I'm not a journalist," Kentris replied.

"So you're not. May I ask why you are interested?"

"It's part of an investigation I'm conducting."

"That's not very specific," Gates asked.

"It wasn't meant to be. Now, about your business with Mr. Lassiter . . ."

"I know you understand that we try and keep such matters

confidential, releasing only as much information to the relevant government agencies as we are required to do."

"I have no interest in spreading the word, nor do I have a lot of time to spend here," Kentris said, looking at his watch. "If I have to get a court order, my whole day will be shot."

Gates shrugged. "Very well; I certainly intend to cooperate. What would you like to know?"

"Let's start with the nature of your business together."

"We are conducting a trial of an experimental drug that Mr. Lassiter's company is developing. The trial is in its late stages."

"What's the name of the drug?" Kentris asked.

"Amlyzine."

"Is it an extensive trial?"

"Very much so. And it has the potential to be a very important drug."

Gates went on to describe the procedure in some detail, actually more detail than Kentris needed at that point. There were 250 people in the trial, half taking the experimental drug, half taking a placebo.

"So the people taking the placebo think they might be doing something to save themselves, when actually there's no chance?" Kentris asked.

Gates nodded. "That's unfortunately the nature of these things; it's the way medical tests like this are conducted in this country. There are good reasons for it, I assure you."

"I'd be pissed if it was my father taking a damn sugar pill."

"It's for the greater good."

"How's the test going?"

"I have no idea," Gates said. "We do not monitor the results as they come in; that would not be proper science. We conduct the study, and then we analyze the data."

"I would like to see whatever information you have related to the study," Kentris said.

Gates hesitated. "You won't know what you're looking at."

"It won't be the first time."

"There will need to be some restrictions," Gates said.

"I don't like restrictions. They have a tendency to feel restrictive."

"Nevertheless, if you don't agree to them I will not give you what you want. You would have to seek your court order, and waste your whole day."

"Let's hear them."

"The names of the patients participating in the study will have to be withheld; the data will have the names redacted for reasons of privacy. You can look at it, but you must do so here, and you must promise to keep what you learn confidential. We have a responsibility to our patients."

Kentris thought about it for a moment; the conditions were something he could live with, at least for the time being. "Agreed," he said. "Though I retain the right to share it with other people who are my partners in this investigation."

Gates was fine with that, and said so. It took forty-five minutes to assemble the information, and Kentris was led to a private room. The books filled with information about the drug study were brought in on a cart, and Kentris was left alone to look at them.

Gates was right; he didn't understand hardly any of it. But if the time came when it was called for, he could bring in plenty of people who would know exactly what they were looking at.

For now, Kentris was pleasantly surprised by the relative ease in getting Gates to cooperate. That didn't necessarily mean that Gates was clean in all this.

It just meant that if he wasn't clean, he didn't view Kentris as a particular threat.

# If Robby Divine burns through his fortune, it

won't be because he spent it on clothes.

According to *Forbes*' annual list, Robby, as he is known to everyone, is worth in excess of a billion dollars. But he is always in sneakers and jeans, even in his Wall Street office, and they look like they came from Target or Walmart. A while back.

I got to know Robby when I interviewed him for a couple of articles I did on the stock market maybe five years ago. His reputation for picking stocks for himself and his clients is legendary, as is his outspoken, forthright manner of speaking. In short, he has always been the perfect go-to guy for financial journalists.

When I called Robby he said to come right over, and within forty-five minutes I was sitting in his office. The same designer he used for his clothing obviously decorated his office as well; it was a dump, with papers strewn almost everywhere. The only area that was cleared off was part of his carpeting, to enable him to putt golf balls into a cup.

After we said our hellos and reminisced about the stories I'd interviewed him for, he asked, "So, did you find your girlfriend yet?"

"Still looking," I said.

He nodded. "Bummer." Then, after making a ten-foot putt, he asked, "So what's up?"

"There's a company called Biodyne, run by Sean Lassiter."

Robby raised his eyebrows a notch; he obviously remembered Lassiter, and probably my contentious relationship with him. "And?"

"He's testing a drug for Alzheimer's. I want to know how much he would stand to make if the test turned out to show that the drug was effective."

Robby looked at me for a moment, then put the putter down and went to his computer. He started punching keys, making notes as he did so. The process took at least ten minutes, a long time when you're just standing there waiting.

"Okay," he said finally. "Biodyne has a market cap of eleven million dollars, which makes it a very small company, even in that world. There are six million shares, trading at around a dollar eighty-five. Sean Lassiter owns eighty percent of the company, meaning four million eight hundred thousand shares. He has a hundred percent of the voting shares, but that shouldn't matter to you."

"So what effect would a positive stage-two drug trial have?"

"Depends on the drug and what it does, and on how successful the trial is."

"Let's say it reverses Alzheimer's symptoms and the trial is very successful." I was probably overstating it, but I wanted to get an outside figure.

"Then the potential is unlimited. A cure for Alzheimer's? You could be looking at a two-hundred-dollar stock. Maybe more."

"Which would mean what for Lassiter?" I asked.

It didn't take him long to mentally compute the numbers. "Just under a billion dollars. And that's just the stock; the drug itself would have mind-boggling ongoing value."

"If it works."

"I thought you told me to assume it worked."

"I told you to assume the trial was positive," I said. "There's a difference."

"So the fix is in?" he asked.

"I don't know for sure. I'm trying to figure out what's going on, and the best way to do that is to follow the money."

He nodded. "There's precedent for this, to a degree. Small companies have exploded in value as the result of successful trials, and some have even gone back down when later trials didn't go so well. But I'm not aware of any where fraud was suspected."

I smiled. "Glad I'm able to expand your horizons."

"And all this is supposed to help you find your girlfriend?"

"Could be."

"Good luck," he said, picking up his putter. "You know, the real shame in all this is I can't even buy the stock. Lassiter has a stranglehold on it, and there's no way he would sell. I hate when I know something but can't make money off of it."

"Sorry about that. What are you going to do for food and shelter?"

He shrugged and made the putt. "Maybe I'll go on the PGA tour. I hear it's a great way to get women."

When I left Robby's office, I went home and knocked out the third installment in the series about Jen and my efforts to find her. Scott had been bugging me to do so, and I could still see the value in keeping the issue in front of the public.

I wasn't really satisfied with the piece when I finished it, because I left out Sean Lassiter. The magazine's legal counsel advised strongly against including him, feeling that in the absence of proof it would give him a strong legal case against myself and the magazine. I went along; the last thing I wanted was to give Lassiter any potential weapon to use against me.

So I filled in many of the details, and while the piece was compelling, it didn't go nearly as far as I would have liked. For instance, while I was positive that Ardmore Hospital was complicit in whatever was going on, the only time I was free to mention the hospital was in revealing that the murdered plumber, Frank Donovan, had worked there.

I sent the piece off to Scott, and he promised to run it immediately. The magazine's circulation was soaring each time one of my articles ran.

Suffice it to say that this was of small comfort to me.

## Kentris knew the look beyond any doubt.

The man waiting in his office when he got back from lunch was a federal agent. He knew it as surely as if the man had a sign on his forehead proclaiming it. FBI agents had a look about them, and this guy was right out of central casting.

"Hello, Lieutenant, Special Agent Emmett Luther," he said, his hand held out for Kentris to shake it. Luther was a large man, at least six-three and two hundred thirty pounds, with a handshake to match.

"What can I do for you?" Kentris asked.

"You've been talking to people about Sean Lassiter."

"I'm not sure I detected a question in there."

"The Bureau wants you to suspend your investigation of Mr. Lassiter. And that's not a question either."

"To tell you the truth, I can't remember the last time I woke up in the morning and gave a shit what the Bureau wanted me to do. So why would I drop the Lassiter investigation, assuming there was one?"

"Because I asked you to, and because our country's national security is at stake."

"How exactly does my asking questions endanger our country?"

"That's not something I can share with you, other than to say it interferes with an ongoing federal investigation."

"You're going to need to be more specific than that."

Luther shook his head. "Not possible. Can we count on your cooperation?"

"No."

"You understand that we can go over your head and have you ordered to stop?"

Kentris shrugged. "Take your best shot."

"You know, it's not a scientific survey, but I have found that the percentage of hick cops who are also assholes is close to a hundred percent."

Kentris smiled. "They weed out the non-assholes at the hick academy."

Luther started to move toward the door, but then stopped. "What is it you suspect Lassiter of doing?"

Kentris shrugged again. "Not sure; it's more of a fishing expedition than an investigation. But based on this little chat, I must be after a pretty big fish."

"You won't be on the case long, Kentris. But be real careful while you are."

Luther's visit had exactly the opposite effect that he was hoping for. Rather than get Kentris to back off, it instead provided him a jolt of motivation. His interest had waned slightly when Gates was apparently so forthcoming at the hospital. But Luther knew that Kentris was asking Gates questions about Lassiter, which meant the feds had some connection to Gates.

Kentris had been around the block more than a few times, and had had his share of dealings, both cooperative and contentious, with the feds. He therefore knew that Luther would not give up, and would probably have the juice to eventually get his way. There was every possibility that before long the mayor would call and order his cooperation.

Which meant that Kentris had to act quickly to find out whatever he could. This case was his, and it was going to be big, and if he had his teeth dug solidly into it, the mayor would see the upside to his department pulling off a major coup. Or arrest. Or whatever the hell was going to be the result.

# "What have you got for me?" Kentris asked

when I picked up the phone.

"What does that mean?" I asked.

"Well, I assume you haven't been sitting on your ass. What did you come up with?"

"Are you familiar with the two-way-street concept?"

"I am," Kentris said. "But it no longer applies here. We've got ourselves a three-way street. The feds are involved."

I started bombarding him with questions about the federal intervention, but he had very few answers. Finally I switched subjects. "Did you check out the license plate and picture of the guy following me?"

"Yeah. Plate was a fake; the number doesn't exist. I sent an alert out on the photo, but nothing so far."

"You're full of good news."

"I need you up here tomorrow morning," Kentris said.

"What for?"

"For one thing, so we can share information."

"What else?'

"You're an investigative reporter, right? Well, it's time for you to investigate."

We spoke for a while longer, at the end of which I promised to drive up the next morning.

When I hung up, Allie, who had come into the room near the end of the call, said, "Update me."

"Kentris wants to see me tomorrow morning. The FBI is pressuring him to get off the case."

"Why?" she asked.

"He doesn't know; all he did was speak to Gates, and Gates showed him everything . . . all the data from Lassiter's drug trial."

"So why does he want you there?"

"He doesn't want to draw too much attention to what he's doing, so I assume he thinks I can learn more by digging than he can. At least for now."

"How can you do that?"

I shrugged. "I guess we'll find out. You busy tomorrow? Because I don't know where I can get another date at this point."

"You think you can ask me out tonight for a date tomorrow morning?"

"That was my plan. Another part of the plan was to stop at a place I know that makes the best blueberry pancakes in America."

She thought for a moment and then nodded. "Seems like a workable plan."

Allie had cooked dinner, not exactly her specialty, but she liked doing it, so I let her. My only regret was that I had to eat it, but she had made spaghetti with meat sauce, and it seemed nearly edible if I swallowed quickly.

While she was putting the final touches on it, I called Craig Langel to tell him about the FBI's attempted intervention into Kentris's work. Craig had many connections with law enforcement, and I wanted his insight.

"If Lassiter's screwing around with a drug trial, that's the FDA's area, and that's federal," Craig said. "It makes sense that the Bureau would be involved if they suspected something. I'll ask around, but I'm sure there would be a tight lid on it."

"See what you can find out," I said. "I'm going to see Kentris tomorrow morning to plan strategy."

"You want me to go with you?" Craig asked, the concern evident in his voice.

"Why?"

"Richard, I don't know if you've noticed this, but every time you take another step, you wind up deeper in dangerous shit. A little personal protection might be a good idea."

"Allie's coming with me. I'm taking her to Aunt Patty's Pancake House."

"Well, that should do the trick. Come on, man, I'm worried about you."

"Thanks, Craig, but I'm fine."

"Yeah, right."

## Allie woke me at seven A.M.

She didn't knock on my door or come in and shake me. She was too subtle for that. Instead she made so much noise in the kitchen that I would have come to if I were in a coma.

I went out to the kitchen and said, "Was there an earthquake in here?"

"Sorry, I was just puttering around."

"Why?" I asked. "We're having breakfast on the road."

"I wasn't cooking puttering. I was just puttering puttering."

"You were trying to wake me up."

She nodded. "It worked." Then, "I'm anxious to get going. You know me, I want to feel like we're getting somewhere."

"That's where we differ," I said. "I want to actually get somewhere."

We were on the road within the hour, crossing over the George Washington Bridge into New Jersey and driving up Route 17 almost into New York State. Allie was quiet most of the way. She'd been a lot moodier since she got back, and it was understandable. I could actually tell when she was thinking about her sister, and I would watch as she tried to shake herself out of her depression. It was amazing how well I was getting to know her, and how much I cared about her.

I reached over and took her hand, then held it. She looked at me and our eyes connected, staying that way until I decided I probably should look at the road. Neither of us said anything, and our hands stayed entwined until a toll booth broke the mood.

The pancake restaurant was crowded as always, and we had to wait fifteen minutes for a table. Patty's was a place that my parents took me to as a kid, and it had not changed one iota in the intervening years. I would go there maybe twice a year as an adult, and the look of the place, and especially the aroma, brought back extraordinary memories. Hopefully they were real memories.

"These are unbelievable," Allie said, once she had chewed enough to clear a path in her mouth, thus enabling speech. "I've got to learn how to make these."

"Or maybe not," I said.

"You don't think I'm a good cook, do you?"

"You're not Aunt Patty."

She took another bite. "That's for sure."

We were back on the road at about nine-thirty, going up route 17 and on to the New York State Thruway. We were about twenty minutes south of Monroe when my car seemed to slow down, and I stepped on the gas.

Nothing happened.

The car had shut down and the motor seemed to be off, even though the key was still turned. It had just died, and we were coasting along, with no power behind us.

"What's wrong?" Allie asked.

"I have no idea. . . . I just filled it with gas yesterday."

I turned the key off and then back on, but it had no effect. At the same time I veered the still-moving car to the side of the road, on the shoulder. We finally slowed to a stop, right near a sign that said there was a rest area one mile ahead.

"Do you know anything about cars?" Allie asked.

"I know how to call Triple A. What about you?"

"Make the call," she said.

I took out my cell phone and immediately noticed that there were no bars at the top; we had stopped in a rather desolate area without cell service. "I don't believe this," I said. "You have any reception on yours?"

Allie checked her phone and confirmed that she did not.

"I'm going to walk to that rest area," I said, opening my door. "I would think there would be a pay phone there. Or maybe cell service."

"You want me to go with you or stay with the car?" she asked.

"Why don't you go with him?" It was a voice I recognized, and I involuntarily stiffened. I finally turned, and confirmed my fear that it was the guy who had been following us. He was holding a gun and pointing it at my chest.

I raised my hands in the air without being told to, and the man frowned. "Put your hands down, asshole. This isn't the movies." He moved toward the open door and said to Allie, "Get out of the car."

Allie opened the door and got out. I was scared to death, but Allie looked more angry than afraid.

Two cars passed by, but I noticed that our captor had his body between the gun and the road; there was no way that anyone passing by would think anything was wrong. That's probably why he didn't want us raising our hands. I also noticed that ours was the only car visible; this guy must have come walking out of the woods alongside the road. Perhaps his car was back there.

Which meant he had known where we would stop. Which meant he had somehow stopped us.

"What happened to your camera?" he asked, a not-so-subtle reminder of the last time we'd met. It also wasn't lost on me that he'd ended that last conversation by calling me a "dead man."

"Let's go. That way," he said, pointing toward the trees. There was a path cut out of them, leading farther away from the road, and that was where he was indicating we should go.

Allie sent me a look that said, *Don't do it.* I considered our limited options. I thought about refusing, but there was so little traffic that he could have shot us there and gotten away without being noticed. I didn't know what he had planned for us down that path, but at the moment I didn't have the guts to force his hand.

I nodded slightly to Allie, and we started walking, with the man behind us. We were about ten feet into the woods when Allie stopped.

"No," she said. "This is as far as we go."

The man laughed. "She's a hell of a lot smarter than you are," he said to me. "But this will do fine."

He meant that we were even more shielded from the road than we had been before. We shouldn't have walked at all, and Allie hadn't wanted to, but she had let me make the decisions, at least for a few moments.

I still didn't see his car or any obvious way the man had gotten there, which didn't mean much to our position either way. The point was that he was there, and he could drive away in our car after he buried us, if he wanted to and if he could get it to work.

"Turn around," he said.

We turned toward him. He still had the gun in his right hand, but now there was also something in his left. It was metallic, and as I looked at it, he tossed it to me. I flinched and didn't catch it, and he laughed at me.

"Pick it up, tough guy," he said, and I did so. It was a pair of opened handcuffs. "Wrap your arms around that tree and put them on. Then me and your new girlfriend can be on our way."

I was thinking surprisingly clearly, though it wasn't doing me any good. I knew that if I did as told, my usefulness in this situation was over. Whatever limited ability I had to protect Allie and myself would be officially gone.

I had to believe that his plan was to keep me alive, or there would have been no reason to cuff me to the tree. He was going to either take Allie with him, or hurt her there in front of me. I couldn't let either of those things happen, though I had no idea how to prevent it.

I wished that I had tried to do something out by the road; the secluded place we were in now reduced our chances considerably. I should have listened to Allie, who was now again shaking her head at me. This time I listened, but it was probably too late.

"No," I said.

"Don't be a hero, Kilmer. Lassiter wouldn't mind if I put a bullet in your head."

I had to assume that he was lying, or he would have killed me already. The fact that he had confirmed that Lassiter was behind this was not a surprise, nor top-of-mind at the moment. I had bigger problems to worry about. "I'm not doing it," I said. "And we're leaving."

He shrugged his disinterest. "Have it your way," he said. He raised his gun up and forward, threatening to shoot.

"*No!*" Allie screamed, and she started to move toward him.

I heard a strange noise, almost like a soft ripping sound, and the man moved farther forward. But it was just his upper body, not his legs, and as he looked toward Allie he had a strange look on his face, as if he were confused.

He fell forward, sort of toppled, and landed facedown in the dirt. He had to be unconscious before he fell, because he made no effort to protect his face from the direct fall.

"Oh my God," Allie said. "What happened?"

"I don't . . ." Before I could finish my thought, I saw a small circle of what looked like blood in the hair on the back of his head, directly centered. It confirmed what I had thought, that the noise represented a shot, perhaps with a silencer, that brought him down.

Simultaneous with that thought was the realization that we could be the next targets. I tried to look through the trees, but couldn't see anything. "Come on," I said, grabbing Allie's arm. "There's somebody out there shooting."

We started to run, not looking back, and not stopping until we got to our car. I quickly tried it and saw that it was still not working, and then confirmed the same thing about my cell phone.

We ran to the rest area a mile away. I'm not much of a runner, but I certainly never considered stopping at any point. Allie wasn't even breathing heavy when we got there.

There was a pay phone, but when I looked at my cell again there was coverage there, so I used that instead. I called Kentris's office, and was told he was in a meeting.

"Tell him it's Richard Kilmer calling. And tell him it's life-or-death."

When Kentris came on the line, I quickly told him what had happened, as well as our location.

"Do you know who it was?" Kentris asked.

"It was the guy who's been following us, the one whose picture I gave you."

"I'll be there in ten minutes," he said. "Lock yourself in a bathroom."

I hung up, and told Allie that Kentris wanted us to lock ourselves in a bathroom. "You okay?" I asked.

She nodded. "I'm getting there. That was pretty scary; I have no experience with things like that."

"Join the club. I should have followed your lead and made him deal with us on the side of the road. When we walked into the trees we lost whatever leverage we had, which wasn't much. You were right, and I'm sorry."

"It's all right, Richard. Once we got there you took a stand. Starting now we need to take a stand against these people." Then she smiled. "Which bathroom are we supposed to lock ourselves in? Men's or women's?"

I thought for a second. "Let's go with women's."

# Kentris showed up with a caravan of four

police cars and two ambulances.

We came out to meet them, and Kentris simply said from the passenger seat of his car, "Get in and lead the way."

Once we were in the backseat, he asked us if we needed any medical treatment. We told him that we did not, though I could have used some vodka to calm my nerves.

We directed him back to the spot on the highway where we had stopped, not exactly a difficult thing to do, since our car was still there. Two more police cars arrived, as well as two motorcycle cops, and they closed off the highway.

We all got out, and Kentris asked, "You never saw the shooter?" Allie and I answered no simultaneously. We pointed in the general direction of where the body was, and Kentris went over to talk to the officers. He came back and told us that the officers would lead the way, and we would bring up the rear with him, while giving directions.

We set off on the short walk in that fashion, behind the group of officers with their guns drawn. It seemed like a military formation, and I was glad we were not leading the way. Everyone walked slowly, carefully, watching for any movement.

Allie and I exchanged eye contact and I knew what she was thinking, because I was thinking it as well. We were walking back to the place where less than an hour before we had thought we were going to die.

We saw the officers ahead of us reach the area, and they stopped. I was surprised that I didn't see more activity, but it was hard to tell what was going on from where we were. There were too many trees.

One of the officers from the front came back to talk to Kentris. "It's clear," he said. "Nothing there."

"Is there a body?" Kentris asked.

"No."

"That can't be," I said.

Kentris told the officers to secure the area, and that process took about five minutes to do to their apparent satisfaction. Only then were Allie and I allowed into the clearing. The body was, in fact, gone.

"He was lying right there," Allie said.

"Could this be the wrong location?" Kentris asked.

I shook my head. "No chance. That's the tree he wanted me to cuff myself to, and that's where his body was. No doubt." I looked toward Allie, and she nodded in agreement.

"You sure he was dead?" Kentris asked.

"I didn't take his pulse, but he had a hole in his head, right here." I showed him the location on my own head. "That would seem to be a tough thing to live through, much less walk away from."

"We've got forensics coming in, but I don't see any blood," Kentris said.

"Look, this happened, okay? He somehow stopped our car, took us back here, and then he got shot. Maybe the guy that shot him took the body, or maybe somehow he wasn't dead. I don't know, but it doesn't make what happened to us any less real."

Kentris nodded. "Okay. Let's go back to the office and we'll take your statements."

"What about our car?"

"We'll have it towed in and checked out."

Before we left I looked around pretty closely at the area. There was truly no sign that anything had happened there. Had Allie not been with me, I would have been once again in the position of swearing that something was real, with everyone else saying it was not. Of course, Garber had raised the possibility that Allie wasn't real. I thought that maybe the truth was that I was home in bed, imagining all of this.

I went toward the tree, hoping the handcuffs would be where I had dropped them, but they were gone as well.

We went back to Kentris's office and both Allie and I gave lengthy statements, answering every question we were asked. We did that separately, but I had no doubt our answers would match. We had lived through the same near-nightmare.

Once we had finished, we sat down with Kentris alone in his office. He told us that the mechanics had reported that the car was tampered with, and that there was a device that remotely shut it off. If there was any doubt that we were telling the truth, that removed it.

"Among the things that puzzles me is that we took a different route than we usually do to get up here, because we wanted to stop at a restaurant. But this was all set up, right down to the knowledge that we'd have no cell phone service. So he had to know what we were doing."

"Looks like he still had a way to record your conversations," Kentris said.

Mark Cook told me that he had successfully dealt with that, but he had also said that there was no such thing as a private conversation. "Why do you think he was going to take Allie?" I asked.

"Maybe to use as future leverage against you," Kentris said.

"He could have just killed me right there; that would have provided all the leverage against me he'd need. But he wasn't going to. He . . . and Lassiter . . . wanted me alive. They're using me for something; I've felt it from the beginning."

"We need to figure out how this ties in to Jen," Allie said. "If we can do that, everything will fall into place."

Kentris didn't answer, but the look he gave told me what he was thinking. There was no concrete evidence that any of this tied into Jen, whether or not he thought she ever existed.

I was getting really tired of people doubting me and doubting Jen. "She called me," I said. "You heard the damn tape. And I identified your murder victim as the man who was presented to me as Jen's father."

Kentris nodded. "Point taken. And just as big a point is that we know the feds are all over this. So something important is going down."

"So where do we go from here?" I asked.

"To be honest with you," Kentris said, "I'm in a tough spot; I'm going to be getting a lot of pressure to back off this. The feds won't let it go. And today doesn't help any."

"What do you mean?" I asked, though I had a pretty good idea.

"You're not considered the most stable guy in the world; you've been very publicly looking for someone nobody thinks is real. And now you've taken my entire department on a wild goose chase after a murderer, except there's no victim."

"You know better than that," Allie said.

Kentris nodded. "I do. But I don't get to call all the shots. There's going to be a limited number of things I can do, so we'll have to pick our battles. If I'm going to make a move, we have to be sure it's the right one."

"Which leaves it up to us," I said.

"Which leaves it up to you."

*These are the people who made it happen.*
That's what Gates thought as he prepared to address them at the hastily called gathering. There were some murmurs of unrest that had been reported back to him, and it was determined that he should do what he could to quell them.

It was amazing that the project had come this far, and in such secrecy. But these were honorable people, and the ones who knew what was happening thought they were doing something that would not only enrich themselves, but more importantly would both benefit humanity and increase the national security of the United States.

Each of the fifty-one people had signed confidentiality pledges, and Gates had seen no evidence that any of those pledges had been violated, even though he had investigators looking for just such violations. But word had come back that some of them were troubled and growing uneasy, and that's why Gates had called them together.

Gates knew how to handle people; it was an instinct he always had. He knew the right things to say and the right time to say them. And this was the time to show it.

"Ladies and gentlemen, thank you for being here tonight. I

know how hard you've all been working, and I thought it was time to bring you together to thank you and provide an update on just how valuable that work has proven to be."

"Our experiment has gone remarkably well, actually even better than we could have hoped. And that's saying something, because, as you know, we set the bar very high.

"We are making history, and the positive effects of our work will change the world for the better. Since day one, our reason for being has been to help people, and you have never lost sight of that mission.

"And you are succeeding. You have succeeded.

"It is somewhat unfortunate that so much secrecy was necessary to protect our work, but any less would have risked our control. There are people, there are countries, that want what we have, many of whom would use it for the wrong reasons. With your help, we will never allow that.

"Many of you know that I have often compared our work to the Manhattan Project, and it is similar in many ways. There is the pure challenge of mastering this new science, and the transformative nature of the work itself. Once we have accomplished our goal, the world will never be the same.

"But there is one major difference. The atomic bomb was born to fight and control evil, it was a terrible weapon used to defeat terrible forces. Our work will be a dynamic, historic force for good, and by keeping total control we can ensure that."

Gates paused to collect himself and make eye contact with many in the group. They trusted him, and he knew that. The fact that he was abusing their trust did not bother him in the slightest. They were going to be well compensated, though nowhere close to what he would get.

"I know that some of you have expressed concern about the events concerning Mr. Kilmer during these last few weeks. While I respect your feelings, I also know that you understand that it is for the greater good.

"And as you know, Mr. Kilmer consented to this process at

the onset," he lied. "The fact that he is currently unaware of that fact is by definition evidence of your enormous achievement.

"So we are nearing the finish line, with great moral, emotional, and, yes, financial rewards awaiting us all. From the bottom of my heart, I thank you. We could not have a better team."

Unbeknownst to the crowd, the Stone watched the entire proceedings on a closed-circuit feed. Gates was of course aware he was being watched, since it was the Stone who had ordered the gathering, and the speech, in the first place.

Things were moving rapidly now; the end game had begun and no risks could be tolerated. It was why the Stone had "removed" Juice from the operation sooner than he had planned. Juice had been a valuable asset, but he had made mistakes, and those mistakes created vulnerabilities. So the man had to be eliminated, and he was. The Stone didn't exactly agonize over it, especially since it was inevitable anyway. The loss of a week or two of life was of little importance.

But the meeting Gates was conducting was of great consequence. It was an unfortunate fact of life that operations like this required a significant number of people to achieve success, and that meant that secrecy was difficult to maintain. The amount of information possessed by each person in that room varied, and was on a need-to-know basis. But indiscretions by any of them could cause major problems.

It was why the Stone instructed Gates to address this gathering. They were in the home stretch now, and every base had to be covered. Soon, the Stone knew, ultimate success would be his.

And everyone in that room would be dead.

**One of the things that the Stone did not**
know was what Marie Galasso was thinking. He was familiar
with her, or at least her background, because he ultimately chose
everyone working on the project. But in his desire to keep his
identity secret, he had not personally met any of them.

Marie was a computer programmer, and as such a lower-level
person in the operation. She actually knew less than most about
what was going on, though she had her ideas about it. But she
showed up every day and did her job, and never had much cause
to seriously question any aspect of it.

Until that morning.

Just before going to work, she had read Richard Kilmer's
third article, and it had thoroughly shaken her. To be specific, she
found one passage particularly jarring. It was the one in which
Kilmer identified the murdered Frank Donovan as having been a
plumber working at Ardmore Hospital.

One of the obligations that each employee had was to write
up a report at the end of the day, specifically summarizing what
had happened that day. Most of it was pro forma, but there was a
special section asking if anything unusual had occurred.

Only once had Marie written anything into that special section, and it was the day she saw the plumber come out of the high-security section, an area Marie herself had never been in. She didn't know how he had gotten in, perhaps it was a blunder, but he had a strange look on his face when she saw him, and he left quickly when she walked over to see if she could help.

Marie dutifully recorded this, but did not think much of it. In fact, she had completely forgotten about it until this morning, when she learned from Richard Kilmer's article that the same plumber and his wife had been brutally murdered.

Marie didn't know what to do or who to talk to. She only knew one thing for certain.

She was scared.

## "My friend wants a gun."

That's what Craig Langel said to a man he called Sammy, and it seemed weird to know that the friend he was talking about was me.

Craig had advised me against going up to Ardmore with only Allie, without him or someone else along as protection. I had shrugged off the warning, and almost wound up dead, or at least handcuffed to a tree.

"Dammit," he said, "you are in over your head here, Richard. You have got to protect yourself."

"I can't have a bodyguard with me at all times."

"Then get a gun."

The idea was horrifying to me, and I immediately resisted. But Craig and Allie were very persuasive, especially Allie. She said I should do it as much for her as for me, since we were always together.

Finally I said, "I'll do it, but there's no way I'm ever going to shoot it."

Craig smiled. "That will reduce its effectiveness somewhat, but okay."

So I found myself at S and R Gunshop in Englewood, New

Jersey, and I let myself assume that the *S* stood for the Sammy I was talking to. Actually, Sammy and Craig were talking to each other and pretty much ignoring me.

"A .38?" he asked.

Craig nodded. "That's what I was thinking."

I shook my head. "Too big. I was thinking a .36 or .37, maybe even a .35." I knew better than that, of course, but I was using humor to mask my nervousness.

Sammy looked at me, then at Craig. "Your friend is a funny guy?"

Craig shrugged. "According to him."

Sammy went into the back and came out with a gun that was probably small to most people, but looked like a bazooka to me. He handed it to me. "Try it for feel."

I took it in my hand, and it felt like a barbell. "Is the safety on?" I asked.

Sammy told me that it was and said, "Let me show you how to take the safety off."

"That's okay. I'm never going to take it off."

"Richard . . . ," Craig admonished.

We went downstairs to a small shooting range that Sammy had set up, and he showed me the intricacies of the gun and how to fire it. I took about twenty practice shots, and he and Craig were surprised by how well I did. As was I.

Once I agreed that it was the gun for me, I filled out a form and Sammy sent it in for an instant background check. I guess that the entire world considering me a psycho was not viewed as a negative, and I was certified acceptable and given a gun permit.

When we left, Craig renewed his offer to stay close to me or get me a bodyguard, but I declined. I patted my pocket where the gun was. "Don't need it," I said. "I'm packing."

When I got back to the apartment, Allie was on the computer, designing gift baskets for her employees back home to make and send out when orders came in. I looked over her shoulder as she did it. "Those look pretty good," I said.

"Thanks. I like knowing that people feel good when they receive them." Then, in a subject-changer for the ages, she said, "Did you get the gun?"

I nodded. "Sure did." I showed it to her, pointing it away from her even though it wasn't loaded.

"Let's hope we can find someone to use it on," she said.

"I think you might be tougher than me," I said.

"That's why we had to get you a gun."

Allie and I spent most of the next day doing little more than hanging out at Ardmore Hospital. We cautiously approached people and asked if they were part of any drug trial. Since it was for an Alzheimer's drug, we limited ourselves to annoying only seniors, but no one admitted to being part of the study.

We did learn that Dr. Gates was out of town, which made our job a little easier. The hospital was private property, and certainly Gates would have been within his rights to have us removed from the grounds if he so desired. Nobody else in authority seemed to notice us, so we were free to accomplish absolutely nothing.

By four o'clock we had had enough for the day and drove back to the city. We planned to return the next day, though it didn't feel as if it would be productive. The problem was we couldn't think of anything else to do.

We stopped for pizza at Sal and Carmine's, on Broadway, on the Upper West Side. Neither Allie nor I were in the mood to go out for dinner, but I certainly didn't want to risk having Allie cook, so pizza seemed the perfect compromise.

It was almost eight o'clock when we got home, and the phone was ringing as we walked in the door. I got to it on the fourth ring.

"Hello?"

"Richard? Philip Garber here."

I was surprised to hear that it was him, though I had asked him if he could find out anything about Lassiter's work. "Dr. Garber . . . good to hear from you. Have you learned anything?"

"Well, despite my best efforts, I may be in the process of becoming 'part of the story.'"

"What do you mean?"

"In your investigation of Mr. Lassiter, have you learned anything about any Canadian interests or connections that he might have?"

"No. Nothing. But the list of things that I don't know is very long. What does Canada have to do with this?"

"Perhaps nothing, and in any event I don't want to say anything until I am far more certain. That could be as early as tomorrow."

"Can I help?"

"No, I can do this in a way that does not ruffle feathers, if I am not mistaken. I will call you tomorrow from Quebec."

The fact that he was going to Quebec, apparently to follow up on all of this, was fairly shocking to me. I gave him my cell phone number, since Allie and I were planning to spend the day in Ardmore.

"Be careful," I said. "If what you are doing turns out to be related to my situation, then you could be dealing with very dangerous people."

He chuckled at the prospect. "Thank you. I appreciate the concern, but my profession is not a breeding ground for heroes."

I told him I appreciated what he was doing, and made another effort to find out some specifics, but he was reticent to discuss it at that point.

Allie and I kicked around for at least an hour what the Canadian involvement in all of it could be, but we couldn't come up with anything. We would find out the next day. Or not.

We arrived at the hospital at nine A.M., and spent the morning accomplishing nothing.

At noon we went to lunch in the hospital cafeteria, which by then we had learned had surprisingly good food. The place was always crowded at that hour, and everyone sat at very long tables. Allie and I found two seats, and she put her bag down on the table to mark our spot as we went toward the cafeteria line.

When we got back, Allie lifted her bag to put it on the floor so that we could set down our trays. As she did so, a small piece of notepaper fell to the floor, and she picked it up and looked at it. After a few seconds, she handed it to me, and I read it:

> *Mr. Kilmer, I need to speak with you about a very important matter. Please meet me in the playground behind the grammar school at five o'clock.*

The note was not signed, and I folded it nonchalantly and put it in my pocket. I looked around to see if anyone was staring at me, but it didn't seem like anyone was.

"Looked like a woman's handwriting," Allie said softly.

I nodded. "I thought the same thing. But I could be walking into some kind of trap."

Allie shook her head. "No, *we* could be walking into some kind of trap."

The afternoon was as unproductive as the morning, except it seemed to take about two weeks to get through. I was both eager and apprehensive to meet the person who wrote the note; it felt like there was a chance that we were going to get help from an unexpected source. Both Allie and I recognized, of course, that it could also somehow be yet another roadblock, or nothing at all.

Another factor that made the day crawl by was the lack of a phone call from Dr. Garber. He said that he would call from Quebec, and I took that to mean that he would do so regardless of whether he learned anything important. But the phone did not ring.

We left at four o'clock, to give us time to learn where the grammar school was and to hopefully check it out before the appointed time. It was only about five minutes away and it was the only grammar school in town.

We drove by and tried to look toward the back. The two side streets were dead ends, so to have driven back there would have been to attract attention if anyone were watching. From our vantage point it just looked like an empty playground, and the school had obviously let out for the day.

It was a perfect place for someone to meet with us if that person did not want to be seen, but an equally perfect place to do us harm.

Neither Allie nor I had any doubt that we were going to go through with the meeting, and I mentally thanked Craig Langel for helping me get a gun. Having it gave me a more secure feeling, even though I kept it unloaded, with three bullets loose in my pocket. I would load it for the meeting.

"You should call Kentris," Allie said. "At least tell him where we're going and what's going on. Just in case."

"I don't want him coming here," I said. "It might scare this person."

She nodded. "I agree. But if we disappear, at least he'll know where to start looking."

I was still reluctant to call him, but Allie insisted it was the way to go, so I agreed and called Kentris's cell phone, hoping to get his voice mail. I did, and left the message about our meeting. The probability was that by the time he heard the message, the meeting would be over. Which was how I wanted it.

We grabbed a cup of coffee, and then went back to the school. This time we drove around to the back, but didn't see anyone, so we stayed in the car. At exactly five o'clock, another car pulled up. It was driven by a woman, and she seemed to be alone.

She parked and got out of her car, looking around warily. She seemed more nervous than I was, which was really saying something.

Allie and I got out of the car and walked toward her. She was standing under an awning in the doorway to the school, so as to stay as much out of sight as possible.

When we reached her, she said, "Mr. Kilmer, thank you for coming. I really appreciate it."

"This is Allison Tynes," I said. Allie greeted her, but the woman just nodded, clearly nervous.

"What's your name?" Allie asked.

"Nothing I say can go any further than the two of you."

I nodded. "That's fine."

"My name is Marie Galasso. I work at Ardmore Hospital; I'm a computer programmer in the annex building in the back."

I had seen that building, but didn't think it was used for anything more than storage. I don't think I had ever seen patients or personnel going in or out.

"What can we do for you, Marie?"

"The man in your article, the one who was murdered with his wife . . ."

"Frank Donovan?"

She nodded. "Yes, Mr. Donovan. The plumber."

"What about him?" I asked.

"I saw him, coming out of the lab. Maybe two months ago; it was late, after most people went home. I was just finishing up." She paused; then, "I shouldn't be telling you this."

"It's all right, Marie. We just want to hear what you have to say. We won't do anything without talking to you about it first."

"He wasn't supposed to be in the lab; nobody who isn't authorized can go in there. I've never been in there myself. I think he might have gone in by mistake. I tried to talk to him, but he left, and he seemed upset. I reported the incident."

"Reported it to who?"

"We have to fill out a form describing what we've done each day. There's a special section to write in if we see something unusual; I wrote that he had been in the lab." She seemed as if she were about to cry, but kept herself together.

"Then what happened?"

"Nothing. I never saw him again. But when I read what you wrote, I knew it was him."

She told us the date when the incident occurred, which was quite a few weeks before the murders. My hunch was that the decision to actually kill the Donovans came when the bugging equipment in my apartment picked up my conversations with Allie about them.

Allie had been letting me do all the questioning, but she threw in one of her own. "And you think your reporting him is the reason he was killed?"

She nodded. "I'm afraid of the people I work for."

"Why?"

"Everything is so secretive, and there are men with guns. Guards."

"What are they guarding?" I asked.

"I don't know."

"What do you do there?"

"I'm a computer programmer; they use me to program chips."

"What kind of chips?" Allie asked.

"They're designed to hold video, but I'm not sure that's what they use them for. They really can hold any kind of data."

"Why did you come to me with this, Marie?"

"Because of your article, because I think I may be the reason that man died. We had to sign a paper saying we would never tell anyone anything about what we do."

"You did the right thing coming to us."

She nodded, then started to say something, but hesitated.

"What is it?" I asked.

"They're doing something to you. I don't know what it is, but they said you were okay with it."

"I'm not," I said, and she nodded.

I gave her my phone number and asked her to call me if she learned anything else, but to be very careful. She gave me her cell phone number, but extracted a promise that I would call only if it was absolutely urgent.

"You won't tell anyone, right? I've got a little girl."

We assured her that her secret was safe with us, and after determining that she had nothing more to tell us, we left.

Allie and I got home at nine P.M., and we were too wound up to eat. Our meeting with Marie Galasso had been hugely important, even if we didn't know what it all meant. What we did know was that whatever was behind Jen's disappearance, as well as what was done to me, originated in that annex.

We talked until almost midnight, and we agreed that in the morning we would tell Kentris what we had learned. We would do so without mentioning Marie's name, and only with a promise from Kentris to tread carefully. If she was right about Frank Donovan, and we believed she was, then she was right to be worried. If it was discovered she was talking to me, her life definitely would be in jeopardy.

We were both exhausted, and we went to our respective bedrooms. I'd been feeling closer and closer to Allie, and I believe she felt the same, but as long as I believed Jen was alive there was no way I would let anything happen again.

I am a big college basketball fan, and I used to eagerly devour the NCAA tournament every year. It was a sign of how preoccupied I'd been with learning the truth about what happened to Jen that the tournament had started and I didn't have the slightest idea what was going on.

I got into bed and turned on the television. I tuned in to SportsCenter, and they were talking about the tournament. Penn had upset North Carolina, and three talking heads were debating whether it was the biggest upset of all time.

There was a knock on the door, and before I had a chance to say anything, it opened. It was Allie, but the look on her face said that she was not there with any amorous intentions.

"Turn on CNN," she said.

I did so, and they were showing some ships at sea, obviously shot from a helicopter. But that wasn't what caught my eye; what I noticed was the legend emblazoned on the bottom. It read:

*Prominent psychiatrist lost in plane crash.*

Allie and I listened to the newscasters saying that the victim had been piloting a private plane that had gone down ten miles off the coast of Maine.

And then they showed a picture of Philip Garber.

The most recent person to die because he knew me.

# I was planning to call Kentris first thing in

the morning.

That became moot when he called me at three A.M., and it was a sign of my level of stress that he didn't wake me. I was already wide awake. "You hear about Garber?" were the first words out of his mouth.

"Yes."

"Is it connected?" he asked.

"I would say that the likelihood of that is somewhere north of one hundred percent."

"You're a real good-luck charm," he said.

I proceeded to tell him about the last conversation I'd had with Garber, and how he was going to Quebec to chase down some pertinent information about Lassiter.

"He gave you no hint what it was?"

"Zero. And I tried to get him to tell me, but he didn't want to say anything until he felt confident it was true."

Kentris had been watching the coverage longer than I had, and he said the NTSB was due to arrive on the scene by morning. They were saying on TV that because the wreckage was strewn over a relatively wide area, it was likely the plane had broken up in the air.

"An explosion?" I asked.

"Could be."

"So what do I do now?"

"You've got to go to law enforcement with this."

"I was under the impression that you were law enforcement," I said.

"No jurisdiction here; it happened off the coast, so it will be federal. But you have no way of knowing that, so you should go to the New York cops."

"They have nothing to do with this," I said.

"Exactly. They'll send it on to the feds. Then we'll see what happens. That will tell us a lot."

I told Kentris that I had reason to believe that whatever was going on at the hospital was happening in the annex building, though I didn't even hint at how I knew that. I was not going to be responsible for anything happening to Marie Galasso; I had done enough damage already.

My confusion at what was happening, while ever-present, was giving way to a barely controlled rage at Sean Lassiter, who I was now certain was behind this.

I told Allie about the Kentris call when she woke up in the morning, and while she agreed I needed to go to the cops and tell them about my conversation with Garber, she had no confidence that it would go anywhere. "Nobody's going to help us with this, Richard. Whatever can be done, we have to do ourselves."

It was incredibly comforting having Allie around; she was the one person I felt I could completely trust to have my back. I knew how difficult it must be for her; we had started this process each looking for a loved one, and thinking they were the same person. I was still searching, but her search had come to a crushing end. Yet she retained her energy and determination to help me find Jen.

Or to learn what had happened to her.

I was experiencing a strange sensation, and it was bothering me quite a bit. It wasn't that I was forgetting Jen; she was still a vivid and powerful presence for me. It was more that certain events in our life together were becoming vague. For example, I would see a certain movie was going to be on television, and I couldn't remember if I saw it in a theater with Jen, or with someone else.

Speaking of movies, I'm a sucker for romantic comedies, films that others might call "chick flicks." There's a scene in one of those films, *Sleepless in Seattle,* in which Tom Hanks's young son bemoans the fact that he is having trouble holding on to memories of his deceased mother. That is how I was starting to feel about Jen, but I wasn't eight years old.

I wished I was.

I called the New York Police Department and was transferred to four different people before getting someone willing to hear my story. It was a limited story, simply relating to my contact with Philip Garber, and I did not mention that I was none other than the "psycho" who had been writing the articles about his missing girlfriend.

They asked if I would come down to the precinct on West Eighty-fourth Street and talk to Detective Will Bortz, and I agreed to do so. When I got there, Bortz was busy, and I was forced to wait for forty-five minutes. I was in the process of leaving my phone number with the desk sergeant and taking off when word came out to me that Bortz was available to see me.

Bortz was about forty, tall and thin, with blond hair, a look more suited to Venice Beach than Manhattan. He moved and talked quickly, and greeted me in a manner that said, *Let's get this over with.*

"Thanks for coming in, Mr. Kilmer. I hear you've got information about Philip Garber," he said.

"I do."

"Okay. Talk to me and then sign a statement. What have you got?"

"I spoke to him about eight hours before he died. He was investigating something on my behalf, and he was flying to Canada because he had some information."

"Investigating? He was a shrink."

"I know that. I'm a writer, working on an article related to his field."

He looked at his notepad and said, "Kilmer. You the guy looking for his girlfriend?"

"I am."

"This Garber thing relates to that? He was your shrink?"

I was annoyed that Bortz seemed to think I was a nutcase, and was using the fact that Garber was a psychiatrist as evidence of it. "He was not my shrink. He was consulting with me."

"Right," Bortz said. "Consulting. What was the information he was going to Canada for?"

"He wouldn't say."

"Why not?"

"He wanted to make sure it was accurate first," I said, wanting nothing more than to get out of that room.

"Then what was he investigating?"

"Sean Lassiter."

"Who might that be?" Bortz asked.

"I'm working on a story about Lassiter possibly manipulating a drug study."

"Why would he do that?"

"To make a billion dollars."

Bortz stopped to think about that for a few moments, and then said, "How does that find your girlfriend?"

"It probably doesn't."

Bortz nodded. "Somebody will be right in to take your statement. Thanks for coming in."

Moments after I left his office, I got a call from Robby Divine. "I've been looking into this Lassiter drug trial," he said.

"Thanks. What did you find out?"

"The drug cleared phase one, which is a pretty low bar, and therefore has very little effect on the stock. All that does is move it on to phase two."

"Which is going on now?" I asked.

"Which has been going on for a while. The street expects the results next week."

"And what happens if it's a big success?"

"Then Lassiter becomes much richer than me. And I hate when anyone is richer than me."

"Maybe I can organize a benefit dinner for you," I said.

"Don't bother, because you know what the problem with money is?" he asked. "You can never have all of it."

# The Stone felt like he should have been worried.

He was closing in on a historic achievement, one that would both change the world and enrich him beyond anyone's wildest dreams. It was within his grasp, almost there, but he'd be damned if he could find anything to be worried about.

Everything was going exactly as it should, which had basically been true from day one of the operation. There were a couple of minor glitches, but he had put the proper people in place to deal with them, and they had done so effectively.

Now it was out of his hands, the remaining events would proceed as they would proceed, but it was hard to see how anything could go very wrong.

The only people who even had suspicions about what was going on were Kilmer, Kilmer's new girlfriend, and the small-town cop, Kentris. Kilmer's progress had been of the Stone's design, and it had been carefully monitored every step of the way. The girlfriend was of no significance, and the cop didn't have the resources or the knowledge to get in the way. At least not in a time frame that would matter.

There had been more killings than the Stone would have

liked. Not because he had any moral qualms; most of those people and many more would have soon died anyway. It's just that deaths attract attention, and they came at a time when the Stone wanted to operate in the dark.

But no one except Kilmer had made any kind of connection between them, and Garber's plane going down was unlikely to change that. Perhaps over time the feds could figure it out, but one thing they did not have was time.

The Stone would have things wrapped up very soon, and then they would all be pointing fingers, blaming each other for the disaster they faced.

# "I want to break into a building," I said into
the phone.

Craig Langel's response was to tell me to "shut up." When I did so, he told me he'd come right over. Allie and I used the time to talk some more about the plan that we had come up with; it wasn't particularly brilliant, but it was the best we could do.

Craig was in my apartment within twenty minutes, and his first comment was, "Every bugging device known to man has been used on you, and you're having phone conversations about breaking and entering?"

"Good point."

Allie went into the kitchen to get us all coffee, and as soon as she left, Craig said, "You don't think we should talk about this alone?"

"I trust Allie completely," I said.

"You're the boss," he said, in a way that sounded like he considered that an unfortunate truth.

When she came back in I told Craig that we felt we were running out of time, that we had to start applying as much pressure as we could. "Robby Divine, my Wall Street guy, said that

Lassiter's drug results come in next week. If it turns out like I think it will, he'll have his money. He'll have gotten what he wants."

"Other than the fact that you can't stand him," Craig asked, "what does that have to do with you?"

"Because if he has Jen, then it might be to use her against me; to keep me in check in case I started to become a danger to him. If I got too close, he could play that card, threaten to hurt her. Once he wins, he wouldn't need her for that anymore."

"Richard, I've been on this guy like white on rice, and I've seen no evidence that he has her. Absolutely none."

"We've got nothing else to go on," Allie said.

Craig frowned, his frustration obvious. "Okay. So you want to break into a building. Which one? The White House? Fort Knox?"

"The annex building at Ardmore Hospital."

"Why?"

I wasn't going to share Marie Galasso's name with Craig. Even though I trusted him, I couldn't be one hundred percent sure that he wouldn't mention it to someone else in the course of his investigation. With Philip Garber lying on the ocean floor, I simply could not take the chance. "I've got information that there might be something in there that can help us."

"What kind of information?"

"I can't say."

"Where did you get it?"

"I can't say that either."

He stood up, clearly ready to walk out. "In the face of all this trust, my eyes are filling up with tears."

"Craig, I need your help."

He stopped, thought about it for a few moments, then sighed and sat down. "What exactly are you asking me to do?"

"You're a security expert. You know how to keep buildings secure, and my guess is you know how to get into one if you have to. You certainly would be better at it than me."

He frowned, but said, "I need to know what I'm looking for once I get in, so that it can be done quickly. The first rule of breaking into buildings, in case you're planning on turning this into a career, is to get in and get out."

"I'm going in with you," I said. "And I don't know exactly what we're looking for, but I'll know it when I see it."

"Are you going also?" Craig asked Allie. "Because if so, I'll need to get a date."

Craig's attitude toward Allie seemed somewhat hostile, which I hadn't noticed before. But it didn't seem to faze her.

"No, you two can have a boys' night out. I've got my own plans."

I could see Craig wanted to ask what they were, but was afraid we would use the secrecy card again. So I jumped in. "She's going to keep an eye on Lassiter."

Allie smiled. "A stakeout."

"What for?"

"Because it's better than sitting around here doing nothing. Maybe he'll lead us to Jen, or maybe to something else."

Craig nodded, more in resignation than anything else. "Be careful," he said, and Allie agreed that she would.

"So are you in?" I asked.

He shrugged. "I'll check the place out; if I think there's a way in without us getting caught, I'll do it." Then, "Even though I think this is nuts."

"You're just figuring out that I'm nuts?"

"I've had a hunch."

# It took Craig two days to check things out

to his satisfaction.

He insisted we meet outside, in Riverside Park, to ensure privacy for our discussion. "I can get you in," he said. "We can go tomorrow."

I was actually surprised to hear this assessment; I thought he'd say the place was too heavily guarded. "You sure?"

He nodded. "I think so. After nine o'clock at night the place empties out. The security guard from the main building does a walk-through every forty-five minutes."

"So that's how much time we have?" I asked.

"Well, this guy is not exactly Special Forces; he probably wouldn't notice if the Rose Bowl parade was going through the building while he was there. But there's no sense taking chances, so I would say just under forty-five minutes,."

"What about burglar alarms, security cameras . . . ?"

He frowned. "Who do you think you're talking to? I can handle all of that."

"That's my boy."

We agreed to go forward on our mission the next night, and I went home to get nervous. Kentris called, more checking in than anything else, but I wasn't about to tell him what we had planned.

"You're holding out on me," he said, as the conversation neared an end.

"What are you talking about?"

"There's something you're not telling me. I can hear it in your voice."

"No way. Why would you say that?"

"I'm a cop; I have a built-in bullshit detector."

I kept denying it, but there's no way he believed me. The truth was, it didn't matter if he believed me or not; I was going ahead with it.

Allie was having no luck at all with Lassiter. She had already spent all of two days following him around, which basically consisted of watching him go to lunch. "You want to give it up?" I asked, as she set off for another day of the same.

She shook her head. "No, maybe something will happen today."

"Just keep your cell phone handy," I said. "I may be calling for you to bail me out of jail."

"You don't have to do this," she said.

"Yes, I do."

She nodded. "Yeah. I guess you do." She said she would be back by five o'clock, in time to cook me dinner before I went off to Ardmore Hospital. She kissed me good-bye, not a particularly romantic kiss, at least at first. The second kiss, and then the third, definitely moved the ball into the "romantic" category.

When we finally broke off the last kiss, she just looked me in the eye and said, maybe a bit wistfully, "Life is complicated, Richard."

I smiled. "Mine more than most."

"You know what I mean," she said.

"Yeah. I know what you mean."

Allie and I were falling in love, had fallen in love. We had just moved past my ability to deny it to myself, and probably the same was true for her. I recognized the feeling because I had been in love once before, with the person I'd been spending every minute of every day searching for. A person who may not even exist.

Life was definitely complicated.

It was a really long day; I guess waiting to commit my first felony had the effect of making time move slowly. I expected Craig to have everything under control; he wouldn't knowingly bring us into a situation that had great risk. Unfortunately, the key word was "knowingly."

Allie didn't come home at five o'clock, and by five-thirty I was starting to get worried. I called her on her cell, but it went directly to voice mail. I tried again at least ten times before six-thirty, when I had to head to Ardmore, and then at least another twenty times on the way.

By the time I got there, I was panicked that something had happened to her; I simply could not think of another reason why she would not be answering her phone for almost three hours.

I met Craig at a mall parking lot just outside of Ardmore. We discussed what was about to happen, then drove to the hospital in our separate cars and parked in the main lot. Craig got out of his car and into mine, because we were early. It was nine-thirty, and Craig said the guard made his first pass-through at nine forty-five.

"Allie is missing," was the first thing I said when I saw him.

"Yeah?"

"She didn't come home tonight, and she's not answering her phone."

Craig said that we needed to focus on our reason for being at the hospital. The plan was for him to stand in the shadows near the building, and when the guard finished his rounds, Craig would do what was necessary to disable the security devices. He thought that would take less than ten minutes, at which time he'd call me, and we'd go in together.

"You bring your gun?"

I tapped my pocket. "Right here."

He pointed to the glove compartment. "Now put it right there. We get caught, you don't want them to be able to put 'armed' before 'robbery' in the charge."

Before he got out of the car, he said, "Richard, no matter what happens in there, we need to talk later. I've got something you need to hear."

I didn't like the sound of that. "What is it?"

"Later," he said. "First things first."

The call came at exactly 9:56. I didn't answer it, just got out of the car and walked to the back of the annex, where Craig was waiting. "You ready?" he whispered.

I took a deep breath. "Ready."

I did so and he opened the door. I cringed, expecting an alarm to go off, but there was only silence. Craig was obviously good at this.

We went inside, and Craig had a small flashlight to guide us through the place. The first room we went into was a large one, in the center, with probably half a dozen desks, each with its own computer screen. The desks were basically clean, these were obviously very neat people, and the drawers that I tried were either locked or empty.

Along the outside of the room were five offices. Three seemed not to have been in use, and the other two offered nothing of apparent interest to us.

We went into the other main room, which was the one that Marie Galasso said Frank Donovan should not have been in, but which she reported him as coming out of. This was set up as a small hospital annex, with six beds and a lot of standard hospital equipment, such as intravenous carriers.

There was also what seemed to be an X-ray room, and another room with a sign that read SURGERY on the door. We went inside each, and they seemed to be as one would expect.

The entire time we were in there I was thinking about Allie. With all that was going on, there was no way she would leave herself unreachable, unless something was very wrong. My mind was racing with questions of what I could do to find and help her, although my record of finding and helping missing women I loved was fairly dismal.

We continued to search for anything at all unusual or revealing, but there was simply nothing to be found. Finally, Craig pointed to his watch, silently making the statement that it was time to get out.

I nodded my agreement; we were learning absolutely nothing by staying there, so there was no reason to risk getting caught. I left and went back to my car to wait for Craig, who was restoring the security equipment back to its original state so as to cover our tracks.

Within ten minutes he was back, and he got into my car. "Sorry to put you through this, Craig. Waste of time."

"No problem," he said. "Everybody gets bad information sometimes."

I nodded. "I guess so."

"Richard, I said we needed to talk."

"I remember."

"I'm a suspicious guy; I like to check things out. I can't help it, and even though it can be annoying, it usually turns out to be a good thing I checked."

I didn't like where this was going. "Okay . . ."

"So I checked out Allison Tynes. I knew you wouldn't want me to, so I didn't tell you about it."

Now I was both annoyed by where he was going and fearful of what he would say when he got there. Was he going to tell me why Allie was missing?

"Spit it out, Craig."

"Richard, she doesn't have a twin sister, never did, and she's not from where she said she's from."

It was as if he'd shot a jolt of electricity through me. "What the hell are you talking about?"

"I said it as clearly as I can. She's not who you think she is."

I shook my head. "That's not possible. It is simply not possible."

"I found this out by getting her prints off a glass in your apartment. Her real name is Nancy Beaumont. She's done time for fraud and extortion. I've got the documents here." He handed me an envelope that he had in his jacket.

"No . . ." My head was spinning.

"Richard, I'm sorry."

"You're also wrong. I don't know where you got your information, but it's bullshit."

"Take it home and look through it," he said.

"You don't get it," I said, getting angry at Craig in a burst of classic kill-the-messenger. "Somebody out there has been manipulating everything in my life. Since day one, nothing has been as it seemed to be, because they're out there pulling the strings."

"Richard—"

I interrupted. "Now they're doing it to you; they're setting you up with false information, because—"

"Look through it. Okay?"

"—because Allie is real. I know it, Craig. I know it. You cannot tell me otherwise, so don't try."

# I drove home in a daze.

Craig's revelation was so stunning, so bizarre, so absolutely impossible, that I didn't fully have the power to comprehend it. As I neared my house, I had finally decided that it could not possibly be true. Of course, I was aware enough to realize that a lot of things that could not possibly be true had already come to pass, so I was left with one dominant emotion.

I was scared.

I didn't try to reach Allie on the way home, mainly because I didn't know what I would say if I reached her. I was still very worried about her, but first I needed to get things straight in my own mind.

I stopped on a street about a mile from my apartment and parked there. I turned on the interior light, took a deep breath, and opened Craig's envelope.

It was all there. Nancy Beaumont's prison record, complete with mug shot, except the person in the shot was Allie. Copies of press clippings about her arrest, again with Allie's picture in them. Copies of photographs of the real Allison Tynes, along with her twin sister Julie, from their high school yearbook, but they looked nothing at all like Allie and Jen.

It was all there, but it could not possibly be true. I would not allow it to be true. If a person could be made not to exist, then these documents could be wrong.

They simply had to be wrong.

I drove the rest of the way home hoping that Allie would be there, but not knowing what I was going to say if she was. The most important thing would be not what I said, but what I saw in her reaction; that would tell me what I needed to know.

She wasn't there when I got home, and still didn't answer her phone. I was fairly positive by that point that she was not coming back. What I didn't know was why.

Her clothes and possessions were all still there, which was among the things that puzzled me. She knew where I was going, and that I would be out all night. If her departure was voluntary, there was no reason she would have had to leave those things behind; there would have been plenty of time to pack up her things and take them with her.

I guess that was one difference between Allie and Jen; when Jen disappeared, it was without a trace. Allie left plenty of traces. I was still thinking of her as Allie; I instinctively wasn't buying in to the Nancy Beaumont identification.

But all of this could not be a coincidence; Craig's investigation and Allie's disappearance had to be connected. And the obvious conclusion, were I inclined to draw it, was that she somehow knew that Craig had learned the truth and had run away.

Except it could not be the truth. Not if I wanted to keep what was left of my sanity. I was in love with Allie, and for one of the rare times in my life, I was fine with emotion trumping logic.

At eight A.M. there was a knock on the door. I had been up for two hours, so it didn't startle me, but nor did it fill me with hope. Allie had a key; she wouldn't have to knock. But we have a doorman downstairs, so someone else would have had to have been buzzed up.

I took my gun out of the drawer and put it in my pocket, and briefly reflected that in my fear and confusion I was starting to rely on it.

"Who is it?"

"FBI."

That instantly explained the buzzer exemption; I looked through the keyhole and saw two men. "Let me see your ID," I said.

The larger of the two men took out something and held it to the peephole. I couldn't read it, but it looked sort of official. Since Kentris had told me that they were involved on some level with the case, I figured it was legit and opened the door.

He still had his ID open, and they asked if they could come in. I said that they could, and they introduced themselves as Agent Emmett Luther and Agent Carlos Soriano. Luther seemed to be in charge and did most of the talking.

"You filed a statement with the New York Police Department about Philip Garber."

"Yes."

"That's what we'd like to talk to you about."

It struck me how fast my statement had made its way to federal authorities, and how fast they showed up at my door. I couldn't imagine the bureaucracy would ordinarily move that fast, especially since this was not a matter of life and death. Philip Garber was already dead, and if the news reports were to be believed, his death was considered a tragic accident.

They'd obviously had me in their sights, and when the Garber report came in from NYPD with my name attached, it triggered this reaction and visit.

"Everything I know is in my statement," I said.

Luther smiled without humor. "I don't think so."

The man annoyed me. These people were hovering over this situation and probably knew more about it than I would ever know, but I was sitting there in the dark, and they were pumping me for information.

"Where is Jennifer?" I asked. With what I had just been told about Allie, I no longer knew who or what Jennifer was, but I still needed to find out.

"The way this works is that we ask the questions," Luther said.

"Not anymore," I said.

"This is not the approach you want to take here," Luther said. "It won't end well for you."

"That's okay. My previous approaches haven't worked out so well either. Time to try something new."

"I'm going to ask you again," Luther said. "What do you know about Garber's death that was not in your statement?"

"Nothing. Not a thing. I've been wracking my brain trying to think of something, out of a patriotic desire to help you guys. Maybe if you told me some of the things that you know it would jog my memory; I've had some memory issues lately. You've got my phone number in case you think of something, right?"

Luther didn't say anything, and, after a few seconds of thinking about it, took out his own card and handed it to me. "And now you've got my number. I suggest you use it, before it's too late."

"Too late for what?"

But that was another one of the questions he was not about to answer, and they just walked out.

I wasn't going to update Kentris on every-thing that had happened.

For one thing, I wasn't prepared to tell him that I had broken into the hospital annex building, since he was, after all, a cop. I also had an emotional reaction about verbalizing what Craig had discovered about Allie. It was childish, but it felt like if I said it, that in itself would give it some credibility. Besides, there was nothing Kentris could do about it either way.

What I did tell him when I called was that Allie was missing, and that I was worried.

"Any idea where she is?" he asked.

"She was watching Lassiter; that's all I know for sure. Do I need to file a missing persons report?"

"Wouldn't do you any good. She hasn't been missing long enough; the local cops wouldn't touch it yet. If they ever would."

"What do you mean?"

"Well, it's not like you're married. They'd look at it like you were living together for a short time and she bailed out. Maybe she'll come back, maybe not. But if they filed a report every time something like this happened, they wouldn't have time to do anything else. Plus—"

I interrupted him. "She left her things behind."

"Then that makes it more likely that they'll take it seriously, but not much, and not yet. Especially in this case."

"What does that mean?"

"Richard, you have some recent experience with reporting women missing. Your credibility in that particular area is not exactly through the roof, you know?"

I didn't respond, because I knew what he was saying was true. If I reported another woman missing, one who looked identical to the pictures I had put out in the media of Jen, they would laugh at me. And they would probably be right in doing so.

"I'll tell you what," he said. "I'll send out the report. It will have the same effect as if the local cops did it, though that is close to nothing."

"Thanks," I said.

"I still think you're holding back," he said.

"Nice talking to you."

I spent the rest of the morning trying to figure out what to do next. Whether or not Allie was who she said she was, she was probably with Sean Lassiter. Either she was part of his conspiracy, which I still found impossible to believe, or he had done something to her, since she was supposed to be following him the day she disappeared. It was Lassiter I had to go after, but I needed to think of an effective way to do that.

For the time being I called Marie Galasso on her cell phone. She answered it guardedly, and I realized she was probably at work. "Hello?"

"Marie, do you know who this is?"

"Yes."

"Can we meet again? I need to speak with you."

She hesitated, and then said, "Yes."

"Same place? Five o'clock?"

"Yes."

It wasn't much, but it was the best conversation I had had in a while.

I drove up to Ardmore, a trip I was becoming all too familiar with. I got there at four-thirty, parked behind the school, and waited for Marie Galasso. She got there at precisely five o'clock, and got out of the car looking nervous. Everything felt the same as the last time we'd done this, except this time Allie wasn't there. Which meant it felt entirely different.

"Hello, Marie. Thank you for coming."

She had her own agenda. "Have you learned anything about Mr. Donovan and his wife? Was it my fault?"

"It was not your fault." I wasn't really lying, since I considered my overheard conversation with Allie to be the immediate reason the Donovans were killed. But I could see the relief in her face when I let her off the hook, so I was glad I had eased her mind. "But that's not what I wanted to talk to you about."

"Okay."

"Last night . . . I was in the annex building."

"I didn't see you there," she said.

"I know, I went in after it was closed."

She seemed surprised. "What about the guards?"

"That's not important," I said. "There was almost nothing in there. The desks were clean; the offices were empty. The place looked almost deserted."

"Really? My desk is always a mess, and that's true of a lot of people there."

"Were you told—"

She interrupted me as she remembered something. "Yesterday? We were all given yesterday off; they said there was a concern about some bacteria they were working with, and they needed to sterilize the place."

Just my luck. "Oh."

"So I guess they cleaned up," she said. "Although it looked pretty much the same this morning."

This was clearly a three-hour round-trip ride and meeting that was a complete waste of time, plus I was exposing Marie to more danger by having her meet with me.

"Has anything unusual happened since we talked last?'

"No," she said, "but by Friday it won't matter anyway."

"Why is that?"

"That's our last day. There's a cocktail party Friday afternoon, and we're going to get our bonuses. This is one time I won't mind being unemployed; I'm glad it's over."

"Marie, is there anyone else I can talk to, someone you trust, who also works there? Maybe works in the other room . . . the lab?"

She thought for a moment. "I don't know . . . maybe Dr. Costello . . . but I don't know. . . ."

"Who is Dr. Costello?"

"He's a surgeon. He's not there all the time, maybe once a week, if that. I don't really know him, other than to say hello."

"So why should I talk to him?" I asked.

"I'm not sure that you should. But he got into an argument with Dr. Gates the other day; he was yelling pretty loud. I think he's upset with some things that are happening there."

"Do you know what he's upset about?"

"No."

"What kind of surgeon is he?"

"He's a neurosurgeon; he operated on my cousin last year for a tumor. It was benign, thank God. She's doing really well, just has a numb area on the side of her face, and her speech is a little bit slurred. You can hardly notice."

"This tumor was in her brain?"

"Yes."

"Dr. Costello is a brain surgeon?"

"Yes."

"What the hell is a brain surgeon doing in the annex building?" I asked, but Marie didn't know the answer.

It was just possible that I did.

# Sean Lassiter could not believe what he was
reading.

A messenger had just delivered the package he had been waiting almost a year for, the results of the stage-two study of Amlyzine. The results that were going to make Lassiter almost unimaginably rich.

But that was not what he was reading.

What he was reading was a four-hundred-page report, the summary page of which said that Amlyzine performed barely better in the study group than a placebo did in a comparable group. What that summary page said, in so many words, was that the drug was a failure and not worth pursuing. And certainly not deserving of getting to stage three.

Lassiter dug into the backup data, poring through it quickly but thoroughly, with a practiced eye. He was hoping, even expecting, to find evidence that the summary page was some kind of bizarre accident, perhaps a mistake by some confused staffer.

But that was not what he found at all. The data supported the conclusion completely, and was perhaps even more devastating than that summary.

Amlyzine was a failure.

Lassiter was under no illusions about the drug's powers; he knew better than anyone that it was ineffective in dealing with Alzheimer's. But that was not what the report was supposed to show. It was supposed to be a ringing endorsement of Amlyzine's value, so dramatic that it would send the stock in Lassiter's company soaring.

This actual report, with the results it was reporting, was going to wipe out what little value the stock currently had. Which was to say that it would destroy him, sending him down a financial hole from which he could never dig out.

If this report were to stand, his last chance was gone.

But still, it had to somehow be a mistake. Gates was in on it; in fact, it had mostly been his idea. He was going to get rich as well; Lassiter had promised him as much. There was no way Gates would have signed off on this report.

Lassiter called Gates at the hospital, but was told he was out. He then called on his cell phone, but got no answer. He kept calling at both places, leaving the repeated message that it was urgent that Gates return the call, a matter of life and death.

Finally, at three o'clock, Gates called back, and sounded calm and unworried. "Sean, sounds like you've been trying to reach me."

Lassiter was somewhat less calm. "You're goddamn right I was trying to reach you! Have you seen this report?"

"Of course I saw it; I signed off on it. It's unfortunate it didn't turn out the way you had hoped."

Lassiter was so confused and enraged that he thought he might be in some kind of parallel universe; he simply could not believe what he was hearing.

"The way I hoped? The way I hoped? Are you out of your fucking mind? You know goddamn well we had an arrangement. The drug was supposed to pass with flying goddamn colors!"

"Sean, I don't know what you're talking about. You're obviously upset, but maybe with more research the drug can be salvaged."

Somewhere in the back of his mind, Lassiter sensed that maybe Gates was talking this way for some other reason; perhaps he feared that the line was tapped. But the front of his mind was so angry that there was no room for this word of caution to reach his mouth.

"You're not going to get away with this, Gates. I swear to God, I will tear you apart."

"Sean, I don't appreciate being threatened like that."

"You are a dead man, Gates. You got that? If this isn't fixed before it goes to the FDA, you are a dead man!"

Lassiter slammed down the phone in frustration and anger, his mind racing for a way to deal with this disaster.

Gates put down his phone and laughed.

# "There must be a God. I'm still richer than
Lassiter."

That's how Robby Devine started our phone conversation at nine o'clock in the morning. My connection to the riches of Wall Street reached me on my cell phone in a doctor's waiting room. There were four signs in the room forbidding cell phone use, almost as many as there were insisting that copayments be made at the time of the visit.

I stepped out into the hall and took the call. "What does that mean?"

"It means the drug test was el floppo. No chance to make it to stage three."

"That can't be," I said.

"Oh, it be. It definitely be."

"It was announced?"

"Announced?" he asked, as if wounded. "Who am I, John Q. Public? I am not without connections."

"And you're positive? Because this makes absolutely no sense," I said, still trying to understand how this was possible. Lassiter's manipulation of the trial to send his company's stock up was the one thing I was positive about, and now that theory had just been shown to be totally wrong.

"Richard, Lassiter's stock certificates aren't worth the paper you wipe your ass with. Whoever gave you your information is not someone you should be relying on for your future investments."

I thanked him and went back into the waiting room, just as I was being called. That, of course, didn't mean I was going to be seeing the doctor anytime soon; it just meant I had made it to stage two of waiting-room hell.

I had never actually bothered to get a regular New York doctor, so I was seeing Dr. Stacy Fairbanks on a recommendation from my across-the-hall neighbor. I had always been slightly uncomfortable with the idea of going to a female doctor, but this time it didn't bother me. My pants weren't coming down, and I wasn't even putting on a paper robe.

It was twenty-five minutes before Dr. Fairbanks came in, smiling and offering her hand in introduction. After maybe twelve seconds of chitchat, she asked what seemed to be my problem.

"Were I to answer that, I'd be here all month," I said. "So I'd like to limit this visit to one specific problem area."

"What's that?"

"My head."

I showed her the area just at the edge of my scalp. "You can see the scar. I cut my head in an auto accident. It bled some, but not that much."

She looked at it, and confirmed that she could see it. "It's healed quite well. Is it bothering you?"

"No, not at all. I just want to know if you can tell if it's a wound consistent with an auto accident."

She pulled back, puzzled by my statement. "I don't understand. You just told me you were cut in the accident, and now you're asking if that's possible?"

"I think it might have happened another way, but I need you to tell me if I'm right."

"What other way?"

"Surgery. And then possibly the cut was reopened sometime after that and made to look like it happened in the accident."

She looked like she had about a hundred more questions, but didn't ask them. Maybe she was thinking about all the other rooms filled with patients she had to see, patients with real, normal problems. No doubt by now she thought I certainly had a problem with my head, but it was not on the surface.

Instead of asking more questions, she just moved forward and checked out my head again, feeling the scar gently with her fingers as she looked.

"If I had to guess, I would lean towards surgical incision, but that is just a guess. It could have happened either way."

"How can I find out for sure?"

"That depends. What kind of surgery might you have had?"

"Brain surgery."

"Mr. Kilmer, I'm sorry, but this is not making any sense."

I explained that it was a police matter, and I gave her Kentris's number if she wanted to contact him. I also assured her that I would be willing to pay for whatever was required to answer my question.

"A CAT scan would probably do the trick," she finally said. "It would at least show the presence of scar tissue, which would be present after surgery of that kind."

"Could you set it up and read it?"

"I can certainly set it up," she said. "Between the radiologist and I we could read it, as long as what you're describing is all you want to know."

"That's it."

I hassled her until she made a phone call that set up the procedure at three o'clock in the afternoon, in the radiology lab of the hospital she was affiliated with. She said I could come in or call her for the preliminary results at five o'clock.

That gave me a couple of hours to obsess and worry about the still-missing Allie, and I did exactly that.

I showed up at the lab at two forty-five, filled out the paper-work, and was called in right away. The scan itself took less than a half hour, and was less uncomfortable than I had expected. I was reminded of the joke that my father used to tell when I was little, that claustrophobia was the fear of Santa. I never thought it was particularly funny back then either.

Instead of waiting, I immediately went back to Dr. Fairbanks's office. The results weren't there yet, and the receptionist told me they would be transmitted by computer. I was offered a seat in the dreaded waiting room, and told that the doctor would call me when she had the results and had gone over them.

It wasn't until five-fifteen that I was called in, and it wasn't by the receptionist or nurse. Dr. Fairbanks herself came out to get me, asking me to come into her office.

When we got to her office, she walked me over to the computer, which had an image on it that I assumed was the inside of my brain. "Mr. Kilmer, you are not aware of ever having had brain surgery?" She seemed incredulous at the prospect, and I couldn't say I blamed her.

"By your question, I take it that I've had the surgery?"

"You absolutely have." She took her pen and pointed to an area on the left of the screen. "You can see the scar tissue here."

"And there can't be any other explanation?" I asked.

"I'm not a neurosurgeon, but I would certainly say no. And my reason for saying that is more than just the scar tissue."

"What else is there?"

She pointed again, a little higher up on the screen, at what looked like a small dark area. "Can you see this?"

"Yes. What is it?"

She looked away from the screen and directly at me. "It's a foreign object lodged in your brain."

**"Based on your previous interest, I thought** you were the person to call," Gates said. "I appreciate your coming over so quickly."

"What have you got?" Kentris asked.

"Well, we've just concluded the drug trial for Mr. Lassiter's company, the one you asked about. You had gone over the data."

"I know which one you're talking about. How did it come out?"

Gates hesitated. "It's been turned over to the FDA and will be announced publicly soon. So I would ask that you keep what I am about to say confidential until that announcement is made."

"I'll do my best. How did it come out?"

"By any standard, it was a failure. The drug demonstrated no efficacy at all."

Kentris didn't know what "efficacy" meant, but by the context in the sentence, efficacy sounded like a bad thing for drugs not to have. "Did that surprise you?"

"I try and shy away from predictions, but in general terms, a failed trial is not a surprise. The majority of them end in this fashion, as evidenced by the fact that cures for intractable diseases are so rarely found. But Mr. Lassiter was certainly surprised."

"What do you mean?"

"Well, it's industry courtesy for the submitting company to get an advance copy of the report, and that was done in this case. I was out the morning Mr. Lassiter received his, and he left me a series of near-hysterical messages. I've saved the tapes, which I can play for you."

"I would have expected him to be upset. Wouldn't you?"

"Upset and professional, yes, but that's not how he sounded. In any event, when I returned to the office, I called him. Because of his tone on the messages, out of an abundance of caution I recorded the call. If I may, I'd like to play a portion of it for you now."

"Go ahead," Kentris said.

Gates moved the mouse on his computer to "play" and clicked it once. A part of the conversation between him and Lassiter came through the speakers.

**Gates:** Of course I saw it; I signed off on it. It's unfortunate it didn't turn out the way you had hoped.

**Lassiter:** The way I hoped? The way I hoped? Are you out of your fucking mind? You know goddamn well we had an arrangement. The drug was supposed to pass with flying goddamn colors!

**Gates:** Sean, I don't know what you're talking about. You're obviously upset, but maybe with more research the drug can be salvaged.

**Lassiter:** You're not going to get away with this, Gates. I swear to God, I will tear you apart.

**Gates:** Sean, I don't appreciate being threatened like that.

234

**Lassiter:** You are a dead man, Gates. You got that? If
this isn't fixed before it goes to the FDA, you
are a dead man!

The conversation ended with the sound of Lassiter slamming down the phone, after which Gates turned to Kentris.

"I don't know if the threat itself is actionable, but it is certainly worrisome."

"Did you know him prior to this?" Kentris asked. "Is this reaction at all typical?"

Gates shook his head. "We've seen each other at business functions, but that's about it. I certainly never oversaw a test of one of his drugs before." He smiled. "And never will again. I've heard stories about him being volatile, but nothing that would have led me to expect this."

"What are you asking me to do?" Kentris asked.

"I don't know, but at the very least I would appreciate any advice you can offer. I'm sure you have more familiarity with this kind of thing than I."

"You can file charges, though that should be with your local police. It may be necessary, but it may just prolong the incident. He might have been blowing off steam, and that would be the end of it. If you file charges, it will be something for you to deal with for a very long time. Having said that, I am not in a position to advise you either way."

Gates nodded and thought about it for a few moments. "I think I'll hold off for now. But may I forward copies of this tape to you?"

"For what purpose?"

Gates shrugged. "I don't know. . . . I'd just like you to have it."

Kentris said that it would be fine, and then left. On the way back to the station, he took time to reflect on his certainty that Gates was lying, and why that might be.

He believed that the test was a failure and that the phone conversation was real. But that was all he believed. He did not see

Gates as an innocent; Lassiter's reaction was such that he probably had good reason to believe the fix was in on the study, and that Gates had not lived up to his end of the bargain.

But that wasn't all he didn't believe. There was no way that Gates chose Kentris to confide in because he was seeking advice, or because of Kentris's previous interest in the case. If Gates were really worried, he would have gone to the local cops, the people he knew would be empowered to take action that could help and protect him.

And either way, as the head of a large company, by now he would have surrounded himself with security guards.

The most logical explanation was that Gates was setting Lassiter up for something, and was using Kentris to facilitate it.

He didn't know what Gates was setting Lassiter up for, but it scared the hell out of him.

# There are a number of advantages to an Ivy

League education. One that most people don't focus on is that it provides one with a group of friends, often lifelong friends, who are usually smart, accomplished, wealthy people.

I hadn't remained close with too many college friends, though the emergence of e-mail had rectified that somewhat. But I had been in a fraternity, and I felt that even though I had not seen or heard from many of them over the years, they would be there for me if I needed them.

I needed at least one of them now, though I didn't know which one.

I dug out my college yearbook, as well as my old copies of my fraternity newspapers that I had kept. Armed with all this, I turned on my computer, went to Google, and started to work.

I made a list of all the names that I remembered as friends or even acquaintances, and looked up each name on Google. By the fortieth name, I was completely astonished by how prominent my classmates already were, in many different fields. As a person known only as a magazine writer/nut job, I felt a little embarrassed by how completely they had outdistanced me. But this was not the time to worry about it.

Unfortunately, I was not finding anyone whose chosen field fit my needs, at least not until I got to name number forty-seven, Daniel Lovinger. Dan was a fraternity brother of mine, though because he was two years ahead of me, we weren't close friends. Basically the only time I remember seeing him was at the Friday night parties, and we were both invariably drunk.

But Dan must have sobered up pretty well, because according to Google he had become a prominent neurosurgeon, specializing in the brain, at Mount Sinai Hospital. I figured he must be good at it, since his name got 467,000 hits on the search.

I called his office, gave my name, and asked for him. The receptionist put me on hold before I could add the phrase, *we were friends in college,* since I didn't think he would remember my name.

I was wrong. He got on the phone, and within thirty seconds we were laughing and reminiscing about times I barely remembered, and he was telling me about other fraternity brothers he had remained friends with.

I finally got to tell him why I had called, that I needed his medical opinion urgently.

"This have anything to do with your missing girlfriend?" he asked, proving once and for all that more people had read my articles than had seen the average Super Bowl.

"In a way, yes, but it specifically refers to a health matter of mine. I have other recommendations for neurosurgeons, but I really need someone I can trust." Dr. Fairbanks had in fact given me the names of top people, but I felt more comfortable with Dan.

"What's going on?" he asked.

"I think I've got something in my brain."

He said I could come right over, and I gathered the CD that Dr. Fairbanks had given me of the brain scan I'd had done. Dan was alone in his office when I got there; it was not a day on which he saw patients, but rather when he worked on research.

This time he was all business, no laughing or storytelling at all. He took the CD and put it up on the screen. "Whoa. Who did the surgery?"

"I don't know."

"You don't know?" he asked, but didn't wait for an answer. Instead he pointed to the very small foreign object. "What is that?"

"I was hoping you could tell me."

He walked away from the screen, sat down at his desk, and said, "Start from the beginning."

So I did. I didn't tell him everything, since much of it had nothing to do with his area of expertise. But I told him all about Jen, and the memories that I had that no one else seemed to share. He knew a lot about it, having read my articles, but he didn't interrupt, just nodded occasionally and listened.

When I was finished, I said, "So I need to know what is lodged in my brain, and whether it explains what has happened to me."

"The only way we're going to know what is lodged in your brain is by taking it out," he said. "But I'm not sure you want to do that."

"Why not?" I asked.

"Well, for one thing, brain surgery always comes with significant risk. Not enormous risk in this case, but it's not something you want to do if you can help it."

"Is it causing any damage?"

"Depends on how you define that. You could live a long life with it, if that's what you're asking. It's not in a particularly sensitive area."

"What area is it in?"

"The main function of that area is memory."

It took a moment for the import of this to sink in, and then I said with understatement, "I've been having some difficulty in that area lately."

"Do you have any idea when this was done? A reliable time frame?"

"Yes. When I was in Ardmore."

"Have you had difficulty remembering events since then?"

"No. Not that I'm aware of. At least if I have, it hasn't been pointed out to me."

"Then whatever this is, it is not interfering with your ability to remember, so your decision is not really a medical one."

He was picking his words carefully, and I was getting frustrated. "Dan, can we cut through this? What do you think this is?"

"I think it's an implant."

"What does that mean? What kind of implant?"

"There is an extraordinary amount of research being conducted in the field of memory," he said. "Much of it is due to the epidemic of Alzheimer's; it's taking away our parents and costing our economy over two hundred billion dollars a year. So the incentive for a breakthrough is rather evident."

I didn't want to say anything, because I didn't want to delay what already showed signs of being a long, professorial lecture.

"There are also motivations rooted in the field of psychology, though more of them are centered on erasing memory rather than restoring it. A childhood trauma, rather than haunting someone throughout their life, could be erased. Does it bother you that you struck out in the ninth inning of the high school state championship game? Wipe it away."

"Obviously there are built-in ethical issues in an area like this, but the really ominous part about memory control is when someone else has that control. Governments can use it to neutralize dissidents, employers can generate complete loyalty from their employees, you could even get your ex-girlfriend to forget you cheated on her."

"But neither of the things you're describing fits my case," I said. "If what I think has happened has happened, then they didn't get me to recall lost memories, or erase intact ones. They've created new ones."

"Yes, it appears that they have."

**"I'll try to make this as simple as I can,"** Dan said, though I didn't really have any hope he'd succeed.

"The brain sends and receives analog signals. It talks to the body in this fashion; that's how we see, and hear, and move, and feel pain. But we, meaning medical science, have only recently been able to participate in that conversation. Believe me, plenty of people have tried, and are trying, to do better."

He went on to describe some examples of how scientists have had success. For instance, artificial cochlea have been implanted in the deaf and restored hearing, and artificial retinas to restore sight are very close to reality. "Those devices communicate with the corresponding brain cells; they talk to the brain and tell it what to do, and the brain does it."

"So maybe this device can tell it what to remember?" I asked.

"Exactly, and once the people creating the device understand the language, it would be easy to do. Everybody in this field knows it's going to happen; I just didn't think the science was nearly there yet."

"But the memories I have are so real, so detailed. . . . How could they have accomplished that?"

"Much of what they would have fed you was real . . . places, people, events. They put on a multimedia show in your head, probably relying on video to some extent."

I literally got a chill when he said that; Marie Galasso had said that the chips she was working on were designed to hold video, among other things.

"But I've got a feeling this has gone even further. The communication with the brain is essentially a mechanical process, the people doing it don't even have to fully understand the depth of it."

"What do you mean?" I asked.

"Well, for example, let's say you own one of those devices that you can download books onto, like the iPad or the Kindle. If you break it, the guy that fixes it only has to know how the device works; he doesn't have to have a knowledge of literature. He's simply a technician."

"So you said this has gone further?"

He nodded. "I would think so, based on what you've reported. They've included a major psychological component, and you have probably been a party to it."

"Me?"

"Yes. Much like in the way you dream. Chances are they've given you most of the facts, like the people and places, and you've filled in the rest. You've made up much of the story, without knowing it. I'm sure some psychotropic drugs helped it along. That's how we remember most things anyway. We recall pieces, bits, and fill in the rest. That's why memory is so often unreliable."

"So the people I remembered interacting with—I might never have met them. And the places I remembered being—I might never have been there?"

He nodded. "That's the way I figure it. The people doing this research would have had to have gotten audio and video of those people and places; then your mind did the rest. If they had control over someone, like your girlfriend, they could have forced her to act things out. Would they have had the technological capability of pulling all of that off?"

I knew all too well what their technological capability was; there was no doubt it was sufficient to the task at hand.

I continued to bombard Dan with questions, and he patiently answered every one. He kept throwing in the caveat that he couldn't be sure this was what had happened unless he removed the implant, and possibly not even then. But I could tell he had no doubts about what he was saying.

"So, do you want to take it out?"

"I don't know," I said. "I don't know. I'm not sure I want to lose those memories."

"That part I can't help you with, Richard. I'm not a shrink."

What I didn't tell him was that he should be glad of that, because the last shrink I brought into this wound up at the bottom of the Atlantic Ocean. I wished I had Philip Garber to talk to now; I felt I needed his perspective.

My head was spinning when I left Dan's office, yet for the first time I could tell that clarity was on the horizon. I believed his theory was accurate; it was the only credible explanation I had yet heard to explain what had happened to me.

I probably should have been focusing on who did this to me, but for the time being I wasn't. I was instead thinking about what it meant to me, and what it said about my mind, and my memories, and my life.

Jen was not real; I had finally come to terms with that fact. There probably was such a person, maybe even an actress, but she was not real to me in the way that I knew her. We did not meet the way I had thought. We did not fall in love, or make love. We did not live together, and I did not ask her to marry me.

The most important person I had ever had in my life was never even in my life.

Or was she?

She was in my mind, with memories as clear and as wonderful as any I have ever had. In that way she was real, and I didn't know if I wanted to give that up.

What is life but the memories we have of it?

I thought about this for hours, which seemed like days. I wished I had somebody to talk to about it; I wished I could talk to Jen.

Or Allie.

I didn't know where Allie fit into this. Craig would say she was probably a key member of the conspiracy that was doing this to me; he would believe she and Jen were the same person. He could be right; maybe she was Nancy Beaumont, and Allie/Jen/Nancy was somewhere laughing at what she and her coconspirators had done to me.

It all made perfect sense, but I just didn't believe it.

I was exhausted, but I was also beyond angry. My mind had been invaded, literally so, and I had been made to jump around like a stupid puppet. I was going to find out who had done it, and make them wish they hadn't.

The best way to find out who was to find out why, but even after all this time I was nowhere with that. I'd been holding on to this vague idea that it had something to do with the trial of Sean Lassiter's drug, though I could never figure out how it all connected. But Lassiter's trial was a failure, and would not be bringing him the fortune he must have been counting on.

Yet Lassiter still had to be the guy. I had been doing the story on him, the one that was going to get me the Pulitzer, and that, plus the fact that he was tied in to Ardmore, could not be a coincidence. Most significantly, the guy who held the gun on us near the highway mentioned that Lassiter was behind it before he himself was killed.

It had to be Lassiter.

Sleep had not come easy for a while now, and this night was not going to be any different. So when Craig Langel called me at almost midnight, I was still wide awake.

"What's going on?" he asked. "I haven't heard anything from you."

"Oh, not much. I just found out that there's a machine in my brain, telling me what to remember."

Craig hesitated. "That's a joke, right?"

"I wish."

"I'm sorry, Richard, but I don't know where to go with that or what you're talking about. I'm going to stay in my world, okay?"

"Okay. What's happening in your world?"

"Something is going down. With Lassiter."

He went on to tell me that Lassiter had a flight booked the next evening to Paris, with a connection to Moscow. "One-way," he said.

"Why Moscow?" I asked.

I could almost see him shrug through the phone. "Beats the shit out of me. But you can bet he's not going there for spring break."

"The project at Ardmore ends tomorrow night. All the workers have been called there for a cocktail party and to get their bonuses."

"Then tomorrow is the day, but for what, I don't know. What do you want to do?"

I still didn't know what was happening or why, but I couldn't let Lassiter get on that plane.

"I want to stop him."

# The operation was not going to achieve
perfection.

The Stone was fairly sure of that now. The ultimate would have been for Kilmer to commit a murder, but that was now unlikely. The emotional component was mostly gone for him, and anger probably would not be enough of a motivation.

But the disappointment struck more at the Stone's ego than at anything else. The winning bidder had been chosen, and the representative was on the way. The buyers would only want final confirmation that secrecy was guaranteed before transferring the money.

That secrecy would in fact be guaranteed that very afternoon, with the deaths of all who had participated. Kilmer would die as well, as would the insurance policy downstairs. And then the Stone could leave the country he hated so much.

So for now he would just wait for the phone calls, confirming that it was over.

It was going to be a long day. Long, but very rewarding.

**Craig and I agreed to meet a block from** Lassiter's house.

He had gotten there early, just in case Lassiter left, so he could follow him. When I was halfway there, he called to tell me that there had been no movement in the house, but lights were on, and Lassiter's car was there.

I brought my gun with me, except this time it was loaded. It made me feel secure, though I wasn't sure I'd have the guts to use it. Unless he had hurt Allie; then I'd blow his brains out.

I parked a block farther away, and walked to Craig's car. I got in the passenger seat, but he didn't even look over at me. He was looking through binoculars trained on Lassiter's driveway.

"Nothing happening?" I asked.

He shook his head. "No, but at least there are no pain-in-the-ass neighbors to deal with."

He finally looked over at me briefly. "I assume you've got a plan?"

I nodded. "I'm going to go in and threaten to shoot him if he doesn't tell me what's going on."

"Brilliant," he said. "You come up with that all by yourself?"

"You got anything better?"

"Nope. So are we ready?"

"Ready," I said. "No matter what happens, even if we have to shoot him, we're going to search that place top to bottom. Today is the day we find out what the hell is going on."

"I hope you didn't bring your gun," he said.

I tapped my pocket gently. "I did."

He put the binoculars down and said, "Richard, listen to me. You—"

"Let's get going, Craig, okay?"

He stopped, then nodded.

"Okay. Here's how I think we should do this—" Before he could finish the thought, his cell phone rang, and he answered it. "Langel."

He listened for a while, and then said, "Shit." About ten seconds later, he asked, "Cause of death?" and then ten seconds after that said, "Yeah. I understand." All in all, it was not a particularly upbeat phone call, at least from his end.

He clicked off the call and turned to me. "You need to hear this," he said.

"Uh-oh."

"I'm sorry to be the one to have to tell you this, but they fished a body out of the Hudson River this morning. It was Nancy Beaumont, or Allison Tynes, or whatever the hell her name was."

The news hit me right between the eyes, and I sagged back into the seat. I hadn't verbalized it, even to myself, but my reaction made me realize that I still had been positive that Allie was one of the good guys, and that she was okay.

And that we'd come out intact . . . and together.

I had no idea how I would deal with the loss; it seemed that I had finally reached my limit. Maybe I would figure it out, maybe I wouldn't, but it would have to wait. Now it was time for revenge.

"Sorry, man," Craig said. "Maybe she was okay; maybe they were just using her."

"Yeah." I was feeling an anger greater than any I had ever felt. "It gives us something to talk to Lassiter about."

"One of us should go in the front door and confront him; the other should go around the back. No need for him to know there are two of us."

I nodded. "I'll take the front."

Something about the tone of my voice made him concerned; I could see it in his face. "Don't do anything stupid, Richard. This is not your comfort zone."

"It's getting there."

He looked like he was going to caution me again, but thought better of it. "Give me five minutes to get in position in the back, then you take center stage."

I nodded my agreement, and he got out and walked toward the house. A few hundred yards away, he ducked in toward the back of the house and out of my line of sight. I checked my watch, waited the requisite five minutes, and got out of the car myself.

I was maybe a hundred yards away when I heard it. It was either a gunshot or a car backfiring, and I sure didn't see any cars around. My resolve immediately turned to near-panic; the shot seemed to come from behind the house, where Craig had just gone.

I wished Craig and I had thought to retain some means to communicate, but my cell phone was back in the car. I debated whether to go up to the front door as planned, but that seemed crazy now. I would go to the back of the house and see if something had happened back there. If not, and everything was okay, then I could go back around to the front, and all we would have lost would be a few meaningless minutes.

I took a quick look at the front of the house, to make sure I didn't see Lassiter and, more importantly, that he didn't see me. He wasn't there, so I ran around to the back of the house. It was a rich person's backyard, beautifully sculpted grounds, swimming pool, and a tennis court in the rear. The son of a bitch lived well.

At first I didn't see anything unusual, and then I heard a

noise about seventy feet from the house. Craig was on the ground, lying on his back, with his head raised and looking at me. There was a red area on his shoulder, and it was widening. He had been shot.

Craig didn't say anything, just seemed to nod to the back of the house, and in a moment I saw why. Sean Lassiter was on the porch, with what looked like a gun in his hand. He was looking toward Craig, so he had his back to me, a situation that wouldn't last for long.

I didn't do anything for a few moments, and Craig seemed to start to panic, since he was lying out there unprotected. Finally, he screamed, "Shoot him! Shoot him!"

"Hold it right there, Lassiter!" I yelled, pointing the gun at his back. "Drop the gun and turn around!"

To my surprise and relief, he did exactly what he was told. I continued to point the gun, and said to Craig, "We've got to get an ambulance out here for you."

"I called 911 on my cell," Craig said. "They're on their way."

"What the hell is going on back here?" Lassiter snarled, apparently undaunted by the fact that I was the only one holding a gun.

"You want to know what's going on? You shot my friend, and I'm going to put a bullet in your head unless you start talking now." I raised the gun; I wasn't going to shoot, I couldn't, but I would have gotten some serious pleasure out of it.

"I didn't shoot anyone. I heard a shot, and I came out here to protect myself. I've been getting death threats."

"Well, then here's another one. You got thirty seconds to tell me everything, or you are a dead man."

"I don't know what you're talking about. Somebody has been playing you, using you to attack me. I hadn't thought about you for ten years."

"You have been systematically trying to destroy my life," I said, but something was gnawing at the back of my mind, something that wasn't implanted in there.

"Really? Why? How? You're trying to tie me in to things I

had no power to do, and no reason to do so even if I had the power. You think your life is ruined? Join the club."

I was experiencing a bizarre sensation, even by my standards. I was holding a gun on someone, someone I'd blamed and hated since this whole thing started, but I was focused elsewhere. Something was just out of my mind's range; it felt like I kept trying to grab it, to make sense of it, but I couldn't.

"Why are you going to Moscow?" I asked.

He laughed. "Moscow? You know something, Kilmer? You really are out of your mind."

And that statement, maybe not the statement but the attitude behind it, pushed me over the edge into clarity. And in that moment I knew the truth. I let my gun drift down to my side and I turned, stunned, and that truth was staring me in the face.

"Put the gun down, Richard. Now."

Craig Langel was standing there, unhurt, gun pointed at my face. "You just figured it out, didn't you? I could see the wheels turning."

"I figured it out," I said, and when he seemed to be squeezing the trigger, I dropped the gun.

"What gave it away?"

"It's all coming together now. They emptied out the lab that night because you told them we were coming. And you knew what route we were taking to Ardmore that day, because I told you we were going to the pancake house. You told your partner we were going to be driving past there, and then you shot him and removed the body."

He smiled as he picked up my gun, using a handkerchief to avoid getting his prints on it. "Not bad."

"You've been the source of so much of this, and you've been lying every step of the way." As I said this, I realized that Craig had been the one to tell me about Allie really being Nancy Beaumont, and about her body being fished from the river. It gave me hope that she was alive, and made me positive she really was who she said she was.

"Well, we can reminisce forever, but time is running out," he said. "Let's go inside."

"For what?" I asked.

"Well, we're all going to die in the next few minutes. With the exception of myself, of course."

# Marie Galasso had debated whether to show

up at all.

It was billed as a get-together to say good-bye and toast their collective accomplishments. Attendance was declared to be mandatory, though the fact that bonus checks were to be given out made that edict mostly unnecessary. Money can be an even greater motivating force than camaraderie.

But Marie had a bad feeling about it, and would have preferred that they mail her the check. Two of her coworkers had coaxed her into going, although the annex building where it was to be held was a place she never needed or wanted to go to again.

She arrived promptly at two; it was contrary to her nature to be late for anything, and she hoped to be first in line for the bonuses so that she could leave early.

The place was set up as a party room, complete with punch bowls and a buffet of hot food. Everybody seemed to be in a good mood, probably pleased with the completion of their job well done and happy it was over.

Marie liked her coworkers and, after a couple of drinks of the spiked punch, was sharing in the restrained revelry. She would miss some of these people, and perhaps would work with them again in the future.

Just not here.

By two-thirty, Dr. Gates had not arrived, so it was obvious to Marie that this was going to go on for a while. He would no doubt give a talk, that was his style, and he might encourage other leaders to do the same. Then the bonuses would be given out. All of it, Marie knew, would take time.

By the time Gates got there it was past three, and most of the attendees were feeling at least a buzz from the punch. That made them slightly less clearheaded, but that was not important.

None of them would have noticed the huge amount of plastic explosives anyway. The explosives were well concealed, placed in the walls and deep in the closets. The timer was actually outside, set against the annex, concealed by a Dumpster.

Gates himself thought he was there to give a talk, praise a job well done, and hand out bonuses. He was actually looking forward to it.

He had no idea that he and everyone else in that building would soon be incinerated.

## Lassiter and I went into the house with Craig

behind us, pointing the gun.

He had us walk through the house toward the front door. When we got to the foyer, he said, "Okay, this should do pretty well. We can set up shop here." He was looking at the room as if trying to judge the position of certain things in it.

"You don't need to do this," Lassiter said. "Whatever they're paying you, I can give you more."

"No, you can't. Believe me, you can't."

"Craig, he's right," I said. "There are better ways to end this."

"Shut up, both of you. I need to figure this out. This has to be done just right . . . sort of choreographed."

"Then why did you want me to shoot him?"

He smiled. "There were bonus points in it for me. But that's okay, it won't be a problem. I'll make it look like you did."

"Craig, I'm telling you—"

Suddenly he got angry. "Shut up! You really think that now, after all that's happened, you can talk me out of it? Are you that stupid?" Then he softened. "Besides, you're just a small part of it. Everything is connected."

"What else is there?" I asked. It was a pathetic strategy, but I figured if I could keep him talking, it would delay the point when he would start shooting. In the meantime, I was inching slightly closer to a statue that was sitting on a tall pedestal. If given the opportunity, I would grab it and throw it at Craig. Among the many problems with this strategy was that it looked as if the statue could be attached to the pedestal, making it quite impossible to lift, much less throw.

He smiled. "Rich, so many people are going to die today that you two will barely be noticed. You'll be on page twelve. The headline will probably be, 'Psycho with Missing Girlfriend Dies in Murder-Suicide.'"

"What are you talking about? Who else is going to die?"

"Everybody who worked on the project." He looked at his watch. "In fact, it's twenty minutes to kaboom."

"What about Allie?"

He laughed. "Her too, except she'll probably be the last to go."

"Where is she?" I asked, but I thought I already knew. I could only hope I lived long enough to tell someone else.

Craig ignored the question. "Here's the way we do it." He directed his next comments to Lassiter. "You get shot up close, as if you were trying to get his gun. Then Richard shoots himself in the head."

He turned to me and held up my gun. "Thanks for bringing this."

He started walking toward Lassiter, who looked petrified. In the process, Craig's back was turned at an angle away from me. If I was going to make my move for the statue, this was the time. But I couldn't seem to direct my arm and body to do it.

Craig was within five feet of Lassiter. As soon as he closed that gap he would shoot, and then he would focus all his attention on me. But still I didn't move.

Lassiter had more guts than I did. As Craig moved forward, he rushed forward himself, closing the gap and grabbing for the gun. Craig was momentarily stunned by the move, and he staggered back a few feet, seemingly attached to Lassiter.

Suddenly a gunshot rang out, and Lassiter fell backward. But I was already moving, finally grabbing the statue and discovering to my immense relief that it wasn't attached to the pedestal.

Craig's taking those steps backward meant I no longer had to throw it at him, I could swing it instead. It was heavy, and it was very hard, much harder than the skull it crashed into.

I hit him as he turned toward me, and he went down instantly, hitting the ground and not moving. I didn't know whether he was alive or not, but every instinct in my body wanted to smash his head again, just to make sure.

But he had wanted me to be a murderer; he said it would somehow provide him bonus points. I didn't want to give him that; I was going to be bigger and better than that.

So I kicked him in the balls.

## Lassiter was dead; I had no doubt about that.

I wasn't sure about Craig, but I didn't bother checking, because I didn't care much either way. If he moved, I was going to smash him over the head with the statue again.

Because of their respective conditions, there was no urgency for me to call 911 and get an ambulance there. Instead I called Kentris, and when they tried to put me on hold, I screamed that people were going to die. That turned out to be fairly motivating, and within ten seconds he picked up.

"What the hell is going on?" he asked.

"There's an annex building behind Ardmore Hospital. It's the small building in the back," I said.

"I know where it is."

"Good. Everybody who works in that building is there now; they're having a going-away party or something. They are all going to be murdered."

"What?" he screamed.

"You heard me. There's no time to tell you how I know, just trust me. You've got to get those people out of that building. You've only got about ten minutes."

"How is it going to happen?"

"I'm not positive, but I think there are explosives there," I said, remembering that Craig had said "kaboom." "They're probably on a timer, or it might be set to be detonated from a remote location."

"Where are you?" he asked.

"Nowhere near there. I've got something else to do. Please hurry."

"I'm on my way," he said, and I believed that he was.

When he got off the phone, I took the card out of my wallet that Agent Emmett Luther had given me. He was based in the Bureau's Newark office, about forty minutes from where I was calling.

Once again the screaming about multiple deaths did the trick, and they patched me through to Luther, who was not in the office.

"What have you got, Kilmer?" He seemed calm; apparently the prospect of mass murder was not serious enough to shake him up.

"Everything. I know it all."

"What does that mean?"

"I know all about the memory implants; I know who's behind it, and I know where he is."

"I'm listening."

"No, listening won't cut it," I said. "I will meet you at Teterboro Airport in a half hour. You have a plane and a bunch of agents with guns waiting there, and once we're in the air I'll tell you where I'm going."

"This is bullshit," he said.

"Then don't meet me," I said, and hung up.

My next call was 911, and I told them that there was a shooting, with one confirmed death and another probable. I didn't know the address, but I gave them the street and told them it was Lassiter's house.

They asked for my name and I gave it, but told them that I wouldn't be here when they arrived.

"You need to stay on the scene, sir."

"Sorry. If you have a problem, call Agent Emmett Luther at the FBI, Newark office."

They were still arguing with me when I hung up the phone. I had to move quickly, or they'd be there and I'd never get out. I quickly felt Craig for a pulse; I didn't want him to get up and walk away once I left. I'm not great at pulse-feeling, but I don't think he had one.

I was four blocks away when I heard the sirens, but even if they drove by me, they would have no way of knowing who I was. I'd have a lot of questions to answer later, and I had probably violated about a hundred laws by leaving the scene, but I didn't care.

Nothing was going to stop me from getting on that plane.

**Kentris immediately knew he was not going**
to make it in time. Not if Kilmer was right about the timing, and
it was quite likely that he was. It was going to happen in less than
ten minutes, and it would take him a minimum of twelve to get
there, maybe longer.

He screamed instructions to two sergeants to call the Ardmore police and the hospital security and tell them that a bomb
was going to blow up the Annex building in a few minutes. The
building was to be cleared immediately, and Kentris was on the way
with a bunch of cops.

He had his doubts that even the phone calls would do the
trick. It takes time to get through to people, and to get them understanding and moving. Then it takes more time to get a crowd of
potential victims themselves to understand and move out in a safe
fashion.

Kentris was in a squad car; others would follow momentarily. He would call on the way and direct that the bomb squad,
ambulances, fire and emergency personnel, and a SWAT team
be sent to the scene immediately, and that the area be cordoned
off.

Then it was out of Kentris's hands; in fact, he believed it was so already. He was close to certain that everyone was only going to arrive in time to help count the bodies.

**Once I was in the car, I did the math in my** head.

My best guess was that the annex building was going to explode in about six minutes, and there was no way Kentris could get there in time. I had very grave doubts that he would be able to get others to do it either.

I had to try another way.

I pulled over to the side of the road and took out my wallet. I found Marie Galasso's cell phone number, and called her as I started to drive again.

There was no answer, and after five interminable rings it went to voice mail.

I didn't bother leaving a message; there was no way that was going to work. Instead, I dialed the number again, and was surprised when she answered just before the fifth ring.

"Hello?" she said, and by the tone of her voice and the boisterous noise in the background, I could tell they were having a good time, probably lubricated by alcohol.

"Marie, this is Richard Kilmer."

"Richard! Today's the last day! Can you believe it?"

"Marie, listen to me. There is a bomb, probably more than

one, set to go off in the annex building in less than five minutes. You've got to get everyone out of there now!"

"What?" she asked, but I know she heard me the first time.

"Marie, you've got to get everybody out of there. There is not a second to lose. Everybody's life is in your hands!"

The tone of her voice had turned to panic; that was better than levity, but not by much. "How do you know that?" she screamed.

"Marie, control yourself. Please believe me, I'm not making this up. The people running the operation want you all to die."

"But Dr. Gates is here."

"He's not running things; he's going to be another victim."

"Oh, my God!"

Click.

She hung up on me. I didn't know if that meant she had heard enough and was going to do what was necessary, or if she thought I was crazy and didn't want to talk to me anymore.

Or something in between.

Except something in between was not going to be close to enough.

**The Stone was watching CNN. He rarely did** that; in fact he rarely watched the news at all. He couldn't trust what they said; it consisted mostly of propaganda or overhyping to generate ratings. That was ironic, because the Stone was in the process of generating a massive ratings boost for CNN and news stations all over the country.

Langel was not going to call him when Kilmer and Lassiter were taken care of, that was not necessary. He would instead come to where the Stone was, to collect his money and clean up the loose ends.

The only way Langel would call was if Kilmer was the shooter, but events seemed to have overtaken that possibility. Once Kilmer learned of the implant and realized his memories of the girl were artificial, the overwhelming need for revenge on Lassiter would be lessened below the level to get him to commit murder.

But you never know.

The real news would come from the television. Once the hospital building blew up, the cameras and talking heads would descend on the wreckage area, and every nuance would be breathlessly reported. That would tell him and his buyer everything they needed to know.

Their secret would be safe; no one working on the physical project, including Gates, would be around to ever reveal it. Only Langel would be left alive, simply because at the moment there was no one left to kill him. That would go on the Stone's to-do list.

Once today's operations were completed, the money would be wired, the material and designs turned over, and the jet readied. If all went well, and it always did, the Stone would be out of the country in two hours.

But this was the calm before the storm, and for the Stone right now there was nothing to do except watch some television.

# Marie Galasso wanted to get the hell out of

that building.

She had no doubt that Kilmer was telling the truth, and she didn't want to be there when he was proven right. But she couldn't just run; she had to get her friends and coworkers out as well.

One glance told her what she already knew. This was a relaxed crowd, talking, drinking cocktails, and listening to music. It was going to take extreme measures to get them up and out in the time required.

"EVERYBODY OUT! THERE'S A BOMB IN THE BUILDING. . . . IT'S GOING TO GO OFF!"

She screamed that three or four times, but it had far less effect than she had hoped. Most people just looked at her, concerned and puzzled, and some even thought she might be joking. But none of them were moving.

"Marie, what are you doing? What are you talking about?" her friend Sandy Miller asked. Marie just screamed at her that they needed to get everybody out of the building.

Marie screamed her warnings again, as loud as she could, but while she certainly attracted attention, she still didn't generate any movement. Most people assumed she was drunk and was handling it badly. How would Marie Galasso have suddenly gotten information about a bomb? It was ridiculous.

"Is this a joke?" Sandy asked, but Marie was on the move and didn't hear her. It was time for desperate measures.

Marie ran to the front of the room and starting turning over all the tables, including the ones with the punch bowl and all the chafing dishes with the food. This created chaos in the room, but still didn't get people to register the fact that they had to get out.

All they were doing was wondering why Marie was going nuts, and trying to decide what they should do about it.

Dr. Gates was in the restroom when he came out and saw what was going on. When he finally realized what Marie was saying, the cold realization hit him in the face. She had to be right, the building must be coming down, and his partners clearly had planned for him to die in the explosion. There was no way he was going to let that happen, and he heeded Marie Galasso's warning and ran out.

Marie had one final idea. She grabbed the gas lighter that was flaming under one of the hot chafing dishes, and she started to set fire to tablecloths, all the while screaming, "GET OUT OF THE BUILDING! NOW!"

She knew that setting a fire in the middle of a building filled with bombs might not be the best idea, but the tables were in the center of the room, and there was no time for the fire to spread enough to impact anything before the time of the explosion.

If Kilmer was right, this was her best chance of saving these people. If not, she would have a bit of explaining to do.

The fire got the people moving, not so much because they understood that there were bombs about to go off, but rather because they didn't want to die in a fire.

Satisfied that she had done all she could, Marie ran out as well. Ninety-four of the one hundred and three people made it out and to safety before the building was obliterated in a massive explosion.

Security arrived in time to see it; the Ardmore police got there three minutes after that, with Kentris four minutes behind them.

The media arrived eight minutes later, just after Dr. Gates was read his rights.

# I heard the radio report about the explo-

sion as I was nearing Teterboro Airport. I had no way of knowing how bad it was, or how successful Marie Galasso had been in
getting herself and the others out of there. The preliminary report simply said that there were fatalities, but then it added that a
large number of employees had escaped the building.

Way to go, Marie.

Teterboro is a private airport, so most of the planes in and
out of there are either personal propeller-driven aircraft or corporate jets. One of the advantages of being on a corporate jet is that
you don't have to go through the check-in/terminal/security/
gate experience. In fact, very often they let cars, mostly limos,
drive right out to the tarmac where the planes are waiting.

A man in a suit and tie was waiting at a fenced gate, and when
he saw me, he opened the gate and motioned me in. He pointed
toward a jet with a half dozen similarly clad men standing next to
it. One of those men I recognized as Agent Emmett Luther.

I pulled the car near the jet, got out, and left it there. I moved
quickly toward Luther, but he and the others were already climbing the steps into the aircraft, motioning for me to follow. I did.

When I got through the door and onto the plane, Luther was standing there waiting for me. Next to him was a man I assumed to be the pilot, since he had wings on his jacket and literally had one foot in the cockpit and one out of it.

In the main passenger area were eight men and two women. I assumed all were FBI agents, but I wasn't sure, and I had a feeling there weren't going to be any formal introductions made.

"Where are we going?" Luther asked.

"North."

"You're going to need to be more specific than that."

"First we have to make our deal," I said. "Before we go anywhere."

"What the hell does that mean?"

"I told you, we're going to do this on my terms," I said.

"Don't fuck with me, Kilmer. I'll throw you off this plane, but I'll wait until we're at thirty thousand feet."

I was not in the mood to argue with him, so I decided to set out the conditions. "I believe that Allison Tynes is being held captive by the man we're going after. His plan is to use her as a hostage if anything goes wrong, and for him something is about to go very wrong. I'm worried about her safety."

"We need to file a flight plan," Luther said. "We can talk about this on the way; just tell me where we're going."

I wasn't having any of that. "First I want your word that her life will be the priority; that every effort will be made to keep her safe and unharmed."

Luther thought about that for a moment, then said, "Okay."

"And I am with you every step of the way. Where you go, I go."

"You think you're a hero?"

"Not even close. But I want to be there to watch you heroes in action, otherwise there's no deal."

"You're a pain in the ass, Kilmer. Okay, you have my word. Now, where the hell are we going?"

"Damariscotta, Maine."

"Who is going to be there when we get there? Besides your girlfriend."

"Philip Garber. He's been behind this from the start."

# I didn't waste time telling Luther how I knew

Garber was behind this.

It didn't matter; I was either going to be shown to be right or I was going to be shown to be wrong. He needed to spend the precious time planning what was going to be done, not worrying about whether he should be doing it.

I took note of the fact that Luther also didn't ask me what it was that Garber was behind. The feds had had their eye on this operation all along, but they didn't have the pieces. My guess was they knew basically what the research consisted of, and maybe even that I was the guinea pig. But they didn't know who was in charge, and they needed that before they could successfully move in.

The truth was it was easy for me to focus in on Garber, at least once I knew that Lassiter was in the clear. Garber told me I had come to see him three times, during which I'd mentioned I was working on a story about Lassiter. That was clearly not true; it was his way of setting Lassiter up as my fall guy.

Also, and even more significantly, he told me that in those sessions before Jen's "disappearance," I had been worried that Jen was a fantasy and was questioning whether I was losing my mind. That was patently false; the truth was that Jen was not in my mind before the implant, and was indelibly there afterward.

. So Garber had to be lying about our sessions. I hadn't remembered them, because they hadn't taken place. His number was on my cell phone bill because I'd called him in the process of chasing down the story I was really on, the story about scientists creating memories. I must have been getting too close, so he made me the story.

I told Luther that I thought Garber would be at a place listed in the phone book as Jefferson Auto Parts, near Damariscotta. It had been listed twice on the phone bill I'd found after Jen disappeared, but it hadn't made any sense.

Garber's plane went down off the coast of Maine, near Damariscotta. I believe he must have sent the plane down purposely, while bailing out before it did. The location would make it easy to subsequently leave the country, and his apparent death would ensure that no one would ever suspect or look for him.

Luther made some calls to get the lay of the land, and I think he spoke to someone in Washington about the strategy they would employ once we got to Maine.

Luther was receiving updates on the explosion at the hospital, and he was good enough to fill me in. There had been nine confirmed deaths, though more were possible. As terrible as that was, it was a relief. I knew how bad it could have been.

I told Luther about the events in the twenty minutes leading up to the bombing, as well as my adventure at Lassiter's house.

"You might be tougher than you look," he said.

"I don't think so."

I asked if he could find out whether Marie Galasso had gotten out, and he asked the question of someone on the phone, then laughed at what he heard and turned to me. "She's okay. She set fire to the place to get everybody to leave. She might be tougher than you look also."

I sat back and reflected for a few minutes on where we were going, and who we were going after. The man who had put me through all of this was there, and if we could get there in time and all went right, he would get nothing out of it.

But my greatest hope, and a hope was all it was, was that Jen was there and okay, and that we would get her out of there.

And then it hit me that I was thinking of Allie as Jen, and of Jen as real, instead of as a metal chip in my brain. And I worried that when all this was over, maybe all the people who thought of me as crazy would turn out to be right.

It was the longest flight of my life.

**Philip Garber was a realist, and what CNN** was saying was very real. All those people had escaped the building, which was bad enough, and indicated something unexpected had happened. But the worst part was that one of those people was Gates, and Gates had been arrested.

Gates would talk; there was no question about that. He had to realize that he was to be killed in the blast, and he would get his revenge. He would reveal Garber's involvement, his leadership, in the entire operation, and he would tell them that Garber's death was faked.

All of that was certain.

The saving grace, of course, was that Gates had no idea where Garber was. He had been smart enough never to share that with Gates, so Gates could not put the authorities on his trail. At least not until long after Garber had left the country.

Langel was the only person who knew where he was, and there was no reason to think anything had gone wrong at Lassiter's house. He assumed that Langel was on the way, as planned, to get his share of the money and kill the woman.

However, this changed the timing. He would close the deal now and leave, before anyone could figure out where he was.

Langel would be out his money, but that was not Garber's concern.

Of course, it would mean killing the woman himself, a prospect Garber did not relish. Ordering a killing was one thing; doing it himself was quite another. He reflected on the irony for a moment; he was that rare combination, a squeamish mass murderer.

Garber called the purchaser, explained what had happened, and why the deal needed to be consummated immediately. The man was upset, concerned about what his superiors, his government, might say.

Garber gave him ten minutes to report to them, but he knew what the answer would be. They would go along with the arrangement. They had to, this was too important to them to lose out on. The ability to control memory gave them that which was most important to people in power: permanence.

Garber took the time to gather everything together. It was remarkable that all the work by all those people could fit into one duffel bag, but it did, with room to spare. When he turned it over, it was not an exaggeration to say that the world would change.

It only took eight of the ten minutes for the call to come in. The money was being wired; Garber could get confirmation of that within ten minutes. Then they would go to the airfield, the handover would be made, and the woman would soon be fish food.

Soon Garber would be wealthy beyond his wildest dreams, beyond the wildest dreams of all but a select few. All he had to do was wait for the money, and then it would be time to move.

Time to get this over with.

**The money was in the account.** Garber had never seen that many consecutive zeroes before, at least not on any financial transaction he had ever been involved in. It was intoxicating to look at, and he could have happily done so all day.

But there was no time for that. The best thing to assume was that they were on to him, even though they likely weren't aware of his location. His customer was just as anxious to get out; he did not have diplomatic immunity, and together they were involved in a most serious crime against the United States of America.

In the moment, Garber had to decide whether or not to change the plan and kill Allie right then. He came to the conclusion that there was no immediate upside to it; there was always the possibility that something could go wrong, so why voluntarily give up a bargaining chip?

They would go to the airfield together, Garber, Allie and the buyer. Then the final piece of the puzzle would snap into place.

Tied up in the basement, Allie knew there was no chance Garber would let her live. He had talked some about what he had done, and his openness and lack of concern that she knew his identity made it clear she would never be allowed to tell the world the truth.

All she could do was wait and hope there would be a chance to save herself. She had never felt fear like that before, but she had to make a conscious effort not to let it overwhelm her.

She needed to be alert to any opportunity, and to act decisively if and when one presented itself.

Garber came downstairs and it was obvious from his attitude that something was up. He had a gun, and he held it on her. "Let's go," he said. "Upstairs."

"Where are we going?" she asked.

"First we're going upstairs," he said. "Unless you want a bullet in your head right here, but dying in the basement seems to lack some dignity, don't you think?"

She did as she was told, and the next step was to get into the car with Garber and a tall man she had never seen before. Garber drove, with the other man in the passenger seat. Because her hands were tied, she was put into the backseat and not viewed as a threat.

Neither man spoke to her, and when she asked questions, Garber angrily told her to shut up. He had still given her no opportunity to escape; it was nearing the time when she would have to make her own.

**Damariscotta's airfield made Teterboro look** like JFK.

Cars were there waiting for us right at the plane as we taxied to a stop, and within ten minutes we were at the target building. Less than three minutes later, the FBI had it surrounded.

True to his word, Luther was allowing me to remain on scene, albeit it near the rear and therefore out of danger. Not surprisingly, he did not seem interested in consulting me on tactics.

The lack of signs of life from the building were worrying Luther, but not nearly as much as they were worrying me. I was realizing just how little beyond a few hints and a lot of instinct I had relied on to bring us here.

Luther wasn't wasting any time; if Garber was not there, he needed to know it immediately. He had his agents move to the building in a pincer movement, though from my vantage point it was hard to know exactly what was happening.

I heard him give the order to move in, and braced myself for the possibility of gunshots. But there were none; all I could hear were shouts.

Luther went in himself, telling me to wait behind. He came out less than a minute later. "They're gone," he said. "Let's go."

"Where?"

"Back to the airfield; we found a copy of a flight plan."

We all piled back into the cars, but I was crushed by the events. "There's no way we'll catch them," I said. "They could have left hours ago."

Luther turned to me. "A phone call was made from the house fourteen minutes ago. We must have just missed them."

Left unsaid was the obvious truth: Garber was playing us for fools.

# Garber saw it as soon as they drove out

onto the tarmac.

There were two planes there. One was the plane they were to leave on; but it was the other he was looking at. On the side of the plane was an insignia with the words, UNITED STATES OF AMERICA.

Federal agents had found him; they were in Damariscotta.

Garber's contact didn't see it, and may not have gauged its import even if he had. But Garber had anticipated the possibility, and he had a backup plan ready to go. He always had a backup plan.

Garber looked in the window and saw the airport employee who worked at the reception desk, the man who was basically in charge of this small airport. He slowed as he passed by and waved, allowing the man to get a look into the car.

Garber then drove the car out to the plane, parking on the far side of it so that the plane was between the car and the airport employee. There was no way he could see them, and no reason for him to be looking in that direction anyway.

They got out quickly, with the car motor still running. The pilot had the plane's engine running; takeoff could be accomplished within seconds. The buyer, duffel bag clutched tightly in hand, quickly ran up the steps into the plane.

Garber held the gun up, pointing it at Allie. "Get on the plane," he said.

"No."

He pointed the gun in an even more threatening gesture, finger pressed on the trigger.

"Get on the plane or die now."

Allie knew that he would be reluctant to shoot her out here; the noise could attract unwanted attention. And once she stepped on that plane she had absolutely no chance. It was time to take a stand.

"No."

# We raced back to the airfield at high speed.

I knew, and I was sure Luther knew, that if Garber was able to beat us back to the airfield, even by five minutes, he would be able to get the plane into the air. From the location where we were, he could be out of U.S. airspace in ten minutes.

At that point there would be only one solution, and it was something I didn't even want to contemplate.

We were not the first car to get back there, and when we arrived we drove right onto the tarmac, where other agents were waiting, along with the man who served as the reception person behind the desk.

"He said there were three of them," the agent said. "Two men and a woman. They took off five minutes ago."

"What kind of aircraft?" Luther asked.

"Gulfstream IV," the man said. "Heading east."

Luther got on the phone and quickly explained the situation to someone I took to be his boss, or his boss's boss. He concluded with, "There's nothing we can do from here, sir." Then, "I concur with that, sir."

When he got off the phone, he turned to me. "Jets are going to be flushed to intercept them over international waters. They'll try to force them back here, where we will be waiting."

"You know they won't turn back," I said. "It would be throwing everything away, and over international waters they'll think they're safe. The jets will shoot them down."

To Luther's credit, he told me the truth straight out. "That would be my guess as well."

"You promised her life would be the priority," I said, though I knew I had no chance of changing the decision.

"It wasn't my call," he said. "But I agree with it. That material cannot be allowed out of the country." Then, "I'm sorry, but when she got on that plane, there was no longer anything anyone could do."

Then it hit me; she would not have gotten on that plane, not without a fight that would have attracted attention. It was like that day along the highway, when we were facing what seemed like imminent death, and she would have handled it the same way.

She would have drawn her line in the sand.

There was absolutely no guarantee or even evidence that I was right, but the truth was that in my mind I couldn't believe that she had gotten on that plane, because I wouldn't be able to stand it if she had.

All the way on the other side of the airfield was a large hangar, and I ran over to the airport employee. "What's in that building?" I asked.

He shook his head. "Nothing; it's empty. We don't use it anymore."

I started running toward the hangar. I didn't know what I would find there, probably nothing, but it was better than waiting around to find out that a plane had been shot down with Allie on it.

I'm not exactly a track star, but I covered that distance faster than I would have thought possible, slowed only by the act of taking my gun out of my pocket. And as I neared the hangar, I saw that the door to it was ajar. A good sign, but far from conclusive.

I should have waited before barging in. I should have called Luther and gotten some agents there to take over. It's not like they had anything better to do. But I didn't. I went through the door without hesitating, and looked around.

"Richard!"

I turned to the left at the sound of Allie's voice. She was standing with her hands behind her, probably bound. Garber was behind her and slightly to the side, arm around her neck, gun pointed to her head. They were about ten feet from a car.

But she was alive. The realization of that flooded me with relief, which was soon competing with the feeling of fear that I would not be able to save her.

The large hangar door was open in the back, and I instantly realized what was going on. Garber was going to make the agents think he had been on that plane, and when they shot it down over the water, they'd feel certain he was dead. He wouldn't have left a flight plan behind for the agents to find if he were going to be on the plane. He was faking his own death a second time, while getting away and into Canada by car. It was brilliant.

But now the look on his face was one of panic, and it seemed incongruous in the moment. He was a man I always thought of as being in control, and I was sure he always thought the same. Now events were closing in on him, and he was having trouble dealing with the sensation.

To me his fear made him more unpredictable and dangerous.

"Put the gun on the floor, Kilmer," he said.

I hesitated.

"*Now!*" he screamed.

"No, Richard, don't," Allie said, but I had figured that out on my own. We were taking a stand together.

"No," I said. "You shoot that gun, and ten federal agents will be in here in two minutes."

"You're going to die, Kilmer," he said, but I didn't hear confidence in his voice. He was trying to figure a way out.

Join the club.

In a sudden motion, he started to push Allie toward the car. They went about five feet, half the distance to it, when suddenly she snapped her head back, hitting him in the jaw with the back of her skull.

He was momentarily stunned, and she was able to get about a foot of separation between them. He raised the gun, but he never got to shoot it.

Because I shot him in the head.

My aim was not perfect; I was trying to shoot him in the chest. But if I was going to miss, it was good that I missed high.

Garber's brains splattered all over the side of the car, and he fell to the floor. Allie ran away from him, toward me, and I dropped the gun. She hugged me and started to cry. I hugged her back, but I was too scared to cry. I don't know which one of us was shaking, probably both.

Just before Luther and the other agents arrived, I looked at Garber's body. He had won, and I had lost; he had turned me into a killer.

But defeat tasted surprisingly sweet.

# There has been no media coverage of the

plane being shot down. I know that it must have happened, because I know it never returned to the airfield. I also know that it never would have been allowed to escape with its valuable cargo, so I can only assume that a blanket secrecy order was imposed.

I am sure that the federal authorities would much rather have recovered that cargo, but it wouldn't be crucial, especially since Dr. Gates and so many others survived the annex explosion. People who are targeted for murder but escape have a natural antipathy for the targeters. When you combine this with an equally natural desire to stay out of prison, I have no doubt that most or all of the key people are cooperating with the FBI.

In combination, all of them would have the knowledge to duplicate the work of the project, which makes the shooting down of the plane less of a scientific setback.

The secrecy has extended to my involvement, though pieces of the story have come out. Marie Galasso, for instance, has become a national hero, a well-deserved designation. She has made the round of talk shows, and her fifteen minutes of fame have stretched to three weeks and show no signs of abating. In this age of ever-present video, it turns out that one of her colleagues used his cell phone to videotape her turning over tables and setting the fire in order to get everyone out of the building. It has become the most widely viewed YouTube video of all time.

In every interview she has talked about her meetings with me, and credited me with informing her of the presence of the explosives. It has made me the target of every journalist in America; I am considered the biggest "get" there is.

But I've turned them all down, which is why I am telling my story in this manner. I'm a writer, so I write.

But the government is not talking about it, to me or anyone else, so there are gaps that I can only fill in with speculation, though I believe it to be informed speculation.

I must have been close to the story early on; it was probably the only truth Craig Langel told, when he said it was "Pulitzer territory." I then became the perfect target for Garber; abducting me and using me as his "model patient" served two purposes. It removed me as a danger, and it made me a perfect success to showcase. I was public proof of the power of their invention.

Ironically, no matter what I did, it fit into Garber's strategy. Whatever stress or danger I put myself under, whatever I learned in my investigation, it all allowed Garber to point to it and say, "See? Even with all that, the memories we have given him remain intact."

Lassiter was similarly in the wrong place at the wrong time. Because of his past enmity for me, he became an obvious choice to use as my adversary, as the person I would naturally chase. Garber also knew Lassiter would become infuriated when the trial was a failure, and his anger would make him the person that the police would look to as responsible for the building explosion.

My hatred for Lassiter, along with the false information I was fed about him, were designed to get me to ultimately kill him, and I have to admit there were times when I certainly considered it.

Other reporters have been gradually digging up information

on Philip Garber. He was apparently a genius, a pioneer in combining biophysics, neuroscience, and psychology. Over the years many of his theories had been shunned, and he had repeatedly been denied financial grants, to say nothing of the respect he felt he deserved. What role that played in his decision to do what he did, I can't really say.

Jen and Julie were, in fact, the same person. Julie was a random victim, kidnapped off an Iowa road because it made it less likely she could ever be connected to this New York operation. Her phone message to me had to have been deliberately recorded by her captors for future use; she was killed months before that call was made.

As I write this, I am all too aware that there is a foreign object lodged in my brain. Dan Lovinger has told me that he is confident it can be safely removed, though such surgeries certainly involve some inherent danger.

But that is not why I hesitate. I hesitate because that little chip is where Jen is, it is my only contact with the six months that we had together. I am aware that the things we shared, the conversations, the reading of *The New York Times*, the laughter, the lovemaking . . . did not happen in the real world.

But they happened in my world, and they are in my mind, residing alongside every other memory I've ever had. The memories of Jen are just as strong, just as emotional, just as personal. They make me happy, and they make me terribly sad. But they are mine, and I'm just not sure that I want to give them up. I want Jen to be a presence in my life.

Unfortunately, the massive explosion in the hospital annex destroyed much of what they call the "work product" of the experiment. Included in that would likely have been tapes of Jen and the other people and places in the fantasy world that had been created for me. It would have been painful, but I would very much like to have seen them.

And then there is Allie. She is still here, living with me. She keeps saying that she should go home, but then she doesn't leave.

I'm glad she stays, so glad that if she ever tries to leave I'll probably handcuff her to the refrigerator.

About a week ago we made love, and have done so every day since. I love her as much as I have ever loved anyone, real or imagined.

The funny thing is, it is Allie's presence that makes me consider having the chip removed. That is because of something Dan Lovinger said to me. He said that Garber and his people could only have given me the tools to form the memories, but that I myself had to fill in the blanks.

I filled in those blanks in the way I would want them filled, and I created in Jen a person I loved and wanted to spend my life with.

Allie is different than Jen in a number of ways, but in some ways she is as close to her as it is possible to imagine. Allie is therefore very much the person that my mind created when it had the chance. In that sense, she could literally be described as my "dream woman."

They don't come along very often.